C000088447

BESIDE
STILL WATERS

Also by Barry Callaghan:

BESIDE
STILL WATERS

Barry Callaghan

McArthur & Company
Toronto

McArthur & Company
322 King St. West, Suite 402
Toronto, ON
M5V1J2
www.mcarthur-co.com

Library and Archives Canada Cataloguing in Publication

Callaghan, Barry, 1937–

Beside still waters / Barry Callaghan.

9 8 7 6 5 4 3 2 1

ISBN 978-1-55278-790-8

I. Title.
PS8555.A49 B47 2009   C813'.54   C2009-900810-6

Cover design by Tania Craan
Interior by Michael P. M. Callaghan
Printed in Canada by Webcom

The publisher would like to acknowledge the financial support
of the Government of Canada through the Book Publishing Industry
Development Program (BPIDP) and the Canada Council for our
publishing activities. The publisher further wishes to acknowledge
the financial support of the Ontario Arts Council
for our publishing program.

for Gabriela

We're all our ages at once, aren't we?
Childhood is like the stone at the heart of the fruit–
the fruit doesn't become hollow as it grows!
The flesh may swell and ripen and soften around it,
but that doesn't make the stone disappear.

–NANCY HUSTON

PART ONE

Toronto, Canada

Adam's mother sat braiding her black hair in front of a big oval mirror. She had bony fingers. A burning cigarette left a long ash in a glass tray, and then she lit another, watching the match burn, staring into the blue flame. She kept the flame alive, building a mound of charred matchsticks, and then she put on her glasses, turned and said to Adam, who was leaning against the leaded window, "Well, let me look at you. What kind of boy are you today?"

"A good boy."

"And what's a good boy?"

"I don't know."

"A good boy is a boy who loves his mommy."

"Can't I love Dad, too?"

"You can, but sometimes Dad doesn't come home like he should. Now, let's pray and go to bed."

"Does God love me?"

"Of course he does. He died for your sins."

"Did I do some sins, Mom?"

"No. No, you're much too young."

"Then he's not dead for me."

"He will be. You'll see, when you get older."

She put him to bed and went down the back stairs to the back hall, the stairs lit by a bare bulb in a ceiling socket, and walked out onto the garden porch and sat down in the dark in a white wicker rocking chair, rocking and humming to herself: *In the wee wee hours . . .*

◈

The hedge at the edge of the Waters' front lawn was heavy with bright red berries. Adam's grandfather said, "Don't eat those berries. You'll die." Adam collected them in his pockets and crept between houses on the street and threw a handful at a bedroom window, and then at another window until a pale face appeared against the glass, staring with wary yearning into the dark, and Miss Klein, whose stone house was covered with ivy, caught him. A woman of forty, she was wearing a white satin petticoat. "You do that again," she said, "and I'll smack you so hard you'll see stars."

That same week, his grandfather died and his mother, Florence, said, "You're too young to see someone dead." She carried him to the neighbour next door. They gave him tea and poured his mother a Drambuie on the rocks before she went to the hospital. There were hand-painted Easter eggs and a photograph of the neighbour woman on the mantel. The woman, a singer with the Percy Faith dance band, was naked in the photograph, sitting cross-legged in an empty room, the walls of the room white, the floor painted black.

Adam stared at the photograph. Years later, he could clearly remember her naked body but he could not see her eyes, or her face, not the face that had put him to bed, but he could remember that her husband, Edmund, who had a pencil moustache, had given him a pocket watch in the morning.

"Well, your grandfather is gone," Edmund said.

Adam curled up in the strange bed and watched the sweep of the second hand, and then he put the watch on the pillow and it lay there like a silver eye and he said, "I guess Grandpa ate some of those red berries."

When his mother came home, she gave him a drawing book. The pages were blank except for black dots, and the scattered dots had numbers beside them. Using a stubby little pencil, he learned to count and connect the dots. He clapped his hands with wonder when the dots became a horse or a house or a man with big floppy shoes holding an umbrella. Then one day, with a Big Boy black crayon, he drew a dot that was bigger than a baseball on the white wall over his bed and when his mother came home, she was furious.

"Why did you do that, you terrible boy?"

"That's Dad," he said, backing away. "He's in the sky."

She took off her glasses and began to cry.

"Adam, sometimes you're all I've got."

"Sometimes you're all there is too, Mom."

He cradled against her belly and said, "I guess I sinned, eh Mom?"

"No, no, it's not a sin."

"Why not?"

"Because it's not. Your dad's off doing what he does, playing his piano, but telling me a dot in the sky is your dad is not a sin," and she put her glasses on and gathered up his drawing books, slipping them between the garter belts and underclothes in her dresser drawer. After supper, she came back from the store with a big glossy book about the stars.

"You want to look in the sky," she said, "then you should know what you're after, what you're looking for."

He studied the stars and tried to stay awake every night for as long as he could, staring into the map that was the dark sky.

As the weeks passed, and his lonely mother chain-smoked, and talked out loud while staring at garage roofs up behind the house, as if there were someone there, he dreamed of winged horses and ships adrift in the sky and planets that wheeled around the spokes of the sun, and he drew the little points of light together on his charts. He sometimes thought that planets wheeled around his room, and he discovered he could squeeze his eyes so hard that he saw little dots of light. He told his mother, "I've got stars in my eyes," and she said, "No, you don't. Your father does. Never you mind who Fatha Hines is. Your father believes he's a better player than the Fatha, and maybe he is. But you don't ever want to have stars in your eyes."

"Why not?"

"Because people who've got stars in their eyes hurt other people." He saw ice come into her eyes. Ice was hard water. Hard water, she had told him, was hard because it was cold. So cold, he thought, that she could hurt his father, and she might hurt him, but then all her hardness turned to tears.

"There's the Big Dipper, Mom," he said, trying to comfort her, "and there's the last star in the Little Dipper. The whole world's up there," holding her as close as he could, feeling the softness and heat of her thighs.

"Not everything," she said. "There's no cross. The fiery cross comes at the end of the world."

"What's the end of the world?"

"When everything's nothing, except we'll see fire in the air first."

"So, we should be down at the South Pole."

"Heavens, no," she said, laughing.

"Why not?" he said. "All they've got in the sky is a Southern Cross."

With his magnifying glass, he searched his glossy star maps, looking for points of light in the north that could connect into a cross, but finally he folded his arms at supper and said, "I give up. There's no cross where we live."

"Oh yes there is."

"Where?"

"We all carry a cross."

"I don't like that."

"You'll see."

Puerto Rico

Years later, when he was almost twenty-nine and a successful foreign affairs photojournalist, he found himself ambling about on the crowded floor of the Casino in the Flamboyan Hotel after coming in on a late flight from Beirut to San Juan. The croupier at one of the six craps tables was crying *New shooter, Saliendo, coming out,* the green baize having the sheen of slime-covered stones in a crossing of river water where a fat woman in her fourties signed a marker for chips, accompanied by a young man wearing a cream suit who carried a riding crop and wore rings on each finger, a young man who had oddly flared, flattened nostrils and was blind and held the arm of the woman as she set four stacks of hundred-dollar chips in the table-rail runnel and Adam watched over her shoulder, curious about the blind man as the croupier scooped the dice toward her. She picked them up. The blind boy opened his eyes – an underbelly fish colour – and said, *"Sol'eri in terra."* She rolled a seven so the blind boy said, *"Se'nel ciel felice."* She rolled a five and made several side bets: the field numbers, the hard-eight and hard-six. The blind boy called, *"Sol'eri in terra."* And she rolled, and then rolled again, and made her five, and this time she said,

"*Se'nel ciel felice,* thank you Jesus." She scooped up handfuls of hundred-dollar chips.

"Praise the Lord is right," a plump man with big fleshy ears said. Others reached over the table, bulging arms and thick necks, bodies bent, all of them suddenly sure that the fat woman had the touch, all except for an imposing man that Adam instinctively shied away from, a lean small-boned man with bird-quick eyes, olive skin shining taut on his skull. Adam, watching him, decided to call him the Bone Picker . . . a man who kept moving from table to table, looking for the cold table, always betting against the shooters, betting against the gift of luck, the gift of grace, always playing the DON'T COME line, hunching his shoulders before each roll, betting on crap-outs as the croupier cried *Saliendo,* the dice caroming around the curve of the table, "Crap," and the shooter muttered, "Shit" as the Bone Picker scooped up 2 to 1 on his chips. But this evening the fat lady kept winning and the Bone Picker was losing, anxiously looking into the face of the blind man as Adam, bemused, began to sing to himself, *The blind man got a letter while he sat in jail, The blind man burned the letter, said love can never fail,* as the players, their fists full of chips, scrambled to get their bets down, and the croupiers chanted: "All bets down, big shooter coming out." The fat woman smiled. She waited, and then said quietly to the blind boy, "Is it a no-go, Nelson?" He nodded. She set down the dice and said, "Cash me in." The players howled. "What kinda Mickey Mouse routine is this, lady, you're red hot, lady, you're hot . . ." "I may be hot," she said, "but I'm not a fool, neither for money nor love."

The croupier shrugged and the dice passed to a portly, pink-faced man. "New shooter coming out . . . fine new shooter . . ." The portly man blew on the dice in his closed fist. "Baby needs new shoes . . . Ten, ten . . . the Big Dick from Boston took out his balls and washed 'em . . ." The Bone Picker laid down a thousand dollars in purple chips on the DON'T COME line. The shooter rolled: "Ace-Deuce, crap." One & One. Snake eyes. Everybody lost, including the Bone Picker, with only the house collecting on a Two as Adam, satisfied because the Bone Picker had lost, feeling wonderfully relaxed, and for some reason, full of anticipation, continued singing to himself, *The blind man in his jail, the blind man got a letter, said love can never fail . . .*

Toronto
Adam, in the year of his first Communion, sat on a needlepoint stool beside the piano and said to his mother and father, "This is my downtown."

"Where?"

"Where we are, Walmer Road," and he told them about one of their neighbours, Mrs. Skinner, who was so drunk one afternoon that her silk bonnet slipped over her eyes, so drunk she couldn't see that her slow-witted fifteen-year-old son had let his trousers fall to his ankles and was playing with himself behind a curtain of climbing sweet peas. His mother and father laughed at the story, but a few weeks later, when the slow-witted son killed his mother with a rake, Web said, "These are wild times, everyone has a boil about to burst." He waved his folded newspaper at his wife. "I like that," he said. He wrote it down in a little notebook. The desk and dresser drawers in the house were filled with notebooks he'd kept over the years, filled with things he liked hearing himself say. He told Adam that he could have his notebooks when he was dead. "You'll be lucky because you'll learn something about your father, you'll get an angle on me, which is more than I can say about my father."

"Your father was afraid of red berries."

"Life is the berries."

Web laughed and poured himself a glass of bourbon. "It is a big old round world out there," he told Adam, "and don't forget it . . . There are strange things for the eye to see, maybe strange to us but just plain ordinary to the people who live there. Like, there's this café in a city called Berlin where I saw raw reindeer meat being fed by naked girls to piranha fish in a tank by the front door. You've got to take all this in your stride, like this is life, as it comes."

Adam asked him why the round world was so flat, and Web said, "Hell, flat's the blues an' I know all about how things go flat." He sat down at the piano. "To really play the blues like your poppa does, you've got to have big hands, and you got to be able to flatten the note." He played a song. "That's your little baby tune called 'Chopsticks'," he said, "except I played it like they played it in the old sporting houses, what they called ragtime, which is what they used to play in Chinese sporting houses, I guess."

"What's a sporting house?"

"That's a house . . . you pretend is a wonderland, but it's not."

"Where's wonderland?"

"Inside your head. That's where your dreams are hiding out. Sometimes it hurts, boy, playing hide-and-seek inside your own head, but that's where most people find themselves most of time, so you make the most of it."

"I play hide-and-seek behind the garages with Gabrielle. Maybe she's hiding in her own head, too."

"Maybe. You never know."

"How'll I find her if she's in her head?"

"If she's It, when you find her, she's found, and then you're It and she has to find you. That's how the game goes."

Then his father said, "The thing that frees you up so that you can feel good at home as you go about in your own city is the ghosts you've got buried that you call your own, like Grandfather. It's the dead, once you've got them, once they come out of hiding, that make you feel at home in your hometown."

Web took Adam to the old burial yard. Several of the Waters had been set down in the yard, some with their tombstones side-by-side, others between crypts, cairns and Celtic crosses under chestnut trees. "It's good," he said, "to be able to stand among your tombstones. In one way, of course, they're nothing to you, they're just these isolated glimpses, little stories and stuff, but in another way, they're really all you've got, back and forth in time, they're not all of you but they're you. I mean, some people don't even know who their aunts and uncles are."

In September, the chestnuts would have been as big as green apples, but since it was winter, the black branches of the trees were sheathed in ice. Web threw snowballs up into the trees, shattering the sleeves of ice so that shards of ice fell glittering in the sunlight.

"You know, I was hanging out here one day after a big squall of a snowstorm," Web said, "what with the snow banked up high around the stones, when these pall bearers appeared, carrying this coffin with a big bell sitting on it, and some navy men and cadets followed along in single file, in lockstep through the snow. It reminded me that back in the old days there'd only been a wagon track through these trees that they had used for the hauling of boats up the hill on the portage through the bush to Lake Simcoe. The story was that a huge elm tree had fallen across the trench and all the wagons had to go under it so that it looked like it was the crossbeam of a gallows tree, leading to a particular place that was then called Gallows Hill. That's just down the road a piece now, the Yonge Street hill. Didn't know that, did you? And it was a hill of blue clay that was used to fire the bricks for the first jail-house, a blue jailhouse, and your great-great-grandfathers are lying down here under where those sailors went, lying here just like they're buried in their own little boats."

Many of the family stones stood along the walkway through the cemetery and some lay flat below the snow, with only the nub of an angel's head showing and letters that needed rubbing to be read when the snow was cleared away, but the rest were lean, elegant slate slabs or little stone steeples and turrets inscribed with dates and lists of names. Adam's favourite stone, a stone that had no dates, was pale brown, between his grandmother and grandfather:

> *You passersby, stay not to ask my name,*
> *I'm nothing at present,*
> *From nothing I came.*
> *I never was much, am now less than ever,*
> *And the idle hath always been my endeavour,*
> *Who, coming from nothing,*
> *To nothing is fled,*
> *Yet thought she'd become something once she was dead.*
> *18__ to 18__*

❦

Several of the large red brick homes on Walmer Road, his street of rich mercantile families who'd gone into steep decline, had been turned into rooming houses for young working men and women who were always in a hurry. Sometimes on Saturdays, unshaven bachelors with little or no money to spend stood on their stoops wearing baggy trousers and old hats or baseball caps, and they stared wryly (and with a little wonder) at two elderly chauffeur-gardeners across the road who would smoke a roll-your-own Navy Cut cigarette and then unbutton their paisley vests, part of their midnight-blue uniforms, before starting in to polish the household cars. Other men sat reading the newspapers in chairs on the lawns, others sprawled over the hoods of their own cars, talking about baseball or fishing. Edmund Alt, the neighbour who had given Adam the silver pocket watch, put his hand on Adam's shoulder and told Web that he wouldn't mind taking Adam fishing. "It's the first spring run. He'll see something he's never seen. The sap's running out of the trees just like candy."

"I don't know if my kid needs to see you guys in the raw."

"Come on. I'm talking nature, I'm talking about trees and fishing."

"And I'm talking booze in the bush."

"Naw. None of that, not like that. A kid should learn how to fish. Pan-fry your own catch . . ."

"The kid doesn't even like to eat fish."

"He'll catch a fish and he'll want to eat it. Take my word for it. It's human nature."

Adam got into a car with Edmund and two of his friends who were sportswriters and they drove north on Highway 69 to a wide shallow river. "On a clear day you can see right to the Moon River basin," one of the sportswriters said, and they set up camp, making a fire in a circle of stones. They sat on their haunches and passed around a bottle of whiskey, talking about books ("The best story about fishing ever writ-ten," one of the sportswriters told him, "is by Hemingway, you heard of him? 'Big Two-Hearted River,' you read that someday now."), and about hooks and bait and how to fillet a fish, depending on whether it was perch or pike, and how carving a duck was not like carving a turkey: "You got to take your shears and scissor right through the breastbone to quar-ter the bird. My father was a tailor," Edmund said, "and I got his shears. The only damn thing of his I got to remember him by and they're perfect for scissoring ducks."

They put Adam in men's high black rubber boots and led him out into the white water, a long rod in his hand, and Edmund helped him to cast and Adam tried snapping the rod so that the fly would leap forward over his head in a looping arc and then he looked around and couldn't find them. They'd gone. They'd all disappeared around a bend. He stood in the river for a long time, bewildered, holding the rod straight out in the air, with no idea where the end of the line was, scared and cold, so he began to sing a song his mother had always sung in the dark when he was a child: "It's a grand night for singing . . ."

He liked to sing. He was in the church choir where he and the boys got dressed on Sundays in black soutanes and stood close to each other in the stalls, and as he stood in the river he squeezed his eyes closed and pretended the lights that flashed in his eyelids were stars. He tried not to topple over in his men's black rubber boots as he sang and he suddenly felt the boys in the choir were all there with him watching as little stars fell like stones into the rush of white water as he sat down on a big rock to wait alone. He was still cold but now he was calm. Being alone didn't frighten him. He remembered being alone in front of the photograph of Mrs. Alt's naked body. With his eyes closed, he stared at her body in his mind's eye, listening to the stillness in the silence. Then he heard the water running over stones. He opened his eyes. He loved stones. The colours were startling when they were wet. He wondered why the colours were hidden and why the water made them alive. The old parish priest, Father Zale, had told him that water was the grace of God, His gift, and Adam had leaned against the church walls listening for voices inside the stones, sure that the iron stains in the stones were the tears of trapped voices, maybe the trapped voices of men and women who had been in the blue brick jail or maybe the tears were the trapped voice of God.

Hoping that he might hear the voice of God, he had often lain down in a pew in the empty church on a weekday afternoon but instead he had heard Harry O'Leary, the choirmaster, practising at the organ. The gently vaulted blue ceiling was covered with hundreds of gold stars as if all his spinster schoolteachers had filled the sky with their approval. He felt, looking up, that he could be anywhere he wanted to be among those stars. The organ's rumbling bass notes shivered him in his bones. Maybe, he thought, that was the sound of God's voice, and he wanted to sing out as loud as he could so that the choirmaster would hear him, and maybe even God would hear him, but he had only a little voice, too small to be heard above the heavy rumbling organ, and so he began to pound the heels of his shoes on the pew to the beat of the music, but then, after the music stopped, the beat of his heels went on: *bunh bunh bunh*, as if he were marching somewhere and he didn't know where, or care. Then he heard the choirmaster coming down the aisle so he stopped marching and held his breath, taking off his shoes, tucking them out of sight under his body, afraid the choirmaster would take his shoes away from him, not just as punishment for making a stupid noise in church, but for marching off to wherever his shoes were going to take him.

He had made his first confession in that church, kneeling in the dark, waiting for the grate to roll away from the wire screen, trying hard to think of something terrible he had done, wanting to be taken seriously, and since he had seen the choirmaster's daughter, Gabrielle, lift up her skirt and spread her legs, he'd blurted it out, spelled it out: "I f-u-c-k-e-d, Father." He'd heard a chuckle in the dark. He'd felt confused, mortified. The priest had whispered, "How old are you, my son? You mustn't try to be bad, my boy, that'll come soon enough, soon enough" (some eight years later he and Gabrielle had become school sweethearts and, after two years, lovers, and not long after that he had stopped going to confession, and then, after nine years of not seeing each other, as they lay in bed in a hotel room outside the town of Ponce in Puerto Rico, laughing under the covers, he told her – whispering in her ear as if her ear were the confession screen: "I F-U-C-K-E-D, Father" – and she said, "Oh, my sweet little sinner, I'd forgotten how beautiful your cock really is and I can't see it under the covers . . .") "so, my boy, say the Stations of the Cross for a penance and try to remember that Our Lord died for your sins."

Adam forgot that his knees hurt. He was pleased. The priest had said that God was dead, that he had died for him, and that meant that he had probably died for Gabrielle, too. As he stepped out from under the confessional curtain, he wanted to tell the priest to go and talk to his mother, to let her know what had happened to God. She'd be happy to know that she was right. Perhaps he and his mother might like to have a cigarette together. Maybe he and Gabrielle would share a Coke and put an aspirin in it and get "a buzz" as they watched the priest build his own little pile of burned matches beside his mother's matches. But then the grate rolled shut SHLUNK and he became angry, he'd been cut off in the dark from the priest's kindness, and he pounded on the grate, whispering, "Open up, I got more sins."

Wearing a starched collar with a white silk bow, he and Gabrielle had taken Communion at the marble altar rail. He had opened his mouth to the pale disc pinched between the puffy white fingers of the other priest in the parish, Father Zale. This priest had promised him that he would swallow the Word of God and that the Word would always speak in him no matter his own silences because "God is the still water within your silence and the day will come when God, the fisherman of souls, will break that silence and speak to you."

Stop traveller, and know
that here lie the remains
of Edgar
son of Maurice and Margaret Waters.
Before he was a year old,
he arrived at puberty and was four feet
before he was three years old,
endowed with great strength,

exact symmetry of parts,
and a stupendous voice.
He had not quite reached his sixth year
when he died, as of an advanced age.
Here he was born and here he gave way,
September 3rd, 1907.

Puerto Rico

In the same week that he'd come from Beirut to San Juan, some twenty years after they had taken first Communion together, Adam and Gabrielle – having met by chance – took a room in a squat, grey stone hotel on the seaside road to Ponce, an old colonial town. With the turquoise wood window shutters closed against the sun, and because neither had turned on a light, they were shadows to each other in the dark.

"Look at us," she said, "like we really know what we're doing here."

"I'd look if I could see you," he said, laughing.

She was sitting on the bed. He stood waiting.

In the morning silence they could hear the breaking of surf on the shore.

"That's the sea?" he said. "It'll be beautiful here beside the sea."

"Whenever I hear the sound of the sea," Gabrielle said, "I feel so free I want to make love."

"With anyone I know?"

"Maybe," she said. "Maybe, maybe."

They both laughed.

"The truth is," she said, "I've always lived as far away from the sea as I could get."

"This is crazy," he said as he sat down on the bed beside her, "the two of us carrying on here in the dark like we hardly know each other."

She put her finger to his lips and for a moment they were silent, they were still, but then she whispered, "Yes. Come on."

She began to unbutton her blouse, but then she said, stepping up and away from him, "Do you remember what I look like?"

"You've got a mole on your right breast," he said, turning on the table lamp beside the bed, "and a scar on your hip you got when your mother spilled boiling water on you. And," watching her as she did a little turn, "you've still got your beautiful long legs . . ."

"A hoofer's legs . . ."

"And you've got beautiful knees. You didn't have beautiful knees before. Do you know how hard it is to have beautiful knees?"

"When I first got to New York," she said, now more open, feeling like herself, "this director told me, he says, 'Gams, you got great gams, girl . . .'"

"How old was he?"

"Sixty. Seventy. He loved Cyd Charisse."

"How old was she?"

"Cyd Charisse is forever," she said. "Like us. I can't imagine what forever is without us being there."

They could hear the rasping call of cicadas in the heat outside the closed shutters.

"I mean, you're the boy I've loved all my life, and here you are, a man, and I want to fuck you. I want us to be lovers like we were lovers before, except right now I feel like a little girl, which is as good as it is bad, so I don't know what to do," but then she stepped boldly out of her skirt and lay down on the bed, her arms and legs open, saying, "How come you're so shy?"

"*Saliendo*," he cried, "new shooter coming out."

He rode her on her back and up onto her shoulders, her knees under his arms until she came and he came.

As they lay catching their breath, sprawled on the bed, he said, "I think maybe I might be falling in love with you all over again."

"I'd love to be in love again."

"Me, too."

"We still make love the same way," she said, "only better."

"What would we do if it was worse?"

"Smoke a cigarette."

"We don't smoke."

"Do you remember the songs we used to dance to?"

"Maybe . . ."

"*See the pyramids along the Nile . . .*"

He took hold of her hand.

"*. . . See the jungle when it's wet with rain – you belong to me.*"

They lay very quietly, saying nothing, getting used to each other again, to the way he breathed with his mouth open, hands folded across his chest, to the way she crossed her long legs at the ankles.

She got up and went to the window, saying, "Let's have a look at what's going on out there." She folded back the turquoise wood shutters.

Outside the window, there was a banana tree, the broad leaves cut back to the joint, a banana black in its ripeness, open at a seam, and a hummingbird hovered in the air, stabbing its long blue stiletto beak into the white pulp.

"It's going so fast it's like it's standing still in the air."

"It can't stand still."

"But it is," she said.

"Maybe it is," he said, "but it can't."

"You're so wonderfully difficult," she said. "What in the world am I going to do with you?"

"Whatever gives you pleasure."

She stepped away from the window, clapping her hands, surprised and pleased, as she found that there was a deep stone bath attached to their room.

"I'm going to fill the bath with cold water. I love cold water baths in the morning."

"You do? That's new."

"Sure, it gets the blood going."

"Makes you sound like some kind of penitent nun."

"If anybody knows, you know. I am no nun."

"By God, you're no nun."

"Penitent, yes, that's possible," and then, opening her eyes wide, tossing her head, as if she wanted him to know that she could be affectionately light-hearted, she asked, "How's your mother? I always felt close to her, she was so pretty. And a little crazy, keeping her matchbook fires burning in front of her mirror."

"She was pretty strange," he said, aroused again by her bare buttocks as she bent over to test the water, "I'll give you that, trying to disappear into her mirror, and sometimes I think she did, though she always came back. But then, you know all about disappearing."

"Maybe," she said as she eased down into the cold water, lying back, the water up to her throat. "I guess I've always been trying to get away."

He sat on the edge of the stone bath, his back to the wall.

"Sometimes in New York," she said, "what I dreamed I wanted to do was show up one morning as a missing person on all the bulletin boards in all the post offices in the country, with a photograph of me that wouldn't look like me, so I could come out of hiding any time I wanted . . ."

"Who were you hiding from?"

"My father. Me mostly, I guess."

"And me?"

"Never you. I've never hidden from you, I just couldn't be there."

Sitting on her haunches in the cold water, she closed her eyes.

"Remember when we were kids," she said, "we used to hold our breath, trying to see who could not breathe for the longest time. I always won," and she took a deep breath, holding it, holding on to holding on, the cords straining in her neck, and then she blew the breath out of her lungs, staring at him as if she had just come from a place deep inside herself, a look of pain embedded in a wonder in her eyes that he had never seen before, a look that took him by surprise as she stepped out of the bath and let him towel her dry.

"My father was the last man I let towel me dry."

She kissed him on the forehead and took the towel from his hands. He wanted to hold her. He loved the weight of her buttocks in his hands.

"After I left, I never wanted to see him again. I sent him a card once from Africa. So he'd know I was alive."

"Africa, what the hell were you doing in Africa?"

"That's another story," she said. "Meanwhile, it's been nine years and who could believe it, here we are, it's like we're six thousand miles from everywhere . . ."

She sang out in a nasal country twang, "Only six thousand miles from everywhere . . . and that much closer to hell."

"Jesus, it's Grand Old Opry time . . ."

❦

The next morning, when he opened the shutters, the hummingbird was there.

"The bird's back," he said. "Still going nowhere fast."

"Quoth the raven, Nevermore . . ."

"That was a black bird . . ."

"They got rights, too."

As they dressed, she said, "I was thinking . . ."

". . . blackbirds?"

". . . the way it was with us before, like, everything was so open, so . . . ready. I don't mean innocence or anything like that, whatever innocence is, but I always trusted you, trusted you'd never hurt me. That's why I let you take my virginity."

"No. No, I didn't take it . . . you wanted it gone."

"Let's just say, blood was shed."

❦

In the walled courtyard to their room, in the shade of *poiu* trees, they ate fresh croissants and drank *maccioti*.

Then he focused his Leica, and took a photograph of her, *click*, and said, "Take off your blouse."

Without hesitation, as if she'd been posing for him in the middle of conversations for years, she did, folding the blouse across her knees.

"Tell me about Africa," he said.

"No."

"Why not?"

"Africa's Africa. That's not for here. We're here, and what I was thinking about when I woke up was the way we always used to meet in the springtime up on the garage roofs when we were still young enough to be goofy, and you'd open up those propeller seed pods from the sugar maples that had fallen all over the roofs and you'd put the sticky pods all over my body like I was this naked angel who had some kind of disease."

"Yeah, well," he said, *click, click,* "while we were playing with your angelic body my mother had her own angel, a little winged lady who hung out up there on the same roofs. She used to sit in her room and talk to her angel."

"Did the angel talk back?"

"Unfortunately, I think so." *Click.*

"Unfortunately?"

"When her angel was talking to her no one else could get a word in edgewise. Jesus, I've had to listen to lunatic women singing their song all my life."

"Lucky you," she said. "The only singing I can hear in the air here is cicadas. With them going on like that, it's going to rain."

"There's no clouds in the sky."

"It doesn't matter, the clouds'll come. And then the rain."

"What'll we do?"

"We'll swim naked in the sea before it rains."

"No, we won't."

"Why?"

"Because we're going into town. We should see where we are."

"I don't want to see where we are," she said. "I want to stay right here and just so we are clear, I certainly don't want to go back to where I was when I was a kid. I don't ever want to go home again."

"But that's why we're here, we were so happy together back home."

"You were happy, and you made me happy," she said, suddenly sounding a little angry, but angry for no reason that he could see as she reached out to touch a tendril of withered buds that was clinging to stones in the courtyard wall, "but my mother didn't kill herself for nothing."

"But that's what we all wanted to know."

"What?"

"Why'd she kill herself? And then you were gone."

"I wouldn't want to say."

He put his camera down, surprised by her tone, an unforgiving hardness. She put on her blouse but didn't do up the buttons. Her breasts were still bare. The *patron* brought them more coffee but she didn't cover herself. She sipped her coffee and said, with a tilt to her chin that he'd never seen before, "You'd be surprised . . . I mean, someone told me once that I've got a stubborn streak in me, staunch, this friend of mine said it was. Strange sound, that word. Staunch." Then she said, taking hold of the tendril, "These flowers are very beautiful at night. They're like blooming drops of water and they only bloom at night, did you know that? And then they die in the sunlight with the heat."

He said he thought she should put suntan lotion on her breasts.

"I love the sun, it's so warm, so fresh, in a hot sun I feel like I'm fresh bread," she said, handing him a tube of Bain de Soleil from her purse.

"I like the nighttime better," he said, rubbing the orange gel into her breasts.

"The wrong things happen in the night."

"Maybe so, but I love the dark hours, the three o'clock in the morning hours in the summer back home, the way the night wind on the air always feels so cleansing."

"The dark, it gets in your eyes," she said. "Don't you know that? They found that out with prisoners, with men who've been locked away a long time."

"How could I be in the dark," he said impishly, "when I'm here with you?" He dropped the tube into her open purse, took a deep breath close to the nape of her neck, whispering, "The heat of your skin is the freshest smell in the world."

"No it's not," she said, drawing his head to her breast. "It's cut grass, the sweetness of cut grass, and you leave it in the hot sun and it dries out brown, drying grass and baking bread, those are the two best smells in the world. That's what I remember from when I was a child . . . And you, I remember you because women remember the smell of the men in their lives, the men they really care about, and I could always smell you, I always wanted to smell you, from when we were just kids, and maybe it's only a kind of nostalgia, but because I felt so easy with you last night, it felt so right to be with you again, even if it is nostalgia, I knew it right away when we made love, I could feel a sweetness, a light rise up in me and it was a light that had the smell of joy in it . . ."

That night as they undressed, she placed a pair of red sling-back shoes on the floor by the foot of the bed, saying that she liked to leave shoes behind in rooms where she had been happy. "So I'll have to come back."

In his bare feet, he tried to step into her slingbacks, telling her, "I did this once when I was a kid with my mother's shoes."

She gave him a playful push. He toppled happily onto the bed, lay there saying nothing because nothing needed to be said, but then got up, seized by a sudden inexplicable dread that somehow things were about to go wrong, that everything was about to come up Ace-Deuce, a sense of impending distress so strong that he heard himself say, "Grief."

"What?"

He stared at her, trying to find the right word for what he was feeling. Surprising her, surprising himself, he kicked her shoes under the bed.

"Grief," he said.

❧

In the morning, he opened the shutters.

"The hummingbird's back."

"Good."

"I wonder where he goes when he's gone?"

"New York."

"No way. There's no banana trees in New York."

"Yes, we have no bananas," she sang out, sitting in the stone bath, splashing water.

"What?"

"It's a great old song, never mind. As old as Cyd Charisse."

"What'll we do today?"

"Make love."

"And . . . ?"

"Dream."

"What'll we dream about?"

"You can't plan dreams."

"I can if I want."

"Watch out."

"For what?"

"The Bogeyman'll get you."

"I've been with the Bogeyman. He's a lousy dancer. And he can't sing to save his soul."

"Gentlemen songsters off on a spree, doomed from here to eternity . . ."

"You're crazy, absolutely crazy."

"Good, let's make love."

The following morning, he woke before she did. He lifted himself up and rested on his elbow so that he could watch her sleep. She seemed to be deep in sleep, which surprised him because he had heard her get up in the night and walk to the window; he was sure that she had stood for a long time staring into the moonless dark. She had then sat down to stare at him and touch his hair, certain that he was asleep, but now she was asleep without a blanket or covering sheet, her legs crossed at the ankles, breathing evenly.

He got up and opened the shutters. He looked, and looked again: "The bird's gone. It's not here," he said in alarm, turning from the window only to see that she was sitting up, huddled cross-legged on the bed, as if she were holding herself in a knot, and she was crying. "Fuck the bird," she said. Then, without another word she got up. She didn't pour her morning cold water bath but got dressed and when he asked her where she was going, she said, "Nowhere."

She closed the door.

Bewildered, he hesitated and thought, realizing that he'd been holding his breath, that his chest hurt, "This is impossible."

He stepped into his trousers and sandals and hurried down the road to the sea, passing a cluster of tall poles tied together, live land crabs hanging for sale from the poles. Even in the very early morning, three black women wearing sweatbands were seated on stools around a fire and an iron pot of *asapao*, each holding a long-handled spoon, stirring a thick soup of shrimps and lobster. Beyond a spur of storm-piled black rocks, he took hold of her by the shoulders.

"Yes, we have no bananas," she cried, shaking, still weeping.

"For the love of God, what's going on . . . ?"

"I can't help this, I can't, it's like something takes hold of me in the pit of my stomach and I just have to get away."

"It's okay."

"No it's not," she said, "it's totally unfair, but maybe it'll be okay for a little while if you say it's okay."

He held their shoes as they walked in their bare feet along the water's edge. She kept singing, "*Yes, we have no bananas, Yes, we have no bananas, Yes . . .*" until they came to a cove of plane trees and satinwoods, where she said, "I could die listening to the sound of breaking waves."

"That is," he said, kissing her hand, trying for playfulness, "the sound of my breaking heart."

"Your heart's not breaking," she said, laughing and stomping her foot in the sand as if she could play at being a petulant girl again if she wanted to. "Meanwhile," she said, "I am a staunch woman. Staunch. I don't break so easy."

"My heart is," he said, "breaking."

"No, it's not. You can't. I won't let you."

"You know," letting a pause for calm fall between them, "you could let me know what's going on with you."

"No, I couldn't," she said, quietly but insistently, following along behind running sandpipers as they skimmed the lace foam of spent waves. "A girl's got to have a little something up her sleeve, a little pocket money, some secrets."

"Still playing hide-and-seek with yourself."

"No. But be careful." She kissed him hard on the mouth. Then pushed him away. "Be very careful."

"Fair's fair."

"Love is always unfair," she said as she stepped out of her sundress, naked except for two delicate gold chains and a gold bracelet. She folded her dress across a low-hanging branch and waded in to the water, pushing her body through the heavy green waves. A breaker swamped her and she rose, gasping, snorting, rubbing water from her eyes as he stripped down and waded in after her. She pushed out farther beyond the breaking of the waves till her chin was at the level of the water, her head seemingly afloat, decapitated.

They fell toward each other, blinded by salt, seeing the sun as a white wafer through the spray. Flocks of frigate birds criss-crossed overhead as they began to flounder, choking on the salt water, going under and then clutching and hauling themselves up for air, coughing and spitting. They lunged back toward the shore, the waves, heavy with sand and pebbles, breaking against the backs of their knees so that they stumbled onto the white sand in the cove. As they stood naked and laughing, he said, "Jesus, for a moment out there I thought we were getting dragged under by the current, the undertow . . . But suddenly it was crazy, I had this feeling like nothing could go wrong, not like I felt the other night when I somehow got swamped by some terrible sense of loss, like the Bone Picker was on me, but it was like when we were making love and this light, a surge of light went right through my body . . . *Saliendo*," he cried, driving his fist toward the sun.

She burst into laughter and said, "Every day you remind me of why I love you," and she kissed him, running her tongue along his lips, laughing seductively, the low laugh he always heard from deep in her throat when they made love. They had laughed a lot, day after day, unable to entirely believe that they could, after so long a separation, nine years, still be so open to each other, so eager.

That night he whispered to her as they lay in bed, sweating and out of breath from making love again, "Catch your breath," and she whispered as they went to sleep in each other's arms, "Catch a falling star."

❧

When he opened the shutters on the ninth day, the bird again was not there and Gabrielle was gone.

She had left behind a sun lotion-stained blouse.

The *patron* said she had ordered a car to take her to San Juan at six in the morning. She had warned the *patron* the night before not to make any noise, not to wake Adam.

"She can be very forceful," the *patron* told Adam apologetically.

In San Juan, he found two of her friends at the Casino hotel, one of whom said, "Yes, yes, she used to sit right here, hour after hour, before you came along," and the other, "Even so, she always said she was going to be going somewhere. . . ."

Angry, feeling deeply humiliated, even insulted, he went walking on the beach in the night. He talked angrily to her, talking out loud, yelling, "We all carry a cross, goddammit." Then he broke into tears, feeling childish and stupid, needing only to find her, determined to find her, so that he could show her his anger, his disappointment, his mortification, and yet comfort her, forgive her, and tell her that no matter the panic or the dread that had driven her to take off on the run alone in the night, he loved her.

No one could say where she had gone. Then a plump brown woman who had worked as her dresser in a nightclub said, "Miss Gabrielle, the day she gone missing, she told me she was going to the village of light."

"The what?"

"That ain't what she called it. She called it *village lumière,* but I be asking her what that meant, and she had this friend, this man called Mio, who says to me it is the light, it means light."

The brown woman tapped her finger to her forehead, indicating that this *lumière* was a serious matter.

"Then Miss Gabrielle up and told me it's got to do with where lepers are living, she says they got this light that shines in their wounds, and I won't never forget Miss Gabrielle saying that," she said, "because then, when I asked her if she knows what she is doing she says, 'I see, said the blind man,' and I said, just like I was back in school, 'I know, said the dumb man,' and she laughed and then she just up and gave me this last steady look and in a New York minute Miss Gabrielle, she is gone."

PART TWO

Gabon

A year later, at L'hotel Flanders en Libreville, Adam showered and put on a madras shirt, a light linen jacket, and went downstairs to the small Five-Star Kansas City Café, a bar attached to the hotel, open to the wind off the ocean. The wind was strong, the skies were clear. A tall young woman in a loose white pleated dress gathered and held at the waist by a rhinestone belt, stood alone at the bar. She had long, hennaed fingernails and her hair hung in narrow braids threaded with bone and ivory beads. Her long neck and high cheekbones gave her a severe, dark beauty. Adam was standing behind her. She caught his eye in the mirror, she held his eye, and, as she turned, he draped his arm around her shoulder and she smiled. Yes, she said, she would take a glass of champagne. Close by her on the bar, there was a small red, yellow, and green flag hanging from a stick in an empty water bottle, the black star of Africa at the heart of the flag. A lizard, skittering along the bar and up on to the water bottle, stretched its neck and slowly became an albino pink, the colour of the glass.

"Like it's disappearing," Adam said.

"We make our own perfections," the barman said.

"It's all in the eye," Adam said, winking at the woman.

"The most perfect thing I ever see," the barman said, running a small towel around the lip of a whiskey sour glass, "was a rat drink coconut water . . ."

"I'll have a whiskey . . ."

". . . and the rat, he go up the trunk of the tree and set out on the coconut and drill himself a hole to sip the water, so when he full up he turn around and whip the rest the water out of the coconut with his tail." The barman poured whiskey into Adam's glass. "So then he nibble the stem some and go in the hole where he don't drown 'cause enough of the water gone and he wiggle around until the stem break so the coconut fall and before the coconut hit the ground he leap out the hole and run off so the coconut break all to pieces without him, so he drink all his water full and take his elevator down, the rat being so smart a rat."

"I like your rat," she said.

"Some say this rat is now so smart-smart in politics," the barman said.

"Some speak too much," she said. "I mek good time instead."

"Where would you like to go?" Adam asked.

She led him away from the elegant ocean-front dining room, whose supper patrons were nearly all white businessmen travelling in central Africa, Cameroon and Congo and Gabon, into a dimly lit service corridor, past an empty convention room where flaccid party balloons still clung to the ceiling. He could hear the beating of a drum, a *boom boom* bass drum. She opened a heavy grey steel door. A steamy, smoke-filled eating hall was crowded with black men and women seated in rows at long tables. They were being served by village boys dressed in kelly-green lederhosen, carrying wide aluminum trays filled with jug beer and sauerkraut and sausages. A big hand-painted banner was slung across the front of the room, with blue and white letters – BAVARIAN BEER – and five paunchy, sweating white men wearing mountain-climbing boots, lederhosen, and alpine hats were playing polkas, with the crowd singing – "Roll Out the Barrel."

"It is joy," she said. "You like?"

"Love it," he said, "I should have brought my cameras."

"I am good girl for hire, yes I mek happy surprise."

She sat down and tucked a linen napkin into the bodice of her dress, beaming as she stared at the sauerkraut heaped on her plate. He knew he should eat something, but he ordered whiskeys with a beer chaser. And while the five bandsmen broke into another polka . . . *oompa pa oompa pa* . . . she ate and asked for more sausage and then led him onto the dance floor, pointing at the tuba, laughing, her dress clinging to her sweating, wet body, bouncing and leaping in circles, her shoulder strap slipping until her breast with its mulberry nipple was bare, and with stern childish glee, she cried, "Polka, polka . . ."

⟨⟩

Toronto

It snowed for three days. Schools were closed. The snow was banked nine feet high along the roads. Some roads were only footpaths. On the fourth day, he began to tunnel into the snow in front of the house, carving out a long hole shaped like a hook, and then several short dead ends off the hook, smoothing the walls so that they had an icy sheen and he could slip easily around turns. It kept on snowing. His mom said she had no idea how deeply he had wormed into the snow until she noticed the flashlight was missing. "It's pitch-black in there," he said, "and cold."

"You've tunnelled all that," she said, staring out the front window, the snow up to the windowsill. "Where in the world did you think you were? It could have collapsed on you, suffocated you, and we'd never have known you were in there."

"I prayed."

"I should say so."

"I thought I was in God's mind," and he showed her a map he'd drawn of God's mind: ה "I heard Harry in there singing."

"Harry never sings."

Adam had met the choirmaster, Harry O'Leary, under a weeping birch in the churchyard, a lean and wiry man with hooded sombre black eyes who paced like a quick long-legged bird, bobbing his black-haired head. Though he wore a pool-shooter's natty, black, straight-last shoes with tooled leather toecaps, he loved eighteenth-century trumpet voluntaries and the operas of Verdi, especially *La Traviata*, the death scene. On Saturday afternoons, he put on a banker's double-breasted blue serge suit and a pearl-grey Sammy Taft fedora and, with Gabrielle, his fourteen-year-old daughter, drove out to Woodbine racetrack to sit at a table with a tablecloth in the Turf Club and have a prime rib of beef lunch from the buffet and bet on the thoroughbred horses. "A horseman under whatever his hat," he told the choirboys, laughing easily, "is your close cousin to a gentleman."

His daughter, Gabrielle, had black hair, too, but her eyes, so wide open with what seemed to be guileless expectation, the pale blue pupils flecked with gold, absorbed all the light in a room. "She's got the strangest eyes," Web told Adam, "you look into them and it's like you're being invited to look into forever."

On Saturday mornings, when the church was empty, she would sit in one of the choir stalls to listen to Harry, and then, when he was finished playing Bach or Gounod, he would stand up and bow to her from across the altar and blow her a kiss and she would cover her face with her hands (Adam had thought she was being shy but years later he learned that she hated that kiss) and then she would stand up, too, beautiful in the stained-glass morning light. Adam remembered how her slit skirt would ride high on her thigh because she had always worn high heels so that she could go to the races with her dad.

Wanting to know what walking in high heels was like, Adam tried stepping into his mother's shoes, but he pitched forward, hitting his head on the wall. He had seen that girls who were short and heavy pitched forward, too, as they walked in heels, but if they had long and slender legs like Gabrielle, when they put on high heels, their legs not only seemed to be longer, but they stopped being girls; they walked with a gait, the gait of a grown woman. *Put on your high heel sneakers*, he'd heard his father sing, *get your wig-hat on your head*. Because he could see that grown women liked grown-up men, and often kissed them, when he walked beside his father or Harry, he tried hard to walk with the gait of a man. When Harry said to him one Saturday morning, "That girl of mine, I love her legs," Adam stretched his stride, trying to stay a little ahead of Harry.

In Harry's choir, Adam stood beside a white-haired boy, Arthur Copter, and he and Arthur and the other boys learned what a clef was and what treble was and they learned to sing medieval chant and the *Regina Coeli* and *Agnus Dei* and *Panis Angelicus*. Then Arthur, who had white eyelashes and pink eyes, left the choir. "He read all the words backwards," Harry said. "He was going backwards when we were going frontwards. His brain was all switched around."

The white-haired boy was chosen by Father Zale to play the Christ in a huge crèche at Christmas. Adam laughed at the overgrown, angelically dressed Arthur Copter nesting his head in the lap of a huge painted papier mââché Virgin. Father Zale cuffed Adam on the ear and took him outside and left him in the snow under the leafless weeping birch. "You stand out here until you switch your brain around, too, until you learn not to laugh at some folks who sing just to keep from screaming or some folks who scream because they can't sing." Adam stood in the snow. His shoes got very wet, his feet, cold. He began to scream at the top of his voice, "EEeeaaa," letting his voice slowly fall. A passing woman asked, "What're you doing?"

"I'm trying to learn how to scream backwards," he said.

"Are you in pain?"

"No. I'm wet. And I have to stand here."

"Nonsense. Why are you doing this to yourself? You're free to go."

"Who are you?"

"Nobody. But I'm telling you you can go."

He went.

He went back to the choir room where he listened to Harry explain that there were several kinds of music – there was choral music and band music and Tin Pan Alley music and Beethoven music – "Da da da Dum" – and then there was opera, and the greatest composer of all operas was a man called Verdi, whose name, he told them, had actually been made up. It was, he said, a cry for freedom, VERDI being graffiti that had been written on all the town walls of Italy by men who were nobodies, by ordinary men – and VERDI meant Victor Emmanuel Re d'Italia – a "cry for freedom that still lurks in a dark gateway." That's the way Harry had said it. "In a dark gateway." None of the boys knew what gateway he was talking about. Adam said that he thought freedom, then, was being able to go backwards through a dark gateway when everybody else was going frontwards.

"That's what my father calls pigheaded," one of the boys said.

"That's 'cause your father's a porker," another boy said.

"Yeah?"

"Yeah. A fatty who smokes a big cigar."

"Yeah?"

"I'll beat your fuckin' brains in."

"Yeah?"

Harry was at the chalkboard paying no attention. He was writing VERDI just below the treble line for *Regina Coeli*.

Adam let out a high-pitched scream – "EEEEEEEaaaa" – the scream collapsing backwards in on itself.

Harry smacked him on the back of the head but then cried: "yeeeAAAAAA."

"EEEEEEEaaaa, yeeeAAAAAA," they cried together, trying to harmonize.

And they began to laugh.

Father Zale ran into the room, his hands in the air against their cry, and then he made a tight little sign of the cross, but he said nothing.

The other boys began to scream, too. They screamed till they were hoarse. Then they stopped and one of the boys said, "Jesus, how mental can you get?" They went home.

On Sunday morning in the sacristy, Father Zale dropped a sheath of embroidered green silk over his shoulders, and angular lanky serving boys, their soutanes too short, followed him onto the altar, bowing toward Harry, who was seated on the oak bench behind the organ. Harry released the ivory-headed stops and shuffled his feet over the pedals. "All together now," he called across the altar to the choir. "B-flat." The *Kyrie* by Gounod. "We got Gounod by the short hairs," the boy beside Adam said, a doctor's son who had taken off his shoes for a quarter in the schoolyard, showing the boys his webbed toes and, after he had touched the toes, Adam had gone home and asked his mom why there were webbed feet.

She had said, "It's where we come from."

"What d'you mean?"

Smoking cigarettes in the afternoon in front of her mirror, she lit match after match, one from the other, burning them in the ashtray, staring into the flame.

"We come out of the water. We were all webbed things once. And the fire's where we're going."

He brought her a glass of cold water and said, "No, we're not."

"Oh yes, we are," she said, and laughed quietly.

❧

Gabon

The next morning, a mist rose from the shore, an acrid, musty smell rising from the elephant grass. Black-and-yellow birds planed from the treetops. Though he hadn't opened his eyes, heavy from too much whiskey, the morning air had the close clingy feel of those summer days of heat lightning back home, lulling days, and he tossed, half-asleep, *naked legs catching the light, your arms thrown back, kisses all over your breasts and belly. The room recedes and then explodes in the salt warmth of your flesh, the salt of your love, your breath against my neck* and then he smelled cigarette smoke and as he opened his eyes he said, "Mother," but saw that the black girl from the Polka hall, who had showered, was standing naked by the open window.

"How come you're smoking, you weren't smoking last night?"

She took a deep satisfied drag on a Gitane.

"The only woman I know who smokes like you, first thing in the morning, is my mother."

"Your mother then must be beautiful."

"A movie star, on the side of the angels."

"De blek women in movies canna not smoke, you never see dem do, but when I wish to, I do so."

"Maybe you're in your own movie," he said, laughing, rubbing the sleep out of his eyes. "Or maybe I'm in mine."

"No, I not think so, no."

The shower water had beaded into opals of light on her dark skin (the first time he'd slept with a black girl, she'd said, "Turn on the light, man, so's I can see you," and she'd run her long finger across his belly and his rib cage, "You got no shadow in your skin, man . . . White folk is like pork fat, all pork fat and no meat. You's scary in a sorta sweet way, like I got a real live ghost in me when you're in me."), and she picked up one of his cameras and said, "How do you have so much cameras?"

"I take pictures. Wherever there's killing I take pictures."

"You tek my picture?"

"If you want me to."

"No. Picture no good. You steal me inside."

"I wouldn't steal you," he said, remembering all the pictures he had taken of Gabrielle in Puerto Rico, the dozen or more rolls of film he'd taken and never developed, a little afraid that if he was forced to see her as the camera eye had seen her, then she might be lost to him, stolen – his dream that he'd held in his heart through all the years, back to their being youngsters together, might disappear as inexplicably as she had disappeared from her home nine years earlier, and now had disappeared from their room in Puerto Rico, leaving him while he'd been asleep.

"You tek me maybe when I sleep?" the black girl asked suspiciously.

"No."

"Good. So why you tek pictures?"

"It's what I do."

"Here?"

"No, in the bush."

"So bad in de bush now, big fighting."

"I'm going to the leper camps."

"It no good to see sick people too many," she said, lighting another cigarette.

"It's a woman I love, that's all. She's called Gabrielle."

"She sick?"

"Who knows . . ."

"And you love?"

She stepped into her high heels and stood brazenly with her hands on her hips. She had a young girl's pointed breasts.

"Yes, very much. It's almost a year since I've seen her."

"Too long time."

"Maybe."

"I tank you love me, too."

"A little."

"Good. I be your today girl for sunshine."

"My mother," he said, laughing and taking her hand, "she told me to never step on sunlight . . ."

"Why?"

"She said I'd break my heart."

On the outskirts of Libreville, Adam waited as a rusting diesel engine hauling an empty flatcar shunted onto a railway bridge over a river, the engine rolling to the centre where it stopped, suspended in silence. The rough logging road on the other side of the river had been corded and crimped by rainwater. As Adam walked across the bridge, carrying his cameras and a garment bag, he had the strange feeling that he, too, was suspended, that he was watching himself take a walk, a long steady walk out of nowhere so that he could at last end up somewhere in a room again with Gabrielle, the two of them together lying in a bed listening to night rain on the roof of a small hotel just as they had done outside of Ponce where she had said, "You've always been like soft night rain to me, this kind of ache I have between my ribs, this sweet ache," and she had let out a cry, lifting her hips off the bed, her eyes full of tears, saying that he had to understand, "Yes," he had to understand that no matter how deep into her own darkness she might sink, there, in that room, with him deep inside her, she, too, had felt – just like he'd said – a rush of light, feeling so happy that she had reached up, into the night, and he had reached up, too, to touch hands, and like a little girl she had cried, "London bridges all fall down," and he had said, "But we can't fall, we're already in bed."

But then, as of the next morning, she was gone, leaving behind only a pair of shoes.

With a red slingback shoe in each hand, he had stood in the room, shaking as if he had a chill, a fever, talking out

loud to himself, bewildered and not just because of the breaking off, without even a word, of their eight nights of intimacy,
their touching of each other – but because of the breaking off
of their shared privacies, the open giving of their deepest
inner spaces – the way she had whispered to him as he had
looked up at her from between her legs, "You have swallowed my soul, you swallowed my sins."

He had drunk himself to sleep on bourbon, shouting in
his sleep, "You're not leaving me here on the front porch of
the dead." He had wakened from his fitful sleep and tried to
piece together every conversation they'd had, tried to get
hold of what had gone wrong when it was clear to him that
everything between them had been so right. He knew that
in his exuberance he often said sardonic and wounding
things, but he could remember only her joy, her ease with
herself increasing from day to day, and those eyes that
always welcomed him, that haunted him. He let out an exasperated cry, EEEEEEEaaaa.

"Yes, she had wondering eyes, you never forget those
eyes," the *patron* at the hotel had agreed, shrugging helplessly, trying to sound helpful. Humiliated but not caring,
Adam had told the *patron* that he was going to find her, "No
question," and – after questioning and probing, deepening
his humiliation, even his sense of insult – he had in fact
found out that this, the road to Lambaréné, was the road
that she had disappeared down, this road that he was following through a muddle of shacks, an old logging road

that seemed like a half-healed scar in a wall of branches, broad leaves, boughs, vines – and beyond the road – all he could see was towering trees that had delicate umbrella tops like monstrous parsley stalks, a vast tangled weight of green with paths and trails that only went deeper into the immensity of the forest, into what seemed to be endlessly the same.

Standing on the shoulder of the road in a shudder of panic, he took a deep breath. "None," he said. "None." He was standing absolutely still. "There's no perspective." He realized that he was talking out loud again to himself. He didn't care. "You can swallow your voice, but you've got to have a point of view. Nowhere's everywhere here. You've got to have an angle, an angle on the angles, some perspective. Without that, mother, we're lost . . ." He didn't know why he thought his mother was listening to him, sitting in front of a mirror, building little fires to herself wherever she was. He held his finger down on his camera's trigger. He began to turn in a circle . . . *click, click, click, click, click.* After a complete turn, he found himself making a sign of the cross with the camera in hand, remembering how he had given Gabrielle a sudden blessing, *click, click, click,* as she had sat bare-breasted in the hotel courtyard, crossing the air in front of her until the camera had *clicked* empty, the camera eye, he had told her as he reloaded, being the only eye that he felt he could trust because it was the eye that had always let him know where he'd been after he'd been there, so that he could say in his darkroom, "I saw that, yes, I was there, right there, because there it is, you can see it, too.

Gabrielle, who had been sipping cold white wine as he'd shot her, had asked, "Do you think I'm really here?"

"You're here – for Christ sake, where else could you be?"

She had said, "Remember in the movies when we were kids, how there was this invisible man? He would just appear and do what he had to do so that he could step into the future, he had this absolute freedom, he could come, he could disappear like there was nothing to it, *click click click click,* still and all, I don't think it can be such a good thing to take so many pictures of me, it's kind of spooky," but he had continued to circle her *click* focusing on her – astonished by her stillness – using up roll after roll of film.

After she had gone, he had stood in their room, staring at those rolls, feeling – not insulted, he'd decided – but betrayed. He had not taken the rolls to a darkroom, he had not wanted to see what he had shot. Because he wanted to trust something deeper. He wanted to trust himself. Since then, he'd seen her every day in his head, he had talked to her, she was there in his mind's eye, and sometimes he talked to her out loud, as he was now, coming to the end of the logging road where he looked up to see two albinos standing down in a ditch holding hands. They were smiling at him because they had heard him say: "I should have seen what was coming, the way you went on about those night-blooming flowers." After he got to the top of the logging grade on the northeast truck route, he looked back to make sure that the albinos' flat noses and pink wool hair had not been an apparition, while he said *yes* and kept talking to Gabrielle, *yes*, so that she was there for him, *I told you yes*, though he could no longer see the albinos.

With red dust from the logging road all over his hair and his clothes, he came into a small town of twisting market streets, shed-like shops and shacks and a Budget rent-a-car depot that was an old Silver Cloud touring trailer that had been mounted on concrete blocks, the tires taken off. Six Mercedes 300s were parked to one side of the Silver Cloud in a small lot. It was late afternoon and the street was crowded with men dressed in perma-press slacks and *galibayas*, sneakers and rubber sandals.

A big man who had the limp little legs of a six-year-old was seated in a box mounted on small steel wheels. With his gloved fist, he was pushing himself across the road, just ahead of Adam, toward the Silver Cloud. There, the Budget man, a man whose head, except for a tuft of top hair, was shaved, sat primly behind an old sewing machine. He was surrounded by women who were down on their haunches under black umbrellas. One was smoking a pipe the size of her thumb. The machine was his desk, they were his wives.

Adam rented a Mercedes 300 from the Budget man, who meticulously filled out several carbon-copied forms. When Adam said he wasn't leaving the town till the next morning, the man sighed and said, "Today then is lost. Of course, tomorrow is perhaps a possibility."

A stray drunken soldier in a greatcoat with one sole slapping loose on his boot whistled and hooted at a passing car. The Budget man, hardly looking up, said, "He will be dead by tomorrow."

As dusk fell, pinheads of light appeared out of the dark green of the hillside forest, pinheads that became a huge electric cross until thunderclouds moved through the valley and in their wake came a downpour so heavy that the town was flooded in rain, the cross darkened by rain and mist.

Toronto

"I'm a dancing woman," his mom said, "all good women are dancing women. The night I met your daddy I was dancing on a table in a restaurant. Isn't that funny? For a lady? We danced and sang songs just like your mom sings songs now."

She had taught Adam to sing nursery songs and jingle songs and then she had taught him to sing sad songs that she could dance to with gaiety while holding him in her arms. "The blues are what give you a little smile when you're all alone, and your mother's been alone too much . . . but I have my nights to remember . . . and your memories of yourself are what keep you going, they keep you alive in your mind, and that's what love is . . . the memory I hold of your daddy in my head is how I know I still love him, and since I've got lots of strong memories then I've got lots of love for him when he comes home . . ."

She lit her little matchbook fires, "Fires so our own personal angels don't lose their way in the night, you know, fires like they do in the movies for airplanes who are landing at night in the jungle," and she taught Adam songs he didn't understand:

> *On a seven hours*
> *On the seventh day*
> *On the seventh month*
> *The seven doctors say*
> *He was born for good luck . . .*

She also taught him another song:

> *We're poor little lambs, who have lost our way,*
> *Baa, baa, baa . . .*
> *Gentlemen songsters off on a spree*
> *Doomed from here to eternity,*
> *Lord have mercy on such as we,*
> *Baa, baa, baa . . .*

"My little lamb, my doomed gentleman songster," she said, sitting with him on the back porch, holding him close. Sometimes she told him about the doomed in their own family, especially a cousin, Christina Waters, a young nurse who had fallen in love with a man in Quebec City. She had lived with the man for a year, speaking only French, but then she had come home to her mother who had bullied her into staying home. And after she had submitted to her mother she had wakened one morning unable to speak, her tongue swollen, dumbmouthed, and she'd sat in a daze as her mother fed and nursed her for two years. But her mother had assured everybody that her love, her special mother's love, would bring her daughter back to talking. And her daughter did in fact wake up on a summer morning and she did begin to speak, but she spoke only in French, her tongue being tied in English, and she never spoke to her mother in English again, but she cursed her mother in French and went back to live with her man and die in Quebec.

Florence also told Adam that she had not only seen her cousin's tomb, the tombstone being a tall, wind-pocked stone angel wrapped in its own wings, but, she said, as they sat on the back porch looking at the row of garage roofs, "One morning, I saw her, and I goddamn well see her a lot, that same angel standing on the peak of that roof right over there. The angel was weeping and moving her lips, like she was telling me a message. And I said to her, 'Are you talking to me, are you talking to me from God?' and that angel there, she shook her head and said, 'No, God's up in heaven, I'm right here in limbo with you.'"

And Florence said she'd asked the angel, "Are you gonna keep all the evil out there away from me?"

"*Honi soit qui mal y pense.*"

At school, when he'd talked to his spinster teachers about angels they gently touched his cheek as if they'd just remembered something ("There was a child once ..."). Telling them that he'd seen a sign outside the schoolroom window that said ADANAC MIRRORS, he'd asked, "What does that mean?" and Miss Hamlin had told him, "That's the country spelled backwards. We live in Adanac country." Then she'd told him to sit on her lap. She was in charge of collections for the African missions, in charge of canned goods and used baby clothes, and Adam, getting on to her lap, had knocked over several cartons of canned soup and the cans had rolled and banged down the school stairs.

"You've bruised all that food," a nun yelled.

"How can you bruise soup?" he asked.

"Don't be so smart. You'll get a good strapping."

It was nuns, not the priests, who punished them. They were dour women who gave off the same sour smell that winter frost gives off as it eases out of the springtime earth. When Sister St. Alban, her chin chafed by a starched wimple, strapped Adam she made him wet his hands with snow. The water, she said, would sharpen the pain.

"Saint Sebastian didn't cry," she said. "In his serene acceptance of pain we are able to discover what love is."

His father told him that anybody who found love in pain was demented. And dangerous, but Adam had been told already by his teachers that he had to read and study the lives of the saints and martyrs; his teachers showed him several Passionals, collections of the mutilations of martyrs; he had been told how the Indians, the Hurons who had lived just a little to the north of Toronto, had picked and plucked the broiled flesh from Father Brébeuf's living broiled bones with clam shells. "They were at war, fighting for our souls there in the bush. Men and women who went victoriously to their deaths." There was a picture of Brébeuf in the school hall, and also a tinted engraving of the lean muscled Sebastian who was tied to a pole. He had long arrows in his thighs, his loincloth was loose, he was staring ecstatically at a gold star. "It is the look of a saint who has seen God. Remember that look." Adam wondered if there had been a tortured martyr for each of those gold stars on the church ceiling. All of them approved by nuns, standing first in their class. Sister St. Alban collected drawings of these martyrs and made her students copy their agonies. She liked detail. Her favourite word was blood: the Blood of the Lamb. One day, she gave Adam a gold star and a prize for drawing. He had drawn Saint Eulalia.

Years later, he read a poem about Saint Eulalia:

> For the breasts of Eulalia
> the consul demands a platter.
> A jet of green veins
> Bursts from her throat.
> Her sex trembles, disarrayed
> like a bird in a thicket.

The prize was a tennis racquet that she said she had played with as a girl, given to her by her father. It had all the strings broken. "You get your own father to fix the strings," she said. "That's what fathers are for."

Adam brought the racquet home and stood it up in his bedroom window and looked through the strings at the clouds, and then, with the racquet close to his face, he looked at his father and said, "You're coming apart." His father laughed. "That's right," he said. "People are always coming unstrung. I'm unstrung, your mother's unstrung, God knows she's unstrung, she's talking to angels up on the garage roofs."

Adam loved the garage roofs, the slopes and sharp angles and tarred and pebbled flats and the tin gullies and rain-gutters. Often after school, he sat on an asphalt roof and stared at the glare of the sun against his own bedroom window. His room seemed on fire. He told his mother about the fire. His mother warned him: "It's the fire next time." But she didn't seem to think that they'd all be burned to a dead crisp. She said no, they'd all be purified, one by one. Like her cousin. The one up on the roof. "Purification For The Nation – The United Sodality Hour," she cried, marching around the breakfast table at eight in the morning. Web was away and – awake since six – she had been drinking. Adam didn't understand purification by fire, but he understood her loneliness. Lonely himself, he liked to sit in a roof gully with a deck of Bicycle playing cards that his father had given him, where he played solitaire. "If the Queen of Spades comes up too soon you always lose," his father had told him. "We've all got a Queen of Spades in our lives." With Gabrielle, "My Queen of Hearts," he played "pick-a-high-card" to see who would take off their clothes first. And in the spring, when the maple trees went to seed – their lime-yellow propellers spinning through the air – that was when he had peeled the seed-pod propellers apart and she'd worn the sticky pods on her nose, and eagerly, with her clothes off, he had put the seed pods all over her body and she had stood with her legs apart and said to him, "Well, look at this."

"But you've got nothing there," he said.

"My mother warned me every boy wants what's there," she said.

"Well, look at this," and he showed her his hard-on, but she laughed and didn't seem impressed at all as they lay down side-by-side to watch squirrels on the run in the trees.

"My father told me," Gabrielle said, taking hold of his cock, "that squirrels are only rats who look good because they live in the trees."

Down below, a couple of men who thought they were alone stood in the dark in an empty garage. They were hiding, too, and then one said, "I got shit-faced drunk." Adam knew it was Al, the Acme Farmers milkman. Al had round wet eyes. "Vaseline eyes," his mother said. Some older boys sometimes slept overnight with Al and they whispered about Al kissing them and how he gave them cases of milk to take home to their families.

After Grandfather Waters had died, mom had given Adam the dead man's long johns, the dead man's underwear. Adam had put them on but instead of feeling warm he'd grown cold and he'd pulled them off and had secretly handed them over to Al because Al had said his legs were cold in the wintertime. Adam had seen the long johns drying one afternoon on a laundry line, flying in the wind, the cod-flap open, empty, and the emptiness seemed somehow to be an insult to his grandfather. Adam had stolen them from the laundry line and hidden them in his father's dresser drawer. He'd stolen them, not just because of his grandfather but because he also loved flying things. He loved his mother's angels (though he couldn't see them), he liked flying kites from the garage roofs. And balloons. He liked blowing them up and batting them in the air. And then blowing them up by touching them with fire from his mother's matches.

One hot April day, he brought fistfuls of balloons to his high school and the other students blew them up while a nun wrote on the blackboard ... THE EXPLORERS OF THE NEW WORLD – PONCE DE LEON ... and when she turned around, the air over their heads was filled with balls of colour being bounced back and forth. She stood stricken. She ran to all the windows, throwing them open, and then, in complete disarray, she waded into the balloons, trying to gather them toward the windows, trying to clear the air, batting at them, but she made them carom away from her until all the students were laughing and she fled from the room.

Her name, as it happened, was Sister Eulalia.

After recovering from her Day of the Balloons, Sister Eulalia had a slight tremor in her right hand. She clasped her hands to keep her right hand still as she told them about Ponce de Leon, a short man, she said, a soldier in a floppy hat. She showed him to Adam. He saw Ponce de Leon standing in a book beside a drawing of a waterspout that looked like a giant celery stalk. "Youth," Sister Eulalia said, "Ponce wanted his youth back." She touched Adam's cheek with the back of her trembling hand. But, "More important," she said, "Ponce had had the courage to come clanking across the sea in an iron suit, sitting down on a poop deck under an umbrella, scowling over old scouting maps of islands and rivers lined with gold pebbles," and, she said, Ponce had taught himself how to read the stars to make the crossing. Adam told all this to Web, who agreed. He told Adam that what was wonderful about Ponce was that he had loved the hills of his own illusions. Adam hadn't quite known what that meant but Web liked it so much that he wrote it down in his book. "He sailed the ocean that men full of good sense and fear said was flat, that men said he'd fall off of, but he sailed into the abyss anyway and disappeared into his illusions."

The next day, Adam asked his mom, "Did you ever worry you were going to disappear?"

"We're all going to disappear."

"I don't mean die. I mean disappear."

"Where to?"

"I don't know."

He was standing in front of a mirror. There was another full-length mirror on an open closet door behind him. He could see tens of images of himself down endless oblongs of reflected light.

"It's like I'm a hundred me's," he said.

"Maybe they're just shadows," she said, hugging him.

"I've got no shadow in the mirror."

"Sure you do, I'm your shadow."

"You're my mom."

"And I'll always be with you in the mirror, especially when you can't see me. I'm your guardian angel."

Gabon

Late that night, the town's only hotel was surrounded by drunken government soldiers. Their tattered greatcoats had been made for the Polish army for Polish winters. On Adam's floor in the hotel, in the murky half-light, several doors to rooms were ajar. Single men sat with their backs to the wall, some in stringy undershirts, some having a last cigar before bed, blue smoke layering the rooms, men who – to Adam's eye – seemed framed and held by their doorways, lonely men posing like the prostitutes he had seen in Hamburg, women sitting in the windows of whorehouses who, he thought, had the same brazen, defiant yet sullen loneliness in their eyes that he'd seen in the eyes of three men he had photographed just before they had been shot. The three had been shot for terrorism in a stony field by two politicians who – as cabinet-ministers-become-assassins – had killed their own prime minister and then, after they had seized power, they held public executions and press conferences to complain about the collapse of the moral order in their country.

"What are ya, a peeping Tom?" one of the single men sitting alone in his room called out to Adam.

Adam's room was so shabby and desolate he opened his camera case and set up a little collapsible aluminum tripod stand at the foot of his bed, positioned a Polaroid camera on it, set the timer and lay down with his hands linked behind his head and took his own picture. "There," he said, "there you are," but watching for his face to emerge out of the whiteness of the Polaroid paper he saw instead Gabrielle's face, and the scar on her hip from the scalding water, and the cold water in the stone bath on the morning when they had assured each other that they were immune to whatever was lurking outside their door in the dark empty corridor of the small hotel. "That's the dark inside of God's mind," he'd said. "I tunnelled in there when I was a kid." They had joked about the darkness of God's mind, and the world that He had made in His image, because, she said, "When I'm with you I feel like a child who has caught hold of the sunlight."

That was exactly how he had felt on the night he'd seen her for the first time in nine years, *like a child who has caught hold of sunlight* as he, standing idly in the lobby of the Flamboyan Casino, had seen her, a long-legged beautiful woman wearing a white silk blouse covered with small red stars. She had made her way through a crowd of conventioneers on the arm of a tall lean man whose left hand was encased in a tight shiny black leather glove. They strode between the singers and out through the lobby.

Adam, taken aback, had cried, "It's Gabrielle, it's you."

The man with the black hand had led her through the lobby's revolving glass doors and hurried down the hotel steps to the crowded street where they had got into a waiting silver-grey Mercedes. Adam had shouted, "Gabrielle," as the sedan had pulled away from the curb.

Head cocked, incredulous, mouth open, he rode the elevator to his room where he opened the ocean-front sliding doors and spread a terrycloth beach towel over a balcony lounge chair.

Slowly, he took off all his clothes, folding them, and lay down on the chair, letting the night wind blow on his bare skin as he stared out into the moonlit spray that shrouded the dark water, seeing Gabrielle's long legs and remembering the perfectly round small black mole on her breast beside her nipple, her "beauty mark," she'd called the mole, and her eyes – always so open in seemingly startled wonder, and behind the wonder, a sadness – and he startled himself by beginning to laugh a quiet, satisfied laughter, a laughter at nothing, satisfied because, as he had told his father, he had come to believe that every day from hour to hour there were doors that appeared and from behind the doors, without warning – whether in malice or sorrow or longing – a hand would be offered, a word said, and you either embraced the moment or you did not, you were either willing to be lucky or not, and suddenly, out of nowhere on this night, incredibly, there was Gabrielle – his childhood love, the woman he'd loved as a young man – stepping out of the elevator door not as an apparition but as herself, and he broke into laughter again, a rollicking laughter as he closed his eyes, hearing against the breaking of the waves in the dark how all the talk back home nine years earlier – before she had run away to New York – had been about the photograph of her mother on the front page of the newspaper. Mrs. O'Leary had killed herself. She had checked into the Park Plaza Hotel where she'd had a whiskey sour with two curators from the Royal Ontario Museum, men she had just met at the outdoor bar of the roof garden café. Then, bidding them goodbye, she had jumped from the roof garden and plunged seventeen floors to her death.

"Astonishing," one of the curators had told the press. "Such a crying shame."

"She knew all about our Chinese collection," the other curator said.

Later, the police said that Gabrielle had taken the train to Buffalo; they had tracked her to a train that crossed the border at the Peace Bridge, and then she had gone on to

New York. She had never written, she had not called. Not that anyone knew. Not for the past nine years. Parishioners had felt sorry for Harry. Adam still felt sorry for himself.

"I guess she's hiding out," Father Zale had said.

"From what?"

"Nothing," said the police, who had refused to treat her as a missing person. "Her mother killed herself, she went away. She's old enough. She's eighteen. She's allowed."

Only Harry, Adam, and his mother had stood at the graveside for Mrs. O'Leary's burial, along with three small boys in red soutanes who had been hired to sing from Mozart and Verdi. Harry had slumped into Father Zale's arms. The priest had said, "There's a lesson in this," but he never did say what it was.

Adam had let a grey speckled stone fall into the hole, the stone bouncing off the box with a loud *clunk*. "Don't wake the dead," his mother had said. "Mrs. O'Leary may come back and tell us things we don't want to know."

❦

Lying on his bed in the shabby hotel room, remembering the sound of that *clunk*, and wondering what story Mrs. O'Leary might have to tell, he heard footsteps in the corridor and then a knock on the door.

"Who's that?"

"Police, open the door."

They were in their thirties and casually dressed. One, with a moustache and a plump belly, stepped back, smiling, as if his presence were a mistake. The other, self-assured, taut, wearing dust-pink jeans, spoke as if his jaw was locked at the latch. He took Adam's passport and said, "You're under arrest."

"You're kidding," Adam said, thinking with sudden dread and then mordant amusement, *Why do I do shit like this to myself?* At the police station, the cop in the pink jeans said to the desk sergeant, "Do what you want with him." After a quick pat-search, the desk sergeant said, "We take your two cameras. And your money. You're carrying a lot of money." As Adam was about to object, the sergeant punched Adam on the breastbone. Then he led him into a dank, damp yard, to the end of the yard, to a high plastered wall with high narrow doors set into the floodlit wall.

"Fucking upright coffins," Adam thought as he was shoved through one of the steel mesh doors. "Upright coffins all over the world." The concrete block cell had small oblong overhead open windows, and a cold damp wind blew through the cell. The walls were painted a glossy black. The toilet was an open hole. The walls were covered with notes scratched into the paint: a drawn skull, a dagger, and Tell Them What They Want To Know – They'll Find Out Anyway. The wind picked up the reek of shit along the floor. Kneeling with his cheek to the concrete floor, he found himself humming the "Dance of the Sugar Plum Fairies," and he remembered the acrid smell of dust in his mother's living-room rug when, as a child, he had marched tin soldiers across the floral patterns. He'd found a sugar plum coated with dust caught in a corner behind grandfather's chair, grandfather dead of an explosion of blood in his brain, BLOOD, his winter underwear with the cod-flap open still hidden at the back of Web's dresser drawer. What did it mean? Adam wondered, *Blood of the Lamb*, to remember sugar plums and tin soldiers as he lay down on a thin, foam rubber pallet on the concrete floor, a pallet sour from puke and the sweat of other frightened men.

Toronto

Adam's high school, a four-storey stone mansion on the bluffs by the lake, had been the first insane asylum in the country. For decades it had remained the parish madhouse, but then, the bishop had made the mansion into a school for boys. There was a small room on top of the mansion's mansard roof, a room with windows on all sides and a widow's walk. Sometimes old Father Zale would sit alone in the light-filled room, staring out over the water where the long tankers loaded with grain moved slowly past a spit of land, the Eastern Gap, to the harbour. In the autumn, before the first snow, a boy was always chosen to chisel and scrape the year's pigeon lime from the slate roof of the little room, his feet wedged into the rain-gutter, his head bobbing against the blue sky.

It was Father Zale who said, "The bird is the symbol of the soul, the lime is the stain we leave in time," and Adam remembered old Father Zale writing on the blackboard,

$$\text{if } x = y = 1$$
$$\text{then } x^2 - y^2 = x^2 - xy$$
$$\cancel{(x - y)} (x + y) = x\cancel{(x - y)}$$
$$[x + y] = x$$
$$x + y = x$$
$$x + 1 = 1$$
$$2 = 1$$

and then turning to the class he said, "There you are – there's life. What's absolutely not true is proven to be true, and until you understand how to find out where the mistake is, and live with it, you understand nothing."

PART THREE

Gabon

In Cairo, sitting beside a hotel Day-Glo blue swimming pool waiting for a telephone call from a Revolutionary Council in Amman, he realized he'd been caught for weeks in one of those pockets of lethargy that he had learned to put up with as a photojournalist, pockets of inaction between surges of energy and exhilaration, when he tried to feel busy by being busy at doing nothing.

He had taken his Nikon X30 apart, cleaning it, blowing away any dust, polishing the parts over and over again, settling into a lethargic stillness as he watched Swedish airline flight attendants sun themselves as they read John Grisham novels. "The blonde reading the bland," he'd said sourly to Eric Carrier, an Egyptian Jew who was the correspondent for *Le Monde*, and Carrier had smiled and said, "Frankly, I find them spellbinding . . . I look into those pale blue eyes and I know that in those eyes there is the light that is in the abyss. It fills me with hope." Adam had laughed, had thought of taking their picture, but instead he ordered champagne cocktails for the women at poolside, waving to them gallantly.

"Make it pink champagne," one of the women cried.

That same afternoon, the sight of the black gull sails of the ancient boats on the Nile had filled him with melancholy, a yearning. The Black Queen! He had known for months that Gabrielle was deep in Gabon, and he had known that he was going to go after her. But he had stalled, he had grown to feel not just betrayed but deeply wronged, and he had begun to enjoy feeling wronged, feeling the poignancy of grief over what had been lost as he looked back into the eye of recollection through the amber of single malt scotch. But then, sitting there beside the swimming pool, waiting, doltish in the afternoon, watching the blond flight attendants drink pink champagne, for the first time in his life he found himself to be lonely in his own company.

He had booked a flight to the west coast, to Libreville, and now he found himself under arrest in the interior, wakened in the morning to a cold gruel, and bullied at high noon by guards who led him out of his cell into a sunless, mildewed courtyard of twenty-foot-high walls. They then went through three sets of steel doors to a small barracks, and upstairs to be confronted by a colonel who had olive-brown skin tight on the bone, the skin of a polished gourd. He was wearing smoked glasses. He said, "You have the right to say nothing if you want to say nothing. But nothing's not very interesting."

"What would you like to know?"

"I would, of course, like to know everything," he said with a broad smile, "but we shall be considerate, we shall wait."

The colonel seated Adam on a wooden stool by the window. "We shall talk about war," he said, again smiling broadly. "I am a student of war, you are a photographer, are you not? Let us talk. Why not?"

Below the window, Adam could see a brick hut with an open oven. The hut faced a graveyard, a path running through the graveyard with wooden markers on either side and two girls who were selling bread at a stand that they had set up on the path, the path ending in a swamp where several men tended grass fires. The grave mounds were well-kept, the earth raked, and there were strange icons on the mounds, a small red sports timer's clock, a licence plate – TJ 199-491 – jars with dried roots tied to them, an empty milk bottle.

The colonel, taking off his cap and putting his sidearm – a Glock .9 – on his desk, as if he and Adam were taking a pause on a stifling afternoon for a casual chat, said that first of all, despite what Adam might expect, he wasn't himself, as a soldier, as interested in the political miscalculations that caused wars as he was in how the technology of killing had got into the way men talked to each other about war.

"Yes? Why not? Yes!" he said, reaching toward Adam.

Incredulous, Adam nodded but said nothing.

"And this was even more true, you may remember," the colonel said, "at the time of the archers and their longbows, those archers who were fighting for someone like Henry the Fifth." He smiled, as if Henry the king were a casual friend, too. "Those archers, they could fire twelve arrows a minute.

Fantastic. Five thousand archers turning the sky into a blue whispering shroud of sixty thousand arrows a minute. That's more indiscriminate than the machine gun ever was, and as a killer, more silent, more anonymous, which is why" – and he paused because two very tall, ebony-skinned men, wearing long white dashikis tied at the waist with black and red cord, had come into the office, bowing their heads, one extending his hand, making it clear that the colonel should continue – "which is why, even going into the Vietnam War, crossbows were still being used by assassins, a silent strike from a long way off of the arrow through the throat which brought to an end" – and he bobbed his head eagerly at Adam and the two men – "to the quarrel, yes, and why not? Why not an end to your particular quarrel, which is where, I can tell you, the word comes from, *quarrel*, from the medieval *quarel* which takes its root, gentlemen, in the medieval Latin *quadrellus*, which is, in fact, the square-headed arrow of the crossbow. And when the killing was done and the quarrel was over, what the archer did was raise his two fingers to make a sign, to himself, as you do to yourself, and to the crowds, as I now make a sign to you, here in this office – like an ancient archer, the sign of your two gripping fingers on either side of the arrow as it was released from the string, the V," he cried triumphantly, raising both arms, "the V, gentlemen, like Churchill himself, I give you victory."

The two unsmiling tall black men in dashikis allowed a moment's silence as the colonel stood with his arms upraised. Then they took their chairs beside the colonel's desk.

"I think we can get this done quickly," the colonel said, as he holstered his sidearm and sat down at the desk beside them.

Astonishing, Adam thought, suddenly fearful. *This is where the war is, in this guy's head.* He realized the colonel's fatigue jacket did not match his fatigue trousers. *How many goddamn armies has this guy been in?* and he straightened up on the stool beside the window, aware that once again in his life he had been blissfully reckless, even more than foolish, stupid, exposing himself to lunatics like this colonel, wearing his disdain for danger on his sleeve. "You guileless guys who go around like you can't get your asses shot off," an old journalist had told him, "it's just a kind of showboating. You think you've got some kinda guardian angel. You'll get yours."

"Our officials of the revolution," the colonel said, as the overhead ceiling fan began, without anyone touching a switch, to turn slowly, "will review your case."

"What case? I only came to the coast three days ago, how could I have done anything?"

"Among your papers is a police card . . ."

"I'm accredited everywhere . . ."

"Perhaps not."

"Anyway, I'm not working, I'm not here to work. I'm just passing through."

"Ah what luxury, what luck, and why not? To just pass through . . . now, when there's this lull in the bestiality."

The colonel smiled but this time with rueful menace as he tapped his middle finger on the desk, speaking in a guttural, unintelligible whisper that at last took on its own music to Adam's ear, and he realized it was Arabic . . . the colonel, whom he'd thought was French, was now talking in Arabic, making some kind of statement, and he wondered how he could be hearing Arabic this far south. Suddenly he heard the word "revolution" and then the word "Islam" and the two tall men bristled and shook their heads and began to speak angrily to the colonel and Adam said helplessly, "I can't understand . . ."

"It is not important. But have you been to Chad?"

"No."

"It's not important."

"But . . ."

"It's not important."

Adam could feel his nerves draw at the base of his scrotum, he had to lift slightly off the chair. *O Jesus, how the fuck could I let this happen.* He crossed his legs, trying to appear calm, even disinterested, sinking into a slouch on his stool. Letting his arms hang loose, he tried to appear indifferent to the men's voices, to their guttural lilt, to their finger-pointing. Always – he thought – no matter where he had travelled he had run into aloof, righteous, bony-fingered men like these who were bent on punishing the defenceless, the half-guilty, while at the same time they were busy cutting deals with ruthless ideologues, those men who had pea-shooter minds, as Adam called them. Impetuous, he had certainly come un-prepared into the world of this colonel, he had been willful once again, leaving himself open to malevolence and men-dacity and to terrors that had, as he'd long since learned, the casualness of the colonel's fatigues – the mismatched insignia of a killer whose only charm was that he seemed to be in the wrong war. He had left himself open to terrors as dreamlike as the actual dream that had, over the years, come to haunt him in his sleep, to punish him, more and more . . . a dream in which he saw a man's big bony hands, a strangler's hands, his bony shoulders in a loose jacket . . . a man, a drifter, who lured him underground into a dimly lit parking garage, between long rows of sleek black and white cars . . . an old car from the fifties, a Cadillac with its twin chrome "Jayne Mansfield" bumper tits, Jayne herself sitting naked in the front seat, her head flying off into the drifter's arms, decap-itated, which – Adam knew – was how she had actually died, and the drifter, he could almost see the dark face of the man as he stood by the hood of the car saying over and over, "Black Snake Crawling . . ." And Adam was so appalled by this drifter who was holding Jayne Mansfield's head by her blond hair, so angry, that he suddenly cracked an iron bar across his skull, a tire iron . . . and then Adam always broke into a sweat and woke up, unbelieving yet utterly convinced that he had killed the man.

The shudder of the tire iron in his hand as it crushed open the drifter's skull had become so believable that he'd found himself waking time and again shivering in his bed, wishing that he knew some way to ward off this dream, ransacking his memory for the face, trying to reason out his actual motive, saying in his half-sleep, as if he were making a logical persuasive point to himself, "It can't be because of Jayne, she's already dead." But the more he tried to draw out the face, to talk to it, to wheedle and cajole it out of the darkness, the more he shrank into revulsion, astonishment, so that he'd leap out of bed, panic-stricken, certain that he was about to be found out, and one night he'd even rushed into the street in the early hours to be near someone, anyone, still seeing the blow, trying to find words to describe the blow, and he'd wept and cried – scaring an immigrant woman on her way to work – crying I AM CLEAN – but in the daytime he could hardly believe that he'd been so upset, so frightened, because he was after all innocent ("Open up, Father, I got more sins"). He had proven time and again that he was not easily upset or frightened, not by the thugs who called themselves insurgents, not by the gun jockeys in the side streets of Beirut who had stuffed the barrels of their automatics up under his chin and hit the action bolts to see if he would flinch. He had not flinched. He'd cried BAM mockingly, though all the muscles in his abdomen had drawn tight, that pull in the nerve endings that took his breath away, leaving him bone-weary, as weary as he was of this tribunal, these stern men who were, he realized, trying him for something he hadn't done in a language he did not know. He began, disrespectfully, stupidly, to hum. The colonel shushed him. Then it struck him that maybe the joke was on him; maybe he was merely off in the hills of his own illusions where the missing face in his dream was his own face, lost in these war-struck jungle towns where war was not just war, but all somehow linked to the war on poverty, the war on drugs, the war on pollution. Maybe his going off was, in fact, not a pursuit of Gabrielle – but maybe he was actually trying to get himself killed, or more accurately, trying to see what it was like to be about to die, to find out what Dostoyevsky had actually thought behind his blindfold as he had waited to be shot, and if that was the case, then these dark gabbling men were not judging him. They were only his unwitting accomplices, they were the unwitting avengers of the faceless man who had decided to hole up in his dream.

At the same time he cried out in his heart that his being there had only to do with Gabrielle, who'd been the cause of his great burst of laughter, and the cause of that shock of recognition in her arms that had nothing to do with anything other than what it was in itself – joy – a joy so intense that it had been painful – a joy that now appeared to contain, as a condition of its moment of realization, its own promise of grief. And that grief was exactly why he was on the road, he was going to look to see if he could find that grief in her eye – and so he kept quiet on the stool, he kept to his self-enclosed stillness as he looked out the window and saw that in the early dusk the moon was already up before the sun had gone down *and why is the moon, the shadow of what is to come, up before the sun goes down?* . . . and he wanted to yell, "Why?" but the colonel said, "They want to know, since you were – according to your passport – in Beirut, did you know a man called Ghassan Kanafani?"

"Yes," he said eagerly. "I photographed him for *Time*."

"How well?"

"Quite well. He saved my life, and . . ." He hadn't thought of Kanafani for years. Not since he'd been arrested by the Saica PLO commandos in Shatila camp in Beirut, and Kanafani had negotiated his release.

"They would like to know who his wife was?"

"She was Dutch. I forget her name, Anni maybe, but she was Dutch. A quiet woman. Blond. *Time* didn't use my picture of her. It was a little strange, his being with her and being . . ."

"Such a revolutionary . . . ?"

"Yes."

"He was a martyr! We are all witness to his pain."

"Well, the Mossad got him, and his niece, too."

The colonel and the two men nodded and scowled. One of the tall black men wagged his finger at Adam. He heard the word *Somalia*, but that didn't make any sense, Somalia had had no part to play in Kanafani's neck of the woods. Suddenly he wondered if he hadn't been too eager, too helpful; it was one of his weaknesses – the way he let his air of detachment become a confident helpfulness that often seemed like vanity, and he knew that some men, in a way he could never understand, hated his openness, taking it as an affront to their need for caution, to the way they had played their own lives so close to the vest; locksmiths of the heart, his father called such men. Perhaps these black men in their white dashikis were just dangerous big-time locksmiths. Perhaps they had hated Kanafani. But he couldn't hate, let alone belittle, Kanafani, though he knew what Kanafani had been – not only a journalist and storyteller but a ruthless killer for the Palestinian revolution – a man who, for no reason that Adam could discern, had openly vouched for him, had sent emissaries to argue before the Saica tribunal that he could be trusted. And so he had come to believe that he owed his life to a man who had not only fought for the rights of the dispossessed, but a man who had also helped to organize the Lod massacre: a remorseless killer who had shown him, a complete stranger, nothing but thoughtfulness and care in a time when offers to kill were being handed around in the streets like business cards, or better still, like dance cards by militiamen and mercenaries who drove their Mercedes through towns. Kalashnikovs or Uzis on the passenger seat, loyal only to their arms dealer, bankrollers of strategic alignment and policies of negotiation. Adam felt a weariness, the weariness that his mother had said that she'd felt one night as she'd sat scissoring paper squares so that she could then unfold them into snowflakes to be burned in a dry holy water font beside the bedroom door:

> *ash is evidence*
> *of the sacrifice we make,*
> *absence of water*
> *the pain in which we partake.*

He rested his head against the colonel's windowpane. He laughed ruefully as he watched the women close down the bread oven and walk away with their baskets strung out on poles, past white mercenaries at the graveyard gates who were eating sugar candy animals, their faces reddened by the sun, just like red-faced Ponce who had told the tribesmen that he was red in the face because he was the son of the sun and he had set up a sundial for them so that they would know at exactly what hour they were going to die, and they had believed him . . . and why not, since they also thought that mountain streams were the magic urine of spirits who spoke to them out of tree trunks. Adam licked his upper lip, still in a cold sweat, but then the colonel and the two men in white stood up.

The colonel took off his glasses. "You are free to go."

"Really?" Adam asked, suddenly remembering a woman he had not known who had told him a long time ago under a weeping willow, "Nonsense, you are free to go."

"Yes."

"Why?"

"The truly dead man," the colonel said, "is the man who never asks why."

The two black men bowed their heads and left, and the colonel said, "It is not easy, being arrested, yes?"

"No."

"Someone must be punished."

"So why me?"

"Nothing personal," and he took out a tin box of cigarillos, each scissored in half. "Smoke? Ah, no, you are offended by your arrest . . . Well, you are free, because my two friends are scrupulous men. Morally scrupulous men. But I will tell you this," and he gave Adam the V for victory sign, "I could have shot you, my friend. Altogether too much gets written down these days. And as for you, you photographers, you are the snitches of history. The fewer pictures the better, that's what I say."

Toronto

Adam had never forgotten Arthur Copter, the little choirboy with white eyelashes and pink eyes who had been told to sit in the crèche, because there had come a day when Arthur had shown Adam a rifle that had a telescopic sight. Arthur's father had given it to him, and he and his father had gone down to the bluffs by the lake and they had fired round after round into the emptiness over the water. "There was nothing to hit, not even a seagull. My stupid father was happy because it was just a lot of stupid empty sky." Adam had watched Arthur kneel down in their family backyard behind the garages to fill a dozen Sheik condoms with tap water. He'd knotted the balloons and then clothes-pegged them to his mother's wash line so that they'd hung like tears among the hollyhocks and then he'd said, "I don't see things so switched around when I've got a gun," and he'd sat on the stoop and fired, letting out a little whoop with each explosion of water, and when he'd finished, he'd said, "It's too bad your father doesn't give you a gun, then we could play real cops and robbers."

"Jesus, we'd kill each other."

"So? It'd be real."

Adam had asked if he could borrow the telescopic sight for a couple of days, and he had carried the sight around in his pocket, putting it to his eye, fixing on doors, windows, *framing, framing,* and it had excited him, seeing how something deep in the distance could be brought sharply into focus, BAM, so that he could observe a thing, a person, up close, intimately, engaged, excited, but unobserved.

"That's how I like to see things," he told Arthur.

"That's all make-believe," Arthur said. "There's no blood."

"That's what I believe," Adam said.

Harry O'Leary, overhearing them at a summer party on the church lawn, had told Arthur that he believed in the blood, too, that love was in the blood, and he loved his daughter, "Yes

I do," he said as he held up a poster, a photograph of Gabrielle, so that all the new and the old choirboys attending the party could see her in tights, dancing in the CYO Junior Dance Championships: Jazz Section. "Belief is in the blood. One day she's going to go to New York and she'll be a dancer and with a little bit of luck she'll knock 'em dead." He rubbed his large hands together. "Even in Timbuctoo, she'll be big," he said. On that same afternoon, the president of the Ontario Jockey Club, an arthritic cripple who attended mass every Sunday in a motorized wheelchair, announced that there was going to be a big international stakes race at the Woodbine track – the San Gabriela Stakes – and he asked Harry if his beautiful sixteen-year-old daughter, Gabrielle, wouldn't like to be there to make the presentation in the Winner's Circle, to present the silver cup after the race and have her picture in all the newspapers. "Oh, this is a big chance," Harry said. "A girl who wants to be in show business should get used to being in the papers, that's what show business is all about, notices."

"She's still a child," Mrs. O'Leary said.

"So was Shirley Temple," Harry said.

On the afternoon of the race, Harry wore a grey silk tie and grey spats, and his wife, a puffy-faced silent woman with her auburn hair gathered in a snood, followed a step behind him. She had a wary, bruised air. Adam thought he'd seen the same puff around the alcoholic eyes of older women on his street, their faces at windows, full of loss and panic, trapped behind glass.

Gabrielle, however, strutted beside her father in her white high heels. Harry said, "They'll eat out of your hand." He stroked her hair. He stroked her hair for a long time, his breath on her cheek, his gaze, tender and moist. But the next day, there was no picture of Gabrielle O'Leary in the newspapers. There had been a midnight fire in the barns and several horses had been burned alive and all the pictures were of the fire in the night. Florence bought all the editions but then she forgot what she was looking for and began to cut out a recipe. "It's sad," Adam's father said. "All Harry wanted was her picture in the paper. Mind you, maybe he's one of those people who doesn't believe he exists unless they get their picture taken."

He wrote that down in a little notebook.

"Maybe you'll buy me a camera?" Adam asked. "And I'll take Gabrielle's picture."

"You want to be a photographer?"

"Maybe."

"It'll let you travel light. You could wear loose shoes, too. Feel real free."

"I could shoot you," he said.

"You'd like to shoot me?" Web asked.

"Sure."

"And your mom?"

"Why not? Except then you'd know I was looking at you."

He hadn't been up on the garage roofs for a year. He'd phoned Gabrielle. She was waiting for him. "I can't believe

I got myself up here," she said. "So much for me in the papers."
She was wearing a T-shirt that said: *I have Vincent's ear – so
talk to me.* They snuggled into one of their old hidden corners, a corner where he had taught her a song that Web had
taught him, a song "for when things get tough, when they're
tough enough," and in honour of Vincent and those who'd
lost their ear, they sang one of their childhood songs:

> *Lulu had a baby,*
> *his name was Tiny Tim,*
> *she stuck him in a piss pot*
> *to learn him how to swim.*
> *He sank to the bottom,*
> *he floated to the top,*
> *Lulu got excited*
> *and grabbed him by the*
> *cock tails, gingerales,*
> *five cents a glass,*
> *if you don't like it stick it up your*
> *ask me no questions*
> *tell me no lies,*
> *if you get hit*
> *with a bucket of shit*
> *be sure to close your eyes*

Then they climbed down from the roof, going through
a broken board fence so that they could avoid Arthur Copter's

back garden. There was a lightning-struck tree there, its limbs sawn off and the bark stripped, a lustrous dead-white tree with fungus shelves at the base and mushroom tents in the spongy earth. One of the boys had said, "It looks like my dad's dead dick." The tree had been known ever since as Dad's Dead Dick and since childhood they'd all been afraid of lightning.

They agreed that since they were no longer kids they should stop going up on the roofs. "We're far too old. Only my mother's angel hangs out up there."

"I don't know," she said, "I was just thinking it's a good place to sunbathe where no one can see us."

He led her into an empty garden shed between the garages. He wasn't sure who owned it. Maybe Mr. Copter. He said that's where he was reading about all kinds of explorers, like Ponce de Leon. And books of stories his father had given him, some by the man named Hemingway that the sportswriter told him about when they had gone fishing, and another writer, Kafka. "I think he must've done drugs. Do you think you could ever wake up in the morning and believe that you were an insect? Or your closest friend could be a cockroach?" The shed had been a little implements house with its own window and rat holes in the floorboards. Adam had swept it clean and painted the walls pale blue. He had painted two old kitchen chairs blue, too.

"When I was a kid," she said, sitting on one of the chairs, "my closest friend was the mailman."

"That guy, he always had a head-cold . . ."

"You didn't know him like I knew him, I thought he was this old drifter with the soul of a dog, a stray dog who if he stayed too long at the door someone would beat him like my uncle Tonton had actually beaten up his mailman for handing him too much junk mail, and he'd left him howling like a dog in pain."

He said he didn't think the mailman was a drifter because he'd known some real drifters down in Christie Pits where he played baseball, the park where lots of old drifters, unshaven and sipping cheap wine, always spoke to him, telling him about the rowing races out on the lake when they were kids and how the rowers were called scullers and the boats were called sculls. One of those old men had died right before his eyes, falling down near second base, trying to scoop the base under his head like a pillow, rolling over on his back, his eyes open, and then he'd begun to shake and flop his arms, trying to wrench his bones free from his heart while the other old men shuffled in a loose circle until the dying man had jack-knifed and lain still, a line of blood coming from the corner of his mouth. Another old man had come close and covered the dead man's face with a newspaper. "Wait'll you see this," he'd said, opening the dead man's shirt, the dead man's smooth hairless body being tattooed all over with fish, fish arced in the air. "What'd you make of that, eh? He wouldn't eat a fish to save his soul." And a red stain appeared on the newspaper and as the stain spread,

Adam said he'd felt a thickening in his throat, a weight of sorrow, and he had wanted to cry but he could not.

As he sat in the shed, telling her about the drifters, moving his hands like flying fish in and out of the floating dust in a shaft of sunlight, she joked with him by making howling hound-dog sounds, but then Mr. Copter suddenly blocked the light through the door: "What are you doing in there?"

"Daydreaming," Gabrielle said.

"You'll get a disease. You'll get sick. Rats."

At the movies, as they sat in the dark, Gabrielle told him solemnly as she let him fondle her breasts, "My mother says men are very greedy." He put his fingers between her legs. Soon, his fingers were wet. She lifted his hand and kissed his fingers. "But then," she said, "I like it when you're greedy." One night, as they went walking home from the movies and passed a hedgerow, he stripped off a handful of red berries. "Don't eat those berries," she said, "you'll die." He laughed, telling her his grandfather had told him the same thing, and he told her how he had thrown handfuls of hard little berries at the bedroom windows of lonely women in the night and she said, "My mother is always looking out the window."

On another night while her mother and her father, Harry, were at the hospital visiting Harry's sick brother, Tonton, they went up to Gabrielle's bedroom where she took off her clothes and Adam, as he stared at her naked body, said, "My mother . . . she says she talks to you, she says she's seen you full of light, full of grace."

"No way."

"She says she sees you and her cousin all the time, up on the garage roofs. A fine little angel."

"You're crazy, she's crazy," and they huddled under the blankets and after she opened her legs he humped his buttocks over her, pushing hard against her, into her, uncertain how deep he was, afraid that he was going to come in her. She lifted her legs, hooking them over his hips, and with a startled cry, she went rigid, and then, after easing him off her body, she sat up in the lamplight. There was a line of dark blood down her thigh and the sheet was stained. She was excited by the blood, she was pleased, and said, "My blood is on your hands."

"Be careful," he said.

"About what?"

"Blood is a bond. I believe that."

"Me, too."

She suddenly drew streaks of blood across his brow and cheeks with her fingers. "There, now you've really got the mark on you, you look like you'd fight for me." He kissed her and pushed her onto her back and entered her again, this time into the blood, aroused by the rank smell.

After that, they made love regularly in the garden shed, lying on an old blanket that had belonged to his grandfather, their legs locked together, gently rocking. Once, someone with a strange dry cough came into the alley. It was like hearing the dry cough of someone dying. It turned out to be Miss Klein, in a chemise, drunk and singing, "There's no business like show business." She did a little pirouette and then sat down in the cinders and whispered, "Vell, mine Gerald, do you like zis dancing?" Adam told Gabrielle that Miss Klein was one of his lonely women, that he had often waited alone in the dark as a child for her lights to come on, he had waited for her to do something private and unsuspecting. "I liked to look into her eyes, so I could maybe see what she was looking for when she couldn't see me, even though I was up real close."

"I like to watch your eyes, too . . . when you come," Gabrielle said, "I'd like to see what you're thinking."

"I don't think I think anything."

"Me, neither, it's all light, it's like painful light and I just want more . . ."

"You're lucky, you can come while I'm in you."

"If you come in me I'll die," she said. "Get some condoms."

"So Arthur Copter," he said laughing, "can use us for target practice."

"He's kind of cross-eyed or something, isn't he?"

One night they heard the rustling of a rat under the floorboards of the shed and they huddled together, afraid of being bitten, and after the rat had gone he licked her nipples and she fondled him. "I'll suck you." She pushed her long hair back from her face. When he came, there was a small pool of semen between her breasts so he cupped his hands and scooped up the semen and was confused, wondering what to do with it, but she giggled and dipped her fingers into his cupped hands as if they were a font and said, "It's full of hormones, it's the best thing for the skin, at least that's what my mother's hairdresser says. Of course, she's almost my age and she didn't tell that to my mother." They cradled each other and she said, "I don't like it out here in the dark any more."

"My mother and father sit in the dark," he said. "They light candles and she says they talk best in the dark because they can't see each other's eyes."

"Talking's for old people," she said. "You're tired when you're old so you sit and talk. My mother talks to herself."

On Christmas Eve, Adam and Gabrielle went to mass and there were steaming overshoes under the hot radiators and the air was heavy with candle smoke and incense. He knelt beside her and they prayed and held hands, listening to the choir. He watched Harry leave the altar during the sermon. Then his face appeared in the glass in the altar door, lean and drawn, and Harry stood against the glass all through the sermon looking as if he was afraid and on the run, and for the first time Adam saw a fugitive look in Harry's eye, a look that upset Adam, a look he'd seen in a stray dog's eye when it was about to turn and run. Adam held on to Gabrielle and they went to Communion together, the silver paten catching all the light under their chins as they drew into a gentle closeness. They strolled home through the silent cold snowbound streets, cradling each other. There were no lights in any of the windows. They walked slowly for blocks until they went into her dark still house, and with her mother and Harry asleep, they undressed by the living room fire and he knelt and kissed her cleft, breathing in her musk and salt dampness. She wet her fingers with her saliva and rubbed her nipples.

"Why do you do that, what do you feel?"

"It makes me tingle more while you lick me."

After they made love in front of the fire, muffling their cries, trying to keep quiet, they sat staring out the window at the stars. "This is terrible, sinning like this after swallowing Jesus."

"We aren't sinning, you can't sin if you're making love."

He gave her his silver watch as a present.

She gave him a ring with a black onyx crown and when he opened the crown he found that she had made a tiny braid from strands of his hair and her hair.

He worried about her saying that they had sinned but he didn't go to confession because he didn't believe he'd done anything wrong. Instead, he told Father Zale that he felt closer to God or, at least, close to the lightness of heart that he thought must be the lightness of the grace Father Zale liked to talk about. He tried to explain himself to Father Zale as they stood under the old trees by the bluff, facing the water, but the priest shook his head and said, "A man might believe anything to avoid God." He had come to love Father Zale, but he was resentful, telling Gabrielle that the priest didn't understand. "Just because you're a priest doesn't mean you understand." She hugged him. "I wish I could believe in things the way you believe," she said. "Though maybe I believe in cockroaches." That same spring, around early May, she grew morose. She wouldn't talk, she even seemed angry. Withdrawing inside herself she watched him while they made love, her body still eager but her eyes unyielding. He was bewildered. She didn't say anything. She lay very still with her eyes closed. But then she opened her eyes, gave him a light kiss, and whispered, "I love you." She closed her eyes and did not open them or move her body or answer his questions until he was dressed, saying goodnight from the doorway. Some kind of loss had come between them, he could feel it. She said: "Ask the mailman." He wanted to cry. He loved her but he wanted to cry. He regretted having given her the watch. "It's like an eye. Maybe I put an evil eye on her."

One morning as a boy he'd walked without warning into his mother's bedroom. She was lifting a chemise over her head, and instead of a strained, sometimes wary woman who smoked too much and played incessantly with fire, he saw a taut bare body, the hollows of her thighs, the quiet unsunned breasts, the wall of her rib cage and black hair against the track of pure white skin.

Later that afternoon, his mother, standing by the sink running tap water over a head of lettuce – her nakedness unspoken – said, "Adam, cut me one of those big Spanish onions."

He began to strip the brown brittle skins to the first wet whiteness.

"Take it down layer by layer," she said.

He made little slits with a paring knife and peeled away sections. His eyes began to water.

"How far?" he asked.

"All the way."

He took away a layer and then another, the ball of onion shrinking in his hands, leaving only flaps and broken layers of onion flesh on the counter. "See," she said. "You can know what you want, you can know where you're going, but when you get down to the heart, there's nothing . . . only the left-over bits and pieces, and your tears . . ." She turned off the tap. "Now, scoop them up and put them in the pan. We'll fry them up good."

PART FOUR

Toronto

It was the coldest January he could remember. After an ice storm, with the black branches of the sugar maples sheathed in ice, Gabrielle had eased a tube of ice from a twig and she had blown across its open mouth, a faint high note. "I can turn music into water," she said, pressing her cold wet hand to Adam's cheek, "and into tears, too." He hadn't seen her since Christmas, and now she was refusing to go out with him, to go with him to join his mother and father at Johnnie Kufu's Club Conqueroo on Yorkville across from the old firehall, its neon lights rippling – THIS WEEK ONLY – RETURNED FROM EUROPE – THE LEGENDARY WEB "SWEET" WATERS.

"I'm unwell," she said. "My whole family's unwell."

"With what?"

"Deeply unwell. Harry's unwell."

He knew that Harry had been conducting the choir every Sunday.

"Yeah, but what's wrong?"

She laughed, a mirthless laugh.

"Ask the mailman," she said.

"That's what she said," Adam told his parents. "Ask the mailman . . ." as they were met by Kufu, a retired light heavyweight fighter. He had been billed as a "White Hope" but had suffered a detached retina while sparring with Muhammad Ali. Kufu, who stared at people with a lopsided grin because of his eye, was effusive as he held a chair for Florence – "Momma Waters," as Kufu called her – at a table close to the small bandstand. "I got a convention of thieves in here tonight," he said, "and you know what's wrong with thieves? Thieves love to steal. No matter how successful. Before they go out with the wife, they got to steal a credit card from someone, or else they won't go. I got a roomful of stolen credit cards tonight."

They were joined by Rufus Paillard, known as Rueful, and Slim Ottis, his father's sidemen who sat like polite grey-haired school superintendents with their brass horns laid across their knees. Adam stared at Rueful's hair, straightened into a combed cap close to his narrow skull, and he wondered why his father would want to stay so long away from home so that he could ride through the shank of the night with such dark men, their black skins shining, bluish, hidden indigos, copper, and mulberry, *and how'd he get his hair like that? shining like tinsel* staring, so that Rueful said, laughing, "They call that conking, boy . . ."

"What?"

"Some black mens conks their hair. You get some lye and lard and if you can stand the burning on your scalp then you can stand in good with the womens." He let out a little *whoooee* whoop and slapped his thigh and sang:

I got me 500 women, gonna get 500 more
Then the sun gonna shine in my door

Web wiped his mouth with his napkin. He massaged his temples as if there were a deep soreness inside his skull, and then he and Rueful and Slim stepped onto the platform to loud applause. For a moment his father sat at the piano, staring into the spotlight, blinded, the lines around his mouth deeper than Adam had ever seen them, lines enclosing a mournful repose as he crouched over the keyboard, and then sang:

One of these days I'm going crazy
Black snake crawling in my brain
Say the black snake crawling
Till he come again
One of these days I'm gonna go crazy

his hands loping along the keys, a solemn detachment in the tilt of his chin, intense yet aloof, lost, so it seemed, in a remembrance, something that made him smile. Adam, seeing that little ruminating smile, remembered the night he'd seen no seam or crack of light coming from anywhere in the house and though the house was in complete darkness he had heard piano blues and had gone down the long hall, what some used to call a railroad hall, feeling for the door into the front living room, staring into the deep shadows, hearing the *dunk*

dunk of bent flattened notes, and then he'd heard his mother's voice moaning low, half-whispering:

> *Tell me how long, how long*
> *That lonesome train's been gone*

and then there was only the sound of breathing, and what seemed like no sound at all for a long, long time. He'd felt a grip of panic, as if a gap had sprung open in the dark and everyone he loved was about to fall through. He flipped the light switch on the wall and found his father sitting at the piano with his arms folded and his mother, wearing scarlet high heels and a pink satin half-slip, sitting bare-breasted on the piano top with her legs crossed, holding an unlit cigarette, staring out the dark windows.

Neither moved. His father said: "Why don't you sit down, son . . . kill the lights, sit down because your mother's singing a song." He turned off the light and they laughed together in the dark, they'd always been able to laugh, especially in the dark, just as he and Kufu were now laughing in the Club Conqueroo, Kufu, with his lopsided grin, saying, "Nice, eh kid! He can tinkle them keys, Sweet can. Ain't nobody plays better on the black notes. Put him on a roulette wheel and tell him to play the black." Adam said the single line of sweat down his father's cheek looked like scar tissue. His mother blinked and said, "Scars . . . Oh Lord . . ." as his father stood up, hammering the keys, his eyes wide open, letting out a high-pitched nasal moaning cry *tell me how long, how long* and threw his arms into the air:

> *I drink to keep from worrying,*
> *I smile to keep from crying,*
> *So's to keep my good woman*
> *From digging what's on my mind;*
> *Someday I'll be six feet in my grave . . .*

As his father stepped down to applause, Rueful took the microphone: "Like the man says, he's Sweet, he's delectable, he's irrepressible, impeccable, sensational, he's Web 'Sweet' Waters," and he blew Web a kiss. The crowd applauded. "Afterwhile child, so stick around, the best is yet to come." That's what Gabrielle had said, too, telling Adam to not look back, "because we're the best, the best is yet to come."

Web sat for several minutes in the stillness of his own quiet, ignoring Kufu, holding Florence's hand as if they were sharing a very private moment of consolation, and then Web smiled, patting his hands together with pleasure.

"You feeling good?" he asked Adam. "Tonight?"

"Okay," Adam said.

"No. Not okay. How you feeling?"

"Relieved, maybe."

"Relieved of what?"

"It's just like suddenly, for some reason, there's a space," as Kufu left the table, "a space in my mind where there's nothing I need to say to anyone, not Mom, not you, not Gabrielle."

"That's good, I like that."

"I don't know whether it's good or not."

"Yeah, but I do. That's what music is, man. And life, too."

"What?"

"The spaces, what's left out. Some guys, when you hear them play, they're filling every hole there is, like grave diggers digging their own graves, but it's the silences, what's left out between the notes, that carries the music."

"Kufu says you play only on the black notes."

"Kufu's cock-eyed. Beware of all one-eyed men."

By the end of the week, his mother was alone in her chair at the window again. "Your dad is gone, he's a gone goose." She was angry. "He didn't play me true." She had a pair of long shears, and taking his suits and sports jackets out of their closet, she scissored an arm from one and a leg from the other. She hung them up again in the closet, tossing the tubes of sleeves and pant legs into the fireplace, sitting on her haunches in front of the flames. "Burn" she said. She lay down for the afternoon. The shears were on the bedside table. After that, the shears were always on the bedside table.

A month later Web had come home and found his clothes scissored. "You cut yourself loose, babe," his father said bitterly, and he went to the Barclay Hotel. Night after night she sat alone in the dark. She would suddenly snap on the light and find herself staring into the mirror. She lit a cigarette and said aloud, "See, I knew you were in there all the time. You can't fool me."

"Dad's not fair," Adam said to his mother, trying to bring her out of herself, out of the mirror.

"Who said life was fair?" she said. "And besides, what's between me and your dad is between me and your dad. The less you know, the longer you'll love us."

"I'll love you anyway."

"That's how it is with me and your dad. That's the joke. We love each other anyway."

In a few days, Web was home again and he and Adam went for a walk. It was early autumn, they had turned up their coat collars against a chill wind and they kept their hands in their pockets as they came up to a church, Our Lady of Sorrows.

"A man should never stand still," his father said.

"But you got to stand for something," Adam said, laughing at his own cleverness.

"When you stand still," his father said, paying no attention to his laughter, "you not only become an easy target but you stop being amazed at yourself, and when you stop being amazed at yourself you know you're dead on your feet. The real killers are practical men, penny-wise, who think they know what's what but what they know ain't worth knowing. Still they'll kill for it because they are stone-cold bored. You should always be amazed at every moment you are alive and you should always be afraid of bored men."

"Don't you ever worry that Mom's bored? Leaving her alone like you do?"

"You mean I should be afraid of her?"

"I mean you should be afraid for her."

By the gates to Our Lady of Sorrows, a policeman was fighting with a man who was swinging a black satchel, trying to club the policeman with it. The satchel snapped open and silver chalices fell out. The man picked up a cup, wheeled and lunged, wild-eyed, at the policeman, who shot him. The thief lay in the snow, blood seeping through his coat. Adam's father knelt down and undid the laces on the thief's shoes and held the man's ankles, looking up at the man's moving fishmouth. "He could've killed me with one of them cups," the policeman said, half pleading as he watched the thief's blood drain into the snow, turning it pink, the colour of candy floss. A young priest came running out of the church. He said the final prayers over the thief and crossed his forehead with holy oil. Then the dying man said, "Y'ain't nothing, cop, nothing. You're a fuckin' zero."

"Rest in peace," the priest said.

"He had it coming," the policeman said helplessly.

"Nice shot," Adam's father said wryly to the cop and took Adam by the arm and walked him away.

They sat in silence in a café. After a while his father said, "I am afraid for your mother. But she'd be afraid for me if I stayed home. What some men want in this life is a quick getaway, in nice loose shoes. I got the shoes."

Ruth Waters
Daughter of Gibson and Alice Waters.
Died June 11, 1888
Aged 9 years, 4 months, and 11 days.
She was stolen from the grave
By Roderick R. Clow,
Dissected at Dr. P. M. Armstrong's office
In Port Hope
From which place
Her mutilated remains
Were obtained and deposited here.
Her body dissected
By
A fiendish man,
Her bones anatomized,
Her soul we trust has risen to God,
Where few physicians rise.

Gabon
Driving northeast from the colonel's office and the burning
swamp fires, Adam followed another twisting logging road
deeper into the bush. The Mercedes 300 skidded on the slick

grades of mud. After two hours he passed a flagpole with a tattered flag he didn't recognize, and clusters of huts – one-room hutches, and shacks, the rust-coloured plaster falling from the lathing, the rib work open – and there were oblong family graves by the doors, concrete pads set above the ground to keep out the white ants. He began to feel a heavy thickening under his skin, a swollen, languid anxiety in the reeking dampness. A black soldier, wearing fatigues, running shoes, and silver sunglasses, stopped Adam's car at a checkpoint and said: "De wrong time dis place, man, mek smart, turn back . . ." He was wearing a headset under his khaki cap and the checkpoint was a disused one-room gas station with a single rusted pump. Adam asked, "What you listening to, man?"

"California dreamin' . . ."

Adam stared into the dust-speckled windshield while the soldier kicked the fenders and all the tires, as if he were a hard-headed used-car dealer in the bush. "Dis is de machete time. Even de trees reach down an' kill you," the soldier said, as if he were making a promise, and let Adam drive on.

After five miles, terribly thirsty, he stopped to get out of the car and stretch and drink his bottled water, tepid and gummy, almost a weight on his tongue as he stood surrounded by the lush green growth feeding on itself, voraciously perpetuating itself. He was sure he could feel the pulse in the dead and rotting foliage. *Death is alive here,* he thought. *So how can I photograph the death that is here, the vital stillness that's between the luxuriance and the dying?* Swallowing more water, he tried to imagine his own death. He had tried before. He couldn't believe in it. Not his own actual death. He couldn't see it. Not in his mind's eye. He knew this was stupid – he knew that death always came after a blind turn around the wrong corner, but he refused to even consider his own death, because he was sure that if he did, he would then die stuck in a place like this – it would be as if he had let the Bone Picker lay his hand on his wrist at the crap tables – he'd end up stuck on snake eyes. "Stuck," that had been Gabrielle's word. "I refuse to be stuck here, stuck in our narrow little town with its two-storey dreams . . .

"You don't know how ingrown this town is," she'd said, "feeding off itself, so mean-spirited. I've never heard my mother sing and my father never sings, he never sings anywhere . . . a choirmaster who never sings, that's a scream. And yet he sits with my uncle Tonton talking about peace of mind, how to keep calm. 'You ain't nothing unless you can keep calm while you're squatting in all this crap,' that's how my uncle talks. Tonton Jackie, they call him, a big man, musclebound, who sings all the time, his arms wide open as if he loves the whole world, like he's St. Francis of Assisi in a zoot suit, but he makes a living by breaking arms and legs and the hearts of anyone who has ever owed him anything, except for Harry. He even beat up the mailman. But he loves Harry because somehow Harry's played no part in Tonton's strong-arm shit, except the fact is, Harry slaps my mother. How do you like that? He slaps my mother and looks at me so forlornly with those moist eyes of his like I should understand him, and I should pity him, but understand what? . . .

"Why my mother, why a woman will let herself be slapped by a choirmaster who never sings while my uncle makes like his own wife is the goddamn Virgin of Perpetual Light is beyond me. Tonton never touches his wife, never, though to be fair, I think Harry never touches my mother either like a lover, at least that's the way I always saw it while he sat playing with my hair and stroking my wrist. I've always wanted out. I've always wanted to go missing, so that I don't smother and die with him putting his hands on me."

Adam got back in the car.

And he kept on driving into the bush.

Suddenly there were single files of children and old people moving along the shoulder of the road, the children leading the old people by short leashes tied to their wrists. He realized the old people were blind from river blindness and their children were leading them out into the maize fields, causing flocks of black big-winged birds to rise and swarm into the sky. The children parked their mothers and fathers alone, one by one, in sections of the fields. It was their work, they were human scarecrows. The children ran back to the road and as some leapt into the river, splashing and squealing, their bodies shimmering in the spray in the strong sunlight, Adam stopped the car and yelled, "No. No," waving from the car window at the motionless black figures in the fields, "you can't do that. Not to your parents. That's wrong," until the children crowded around him, laughing and giggling and prancing, as if he were a mad man.

Toronto

It was late afternoon. His father phoned. He said he'd been in the city for several days, staying alone at the Barclay Hotel. "You're old enough, Adam, to handle these things. You understand the comfort a man can feel in his own aloneness, but it's hard being alone when you're sick."

Adam went for him in a taxi, suddenly afraid that if his father died then, he would have to look into the eye of his own death, he'd be – for a fact – next in line, vulnerable, and his own face would loom up and his own blood would begin the slow drain out of his life. He would be left alone. The question would be, Who could he become when his father had died? A remnant, a repository, someone free at last, free from the years of yielding to his father's waywardness, to his father's lifelong habit of the quick getaway, always doing exactly what he wanted to do, so that – ironically – as a son, over the years, he'd learned to accommodate his father's lifetime of childishness: his father who was now stripping down there in front of him in the cubicle in the hospital's emergency room. But he thought, I don't want to see him stripped down, defenceless: years ago I thought I wanted him punished but now I don't want him defenceless, let alone punished. His father stood barefoot on the grey marble floor, naked, talking about baseball as if nothing were the matter, as if they were in neutral space, all emotion neutered, and neither spoke of a silent unseen tumour, nor said the dread word, cancer, the big C, but only stared at the yellow, purple, pink, sepia blood in rippled layers, a relief map under the translucent skin of his belly. The doctor, a young Korean wearing steel-rimmed glasses, shrugged and smiled as his father sat up on the brown rubber sheet and paper of the examining table, his slightly bowed legs dangling *and his penis is so small*, Adam thought, remembering when he was a child in the bathroom, his father standing over the toilet, his penis between two fingers, thick, so big, so heavy, and now it looked like his memory of his own childhood penis, small, hooded, shrivelled by fear, his only sign of fear. Why am I looking at his penis, when it is actually his bony feet, the long bony yellow toes and toenails that appall me? The hard yellow nails and the thin shins and crinkled blue veins and the flesh hanging loose under his arms like a woman's, the little womanly tits with tufts of hair around the small nipples (Why do men have nipples? What taunting sign of ineffectuality, lost powers?) and laughing lightly, Adam said, "Goddamn, you sure look like the resurrection of the dead to me." The doctor laughed, too, and said, "Don't be so dramatic. You can thank his lucky stars it's only a clogged artery. Like everything that's fairly easy to fix, it looks terrible. What's terrible is what you never see."

Gabon

After a two-hour drive through humpbacked hills, through checkpoints that were only rusted Shell oil drums filled with sand, he shifted into second gear around several half-tracks and armoured cars on the outskirts of the shanty city, M'Begov. The early evening sun was a red opal, the city house walls seemed maroon and sepia, comforting, the colour of dying leaves, and at the central traffic circle there was a bronze statue of a nineteenth-century French general, and though the general's head had been blown off he still saluted the soldiers who went by on the back of a jeep mounted with a 50-calibre machine gun. Two motorcycles drove past, too, men glittering with medals in the sidecars, beefy men with shiny brutal faces. A long, white, empty Mercedes followed the motorcycles, empty except for the liveried driver. The wide river through the centre of town was yellow and filled with sandbars, eddies, and pocket ponds. Adam parked the car in front of a vacated shop in a small plaza by the shore, the windows and the yellow and black Budget sign shot out. The M'Begov Hotel was on an island in the middle of the river. He crossed in a pirogue. Fat old women were gathered on the other shore by the dock, beheading fish. All the heads were kept in a wide basket. *The head, the eyes, the cheeks, are best in soup,* Father Zale once said. The hotel lobby was unlit. There was a coat of dust on stacks of luggage in the lobby, as if it had been there for weeks. The empty barroom was also a tiny disco, the walls lined with grey-blue cardboard egg cartons stapled to the walls as sound insulation. Then, from behind the front desk, a wiry man who wore polished brown boots, shorts, and a white T-shirt lettered with M'BEGOV Hotel and Bar, said, "I am Henri. *Vas-y poupée.*" He carried Adam's bag and black leather camera case up the circular staircase to a room on the fourth floor. "There is air up here," he said. "*L'air absorbant l'absence dans la lumière . . .*"

Adam slept two hours and then went down for a supper of baked whitefish in a small enclosed balcony dining room facing the river. A lean woman with grey eyes who owned the hotel said, "Yes, we are in the middle of nowhere but we make our amusement in many ways, yes, we have a baby gorilla, and like a baby child to us he is very amusing, he laughs just like a human, sometimes he laughs just like my husband, Henri."

She said that her name was Esmelda Waites and that she was the daughter of merchants who had died of blackwater fever before the revolution – "They are all gangs, these freedom fighters, who call themselves militias, and stupid China gives aid to both sides" – leaving her the hotel. She went out to a thatched cage under the house and came back, wobbling slightly on her high heels, carrying in her arms, as if he were a child, a small gorilla about three feet tall. The animal bolted out of her arms and bounded around the dining room from chair to chair, and then clutched Adam's leg, reached for his arm, took hold of his wrist and tried to gnaw his fingers.

Adam held him high in the air by the hands and spun around as if he were dancing with a dwarf, and then the baby gorilla swung his legs around Adam's waist, lips drawn back in a wild cheerless smile. Adam held him under the armpits and began to tickle him and he giggled: then he leapt away, circling behind a chair, peering warily at Adam.

"He is a very strange gorilla," Esmelda said. "You can see in his eyes, he knows he's going to die."

"You're always dreaming of dying," Henri said.

"No. I never dream. Do you?" she asked, turning to Adam. "Do you dream?"

"Just the same dream sometimes."

"I dream," Henri said, picking the gorilla up in his arms. "I dreamed last night of emptying bags of quicklime on all the anthills so the ants wouldn't attack and I'd stay alive for ever, and then a soldier encouraged me when he said to me, 'The best friend a person has is someone who has just died.'"

"Do you think there'll be real fighting this deep into the bush?" Esmelda asked Adam. "You took the road in, you must have seen something."

"Just trees and trees and checkpoints. Some mortar positions down by the river . . . I don't know, after all, it's your town."

"No, it's not," she said, "it's no one's."

"These tribal bush battles," Henri said, "they found a church with thirty decapitated women and children in it the other day."

"You got to be kidding me," Adam cried, and at first Henri thought he was speaking of the decapitated dead, but then he saw that Adam was pointing to the ridge road on the other side of the river, a road that slanted down out of the hills. There, in the dusk, was a truck and flatbed trailer, and seated on the trailer, the polka band from the hotel in Liberville, the five bulky white men in lederhosen and alpine hats, broadcasting as they played over a portable loudspeaker system mounted on the back of the trailer, with a big blue and white banner – BAVARIAN BEER – fluttering over their heads, the bass drum and braying voices and the *phfump* of the tuba echoing through the valley. The trailer truck pulled in behind a cluster of trees and stacks of rusting bedsprings close to a loading dock. Then, the sound system was shut down: a loud echoing *pop*.

"It is what Conrad taught us," Henri said. "At the heart of darkness there is always a German."

"Sounded like a shot," Esmelda said. "What the hell are they doing here?"

"Looking for Doctor Livingstone," Adam said sardonically, pouring himself a Pernod.

They sat watching each bandsman come across the river in separate pirogues, brass instruments gleaming in the dropping light.

An hour later, Adam got undressed beside a narrow, hard cot, exhausted and drunk on the Pernod. The floor was bare concrete, painted sky blue. He laughed as he walked across the sky and leaned against the balcony railing and tried to look far, far away beyond the tree line. He heard croupiers calling *Saliendo*, through the trees, and so he came in and shut the louvred window, propping a chair in the blue that was turning overcast under the handle. He closed the light. Sweltering in the humid heat, his head spinning as he listened in the dark to the bird ruckus in the trees, he lay thinking that they must be hummingbirds, that this had to be where hummingbirds came though he'd never heard a hummingbird sing, not at the banana tree outside their bedroom window, wondering whether the birds had followed Gabrielle, too, and would she be excited to see him now that he was getting close to her. He opened his eyes in the dark and growing more confused, more restless, he rolled onto his side and turned on the small bedside lamp only to have long tubular, wide-winged insects seeking the light come in through the loose window casement, insects with arrows in their thighs, wobbling toward him, chanting

> *the consul demands*
> *a platter for the breasts*
> *of Eulalia . . .*

PART FIVE

Puerto Rico

On the morning after he had got a glimpse of Gabrielle in the lobby of the Flamboyan, he went for a walk along the ocean beach behind the Casino. The retreating waves had left air holes, little dots in the sand, breathing holes for buried clams. "I'd lose my mind connecting these dots." Hoping that Gabrielle was actually staying in the hotel and that she would be out among the women greasing and sunning themselves on the cedar-slat chairs that were clustered around the hotel swimming pool, he passed two slim, hipless airline stewards who were playing shuffleboard on a concrete pad that had been laid in the sand close to the chairs by the pool. The stewards, wearing matching powder-blue leather clogs, giggled and clopped back and forth, using their shuffleboard rakes to shovel little wooden discs along the pad.

"Did I ever tell you," one called out, "about the queer cowboy who kept putting his chaps on backwards."

"Yes, you did, my dear, yes, you did. And I know exactly who you had in mind."

"Whom! It's whom."

Gabrielle was there, just to the left of the shuffleboard pad, lying asleep on a chair facing the sun. He circled around her. She was long and lithe – her legs crossed at the ankles – just as he remembered her, the way she'd always slept. Yet, somehow, she was more womanly; just as beautiful but more settled into a lush sensuality, her breasts heavier, her hips fuller.

He stopped and stood between her and the sun. He could feel the stinging heat of the sun on his neck. He waited to see if she would feel the presence of his shadow on her body. She did not stir. He leaned close to her and said in a low monotone, "Who knows what evil lurks in the hearts of men."

Her lips parted, not in a smile but in startled pleasure.

"The Shadow knows," she whispered, opened her eyes, took a deep breath, and cried, "Incredible. My God!"

He sat on the edge of the cedar chair and folded his hand over hers. "Who'd have thought, eh?"

"Not me," she said, shaking her head. "And not the Shadow . . ."

"Only, long-time lovebirds like us would know who the Shadow is," he said, touching her cheek.

Two women in pink bathing suits were sailing a Frisbee across the pool, the still water lying like a turquoise lozenge in the red sun. The Frisbee fell into the pool and lay on the water. Gabrielle and Adam stared at it. The women stared at it. Then they went back to their chairs.

"Want a hello drink?" Adam asked.

"It's still morning."

"It's nearly noon."

"I never drink in the morning, it's no good," she said. "My mother drank in the morning."

"Your poor mother. You never wrote," he said, "you never came back home."

"Once, I did, to see my uncle Tonton."

"You didn't come round to see me . . ."

"No."

"Or Harry?"

"No."

She plunged the fingers of her hand into her thick black hair.

"But I went where I knew I could watch him, up on the altar with his choirboys. It made me want to cry. And there you were at mass, too, just a couple of pews away. I stared and stared at you, thinking maybe you'd feel me staring and turn around" – and she paused, tilted her head, not hiding her quick look of appraisal – "you, with that air of yours, always so open, yet unapproachable, that's what I remember, following you out of the church, sometimes getting up real close behind you . . . like we were back playing a kid's game . . . though I knew you wouldn't look back, you were always so self-absorbed, weren't you, except you're not self-absorbed like my uncle Tonton is, he concentrates on hurting people and I don't think you've ever hurt people. Have you?" She closed one eye and this time stared hard at him, and then smiled. "Anyway, at a stoplight when you turned and crossed the other way from me I blew you a kiss and felt my head spin a little, like I was making a mistake, I should have spoken to you . . ."

"So how come Harry never went after *you*?"

"I never let him know where I was."

"Never?"

"No."

"Didn't you ever want to talk to him?"

"No."

"Or me? We talked and talked to each other all the time."

"I used to talk to you in my head. You'd be surprised how long I can talk to myself, and how long I've talked to you."

"I guess so."

"You guess so what?"

"I'd be surprised.

"I guess you would. So what're you doing here?"

"Me?"

"You."

"There's a newspaperman here I like, a guy called Kennedy, William, and his wife who's from here, and now that I think of it, she's a dancer, too. Anyway, I came in from Beirut so that we could do a story together on Cuban exiles, and now that we're done I'm just hanging out for a few days . . . And you?"

"There's this special little hotel in town," she said, "the El Convento it's called – it actually was a convent – and my friend Mio owns a piece of it and he wanted to start a supper club in the hotel with a particular kind of singer and the

kind of dancers you wouldn't expect with this singer, six
hoofers, like Radio City Rockettes, except these are male
dancers, so I choreographed the show, and it's a big success
for him, these boys high-stepping in a convent, and the singer
was a local opera star, so it's all kind of beautiful and strange.
She closes her set every Saturday night with the death scene
from *La Traviata* . . ."

"Jesus, Harry would like that."

She shook her head and sighed.

"Harry, Harry," she said, drawing her big beach towel
around her shoulders, suddenly silent, reflective, before saying, "All my childhood, you know, Harry gave me big spinning tops, that's how he was, with flowers and clown faces
painted on them . . . and you pushed the handles down so
that the tops whirled and hummed. All the way to my tenth
birthday he gave them to me, magnolias and clown faces . . .
and so there was this one night, in New York, when I was in
a small off-Broadway one-act Balanchine, I actually was dancing a clown's part and this clown had the face of a flower, his
face whirling and closing in on me like a flower closes in on
itself at night . . ."

"You danced for Balanchine . . . ?"

"A little associate group, not the Company, it was so perfect, being on that stage like a flower in the dark, it is perfect,
the way a spotlight can look like a big spinning flower, and I
shut my eyes and felt filled up with magnolias spinning in
the eyes of all the audience . . ."

"So you never stopped dancing . . ."

She seemed to be intrigued for a moment by the airline stewards, but then she said, "Only for a little while."

"Why?"

"The thing is," she said, as she shrugged off her towel, lifted his hand that had been folded over hers, and brushed the back of his hand with a kiss, "when I was a little girl . . . when my mother went out playing bingo or something, Harry used to sit with me while I washed in the tub. Then he'd braid my hair into two pigtails. Sometimes he'd circle them into a crown on top of my head, and sometimes he'd drop them down over my breasts that were just beginning. You never saw me when I had no breasts, did you? You don't know how strangely painful it is, your breasts beginning, like your bones are being moved."

"No, I never saw you when you had no breasts."

They both laughed.

"The way it worked out, I ran away, I had to run, I really did disappear, so that's the way it was, I just couldn't be in love with you back then."

"And now?"

"Come on. We just said hello."

"And?"

"Now is now. Hello. I like it down here in San Juan." She stood up. "It's kind of my secret life. Like you've always been a secret in my life, too. Like my father had his secret life."

One of the airline stewards let out a squeal and swung at the other with his shuffleboard rake.

"You bitch," he cried.

"Me, a bitch! A slut like you calling me a bitch!"

"Girls, girls," Gabrielle called, laughing at the two stewards while looking at Adam with an assessing eye so bold that he was surprised, "but you've become a really handsome man. Looks to me like there's something truly elegant in you."

"Really."

"Silence," she said.

She turned to walk toward the hotel, but then paused. "You've always given off silence." She kissed him on the cheek. "Come on. Walk with me. There's something about silence in a man. No excuses. You share that with Mio . . ."

"The man last night?"

". . . except he can also be very cruel."

Gabon

Adam woke in the M'Bgov Hotel with the first light. He had been dreaming of the wild, cheerless smile of the baby gorilla. Cocks crowed. Esmelda knocked on his door. She had brought him hot coffee and fruit. He peered through the shutters, listening to the rippling call of parrots. A milky steam rose out of the earth, a steam that turned acrid yellow in the sunlight and spread like rags over the water. The sun, suspended low in the sky, was clearing the bush, turning the river into a sepia flutter of mirrors. It was a light lacking joy. Then, with a sudden wind, dogs began to howl and the cocks crowed again. There were bursts of gunfire across the river in the bush, the island basin had become an echo chamber. A muezzin made his nasal call to prayer over the loudspeaker in a small minaret, sun-bleached blue shutters were pushed open, and someone threw a red and black rug over a wrought-iron balcony railing, airing a room.

Between bursts of more AK-47 fire there was a distant, faint wailing, like hundreds of keening women, but it was the hysterical screeching of thousands of yard hens. Adam had heard this screeching of hens in the streets of Beirut and Amman, terrified hens caught in the crossfire between snipers. Once, he'd been caught, too, trapped down a blind alley, and he had lost his left little finger to shrapnel. In excruciating pain, in shock, he had fallen to his knees, head down in a silent scream. He had almost passed out as he searched for his finger in the rubble on the street. He had not succumbed to panic, to the listless surrender of the self that he had seen in panic-stricken men. He had not panicked, even as he accepted that a part of himself was lost forever. Instead, his eye, his almost driven need to focus on what he was looking at, his need to get the significant and telling picture, had quickened – "With a mad kind of fucking clarity I was sure my finger was just waiting to be found and I was going to put it in my pocket for safekeeping" – as it always did when he was under pressure: "I see like baseball players say they do when they sometimes see the ball, big as a cantaloupe . . ." He had been praised early on for what editors said was the gravitas of his style – images cropped so that a face or a hand in the air always seemed charged with its own inner intensity, an implied narrative emerging out of layers of darkness, "a sable light," his father had told him, "like laughter heard across dark water," laughter whose tones Adam could feel, Adam could hear. "Sometimes when I'm shooting it's like my father playing on the black notes. I'm not crazy, I'm not morbid. Cole Porter composed all his love songs only on the black notes."

He hurried down the dark hotel stairwell to the first floor past two women hiding in a kitchen alcove, and out into the glass-enclosed dining room where the light startled him. One of the long windows, cracked from top to bottom, had not been washed for weeks, perhaps months. There was a line of dirt in the crack, a line that seemed, as he tilted his head to the angle of the crack, to mark a geological shift in the air, a marking of dread in the air. He could feel it, by God, the hand of the Bone Picker had been laid on him: maybe it was, laughter of all laughs, the Bone Picker and not Gabrielle who would be waiting for him at the end of this road, Gabrielle, who didn't even know he was coming – as he ran into the dining room crying, "Craps, you lose, *Saliendo*," startling the heavy bulbous men of the polka band, who were wearing blue shirts and white shorts and striped knee socks. They were sitting around a table, pointing across the road to two men with rifles who were running from house to house, the band's tuba and trombones lying on the floor in the sunlight.

"*Und morgen die ganze Welt . . .*"

"Sorry, I don't speak German."

"Come see the crazy nigger show."

A squat armoured car, flying a small flag with a black star on a yellow field, moved down the hotel street, a 50-calibre machine gun mounted on the back. Henri, who drank Pernod with water in the morning, said he had heard that counter-revolutionary guerrillas were in control of two hills to the southwest. "There's been big trouble, *mon ami*," he said. "These are men of sacrifice, so they say of themselves. They are their own nemesis. Many tied explosives to their bodies and threw themselves into the tanks and others lay down in the path of the tanks. *J'en viens à être ce que je fais.*"

Henri was lean and had long delicate fingers. Sitting in a canvas chair, he spread his legs, and they began to flap apart like the wings of an awkward bird. His right arm hung limp to the floor. Outside, government troops mounted a mortar position beside the hotel. Five small tanks pelted the dense bush on the southern hill. The shells made a sucking, draining sound. Houses broke open, expelling balls of white smoke, and then a yellow smear settled over the hillside.

The troops, all running awkwardly as if their boots were too big, moved in a 105 howitzer rocket rifle on a Jeep truck, the long thin insect-like barrel casting recoil as a concussion through all the houses and the hotel, shattering the windows in the dining room, where a tall man, beefy through the neck and shoulder, tufts of black hair on his knuckles, cried, *"Mein Gott, diese wahnsinnigen Dschungelkaninchen werden uns ermorden!"* Henri hardly flinched: *"Répandez leur sang . . . qu'ils dorment . . ."* But the musicians, clutching their horns and the tuba, barged into the hallway, trotting to their rooms.

"I brought you a revolver," Esmelda murmured to Henri.

Adam went to his room of unpainted plaster walls, a lamp on a hook by the bed, and an old stained sepia photograph of Victoria Falls hanging over a washstand. *Livingstone was here . . .* In a stark light, everything was angled, hard, sharp – *where did that blue sky go?* Laughing at how drunk he had been the night before, he pulled the tilted chair from under the handle of the louvred window: the sun bounced off the corrugated tin roofs of shacks. With each break in the firing, he heard the hysterical hens. The sprawling shack city to the southwest was on fire, and he could see down an incline under a dwarf palm a curled body, an ember of flesh surrounded by a litter of brass shell casings. He took out his camera. Henri appeared at the door. "The army says there is a guerrilla spotter in the hotel, a maid or someone . . . they will shoot anyone they see in our windows."

Four infantry trucks pulled up beside a stone retaining wall, part of an unfinished building. Within a few minutes, incoming mortars from the south blew out the wall and two trucks, bodies catapulting into the air. Adam went to the window: *Click click click. What a life,* he thought with wry satisfaction, *the shooting starts, I get busy.* A gunner wheeled and pumped jackhammer rounds into the hotel, tearing a foot-wide hole through Adam's bathroom wall. *Like I'm fucking out of my mind.* He sprawled on the concrete and waited for the night so he could drag his mattress into the hallway.

Puerto Rico

As they had left the beach of sunbathers at noon, Gabrielle had promised to join him in the evening. Carrying his camera, he was stopped at the door to the crowded casino by a doorman. "Gambling, sir, is a private affair. Can't interfere with the patrons now, can we." Adam smiled, saying, "Well, we could, because interfering is my life, but we won't," and as he handed his Leica to a checkroom lady he saw that Gabrielle was coming down the stairs from the casino dining room and she was carrying a silver ice bucket that she had taken from a dining room table. But the man with the black hand, Mio, was beside her. He was clean shaven with a sallow cheek, had a stoop, and an air of menacing reserve. Adam could see that his left hand was, in fact, encased in a hard shiny black glove; he held his right hand, wrapped in a large white table napkin, down in the ice bucket. Before the startled croupiers could stop him, Mio had eased in beside Adam at the table. Gabrielle was laughing, she was holding the bucket for Mio but she was smiling at Adam, as if this were a joke she had arranged for him. "Sir . . ." the pit boss said sternly, but a bosomy, good-looking woman in her forties wearing a scoop-necked dress called across in a drawl, "Leave that man be, he's gonna make the rooster strut. You just hold on an' roll them bones, boy."

Mio waited. The Bone Picker had backed off and disappeared. The stick man whipped the dice to Mio who, as he unwrapped his ice-bucket hand, said to Gabrielle in the rasping voice of a man who has a parched throat, "I roll, you bet." Then he said to himself, *"Was hab' ich getan, dass ich so leiden muss?"* He clamped his ice-cold hand on Adam's arm and whispered, "You don't bet . . . not on me." Adam felt the weight of two men behind him. Mio threw the dice backhanded . . . eleven . . . and came back with a seven, and one of the burly men cried, "The hand, the hand is here."

In the crush around the table, with bets and backup bets being called, Adam stood silently, uncertain and a little unnerved, but Gabrielle winked at him. *She's drunk,* he thought. They stood waiting for the croupiers to get the bets down after each of Mio's winning rolls. He seemed immune to caution, or to the collapse in conviction – that failure of faith in the self – that comes with caution, and he told

Gabrielle to double the bets, slowly wrapping and unwrapping his hand in the ice-cold towel . . . but, as he was about to roll for his fifth straight pass, a man with little black hairs in his pocked cheeks smacked a stack of chips down on the line, snarling into the moment of silence, "He's wrong, he's coming out wrong." Mio hesitated: the man's snarl had had its own force, but Mio let out a little whoop of rasping laughter and said, "Don't be ridiculous." He rolled a seven, whispering, "The hand is on you . . ." The woman in the scoop-necked dress leaned toward Mio, "Touch me, touch my tits for luck, you got it all." The Bone Picker, who had returned to the table looking stricken, said, "I like that, that I like," as Mio, bemused, and then brazen, drew his ice-cold forefinger down between the woman's breasts, deep into the cleavage so that she shuddered. The Bone Picker quietly stacked his last two rolls of hundred-dollar chips on the line, some five thousand dollars. Mio took up the dice, blew on them in his fist, and rolled, a five, and then a follow-up seven, a loss, and then – as the Bone Picker let five thousand ride – he rolled another loss.

"Whyn't you keep your tits outta this?" a man yelled.

Mio turned to Adam and said quietly, "You'll excuse me. Coming to play beside you tonight was only a harmless whim." He walked through the crowd, leaving one of his men to go to the cage to cash in his winning chips, and Gabrielle, holding the silver bucket filled with sloshing ice, laughed as Mio went out the door.

"What was that all about?" Adam asked.

"You saw it," she said, passing the ice bucket to Mio's other man.

"Yeah, but what was it all about?"

"Really, I thought you were smarter than that."

"You mean he was just doing a number on me!"

"What did you feel when he put his hand on you?"

"I wondered what you felt."

"When?"

"When he puts his hand on you."

"Safe," she said, taking Adam's arm, and they walked up a short flight of stairs to a patio facing a swimming pool with only underwater eye-lamps in the walls giving off light. At poolside, the Bone Picker had taken off his jacket. He was walking in a tight circle, mumbling and muttering to himself, and when he saw Adam and Gabrielle, he rushed forward and took Gabrielle by both arms, crying, "Jesus H. Christ, I came back. My whole bloody life was down the drain and I made it back on that crazy guy blowing his roll, like I came back from the dead . . ." He whirled and with a whoop of joy, luminescent in the strange underwater light, he took off fully clothed into the water and after the explosion of spray he bobbed in the water, dog-paddling, giggling.

"Poor man," she said. "He'll probably live in some woman's life like that for a long time."

"It'd be nice to live in a woman's life."

"You worried about me or Mio?"

"He's your man?"

"Not the way you think. Otherwise he just might kill you."

"So who is he?"

"A man who loves me and a man who wants no one . . . or, maybe it's the other way around. He wants me and loves no one."

"You love him?"

"We've never been alone in the dark."

"You've never been alone?"

"He was a child during the war, he was buried alive. I told him that you were my first love. He's impressed by love, he respects it, he's even a little afraid of it, and I told him that the blood of my innocence was on your hands." She laughed. "The blood of my innocence, I like that," she said, "it has a certain ring to it." The man was swimming on his back, still giggling. "Shall we throw him a rope?" she asked.

"No. If he drowns he'll drown happy. Bone Picker drowns in a fit of happiness," he said as if he were reading a newspaper headline out loud.

They walked through a white filigreed iron gate onto the empty nighttime ocean beach, the waves breaking in the full moonlight.

"It's not like you weren't my first love, too," he said.

They lay down on chairs close to the water line, the screen of lights from all the hotels on the strip hanging in the air behind them, and they lay looking up, listening to the roll of the waves. "You want to know why," he said, wanting to say something unexpected, something interesting, given the years that they had not seen each other, "all the ancient wise men looked so long at the stars? They were the only things in their lives that were fixed, that was their clockwork. The stars were what they could count on, and connect little figures and stories to. But even so, in their heart of hearts they knew all the arranging of the stars was an illusion and all the little stories were only lies covering up the dark empty truth," and he took her hand, lightly kissing her fingers, "and that's why shooting stars were so special. Stars that shot through the system, and magic men followed those stars, ending up delirious in the hills of their illusions . . ."

"Aren't you something," she said. "Delirious . . ."

"Well, maybe just excited . . ."

"Are you excited?"

"Delirious."

"I like that," she said.

Lying on their chairs, salt spray on their lips, and looking out over the dark water, they saw lights, suspended rows of lights moving in the air, cleaving the night sky. "Look," he said pointing at a large cruise liner on the moonlit ocean. "He's out there on the poop deck, sitting cross-legged in his old iron suit, searching the scouting maps spread on his knees, following his star, my old plunger man, Ponce."

"Yeah, but he *was* old, we're still young, too young to have to tell lies to each other, let alone ourselves."

"Who's lying?"

"So let's go away, then. Follow our star. There's this wonderful little hotel outside the old town of Ponce . . ."

❦

Albert Waters
1901–1951
A Sailor on an Outrigger
He Had Wanted
To Be
But Steamships
Made Sail
Arbitrary
So
As Tailor and Outfitter
He Went Down to
The Sea

Toronto

In early December, his father came home from his tour of the west coast. It rained all week. The storm sewers flooded and there were pools of wet light on the road. He and Adam sat on the back porch wearing heavy sweaters. They were silent for a long time. There was a new grey streak in his father's hair and his eyes were hooded by loose flesh. "I never really knew how to talk to you as a child," he said. "But now you're a man, a young man, and I assume I have something to say, but not necessarily."

A raccoon had come into the driveway, snout down, scurrying toward the garbage cans on the other side of the house. "Look at him, he knows we're here," his father said, "yet he's absolutely indifferent, that hunch in his back . . ." He struck a match and the coon disappeared. He had taken to smoking a pipe, but the stem had snapped earlier in the week and now it was held together with a piece of copper wire left over from some plumbing work done years ago.

"I had a friend back about ten years," he said, "a sculptor, his name was Kosso, an Israeli, and one night he told me that all the looting in ancient ruins was no more than garbage picking and it was good pickings because if you really wanted to know about how men lived, who they were, then you just needed to look in their garbage. I suppose he was right, if you think that all men are kind of like coons, some more ferocious than others. It seemed somehow right to me that he did his sculpting in stainless steel."

His father had been down at the courthouse all week, at Osgoode Hall, because a friend had been arrested at the border for possession, and then, after his friend – FRANKIE REKH AND HIS REKHING CREW – a trumpet player who blew two trumpets at once and led an R&B band featuring a black transvestite blues singer – had been freed on bail, he'd stayed around the courthouse, intrigued by an inquest, a story that had caught his eye in the newspapers: a Serbian boy who had been shot by a cop down a back alley. He was fascinated, he said, because everyone in the old oak-panelled courtroom wanted to avoid any trouble for the police. "Even the boy's mother wanted no more trouble and she was looking for a way out. She just wanted to get on with her life, and this getting on with life was bigger for her than any idea of vengeance, let alone justice. She wanted to keep her snout down. She'd turned into a coon. Maybe there's some coon in all of us."

"You got some coon?" Adam asked.

"Well, when I was the only white man around this town playing what your good decent folks called nigger music, they used to call me the boon coon, but that's a different story. I just kept my head down and sang the song."

"Has Mom got some coon?"

"Your mother has bare-faced audacity. The last time I went on the road she said as solemn as a saint, 'Web, you're a good man,' and I tried to laugh. But to tell you the truth, I didn't like her for saying that. It was the first lie she'd told me in years."

It began to pour rain again. There was a strong wind and the rain blew in on the porch.

"Unless you want to soak yourself, we'd better go in," he said, "but don't wake your mother."

They sat in the kitchen.

"You know what old Rueful asked me the other day?" He handed Adam a glass of Armagnac. "He wanted to know if I didn't have a view of myself, some perspective, and I said God no, and I don't want one."

There was a loud clatter of cans in the alley.

"Damn coons, they've knocked over the garbage again."

"What ever happened to your friend?"

"Rekhing?"

"No, the sculptor."

"Last I heard he gave it up and went off into the desert."

"And you've got no view of yourself?"

"Nope."

"You wouldn't lie to me."

"Not necessarily."

Gabon

Night came, with no electricity or water. Adam stretched out on the cold concrete floor and listened to the pumping shellfire and snipers. No candles could be lit in the rooms. He had put night film in his camera. Both the guerrillas of one tribe and the army of another tribe had fired into the hotel. Down along the lava-rock roads, they were burning each other's villages, continuing (according to short-wave BBC radio) to decapitate women and children in the river valley to the east.

Adam spread his thin mattress at the end of the corridor and pulled himself on his belly out onto his room's small balcony. An animal was screaming in the trees. Red tracers streaked across the sky. A phosphorous shell exploded, there was a cloud of searing white light and then a ball of luminous smoke, as if lit from within. Heavy machine guns raked houses in the dark – or fired blindly into the bush. A house came alive, like a twisted white face, hollowed eyes, the doorway a gaping mouth. He turned and crawled back into the room, thudding mortar fire rattling the french doors, and went to the other end of the dark hotel corridor that was crammed with mattresses, where the bandsmen and a consultant for a pharmaceutical firm were lying awake, their short-wave radios losing connection as voices spluttered and then drifted away. One of the bandsmen, drunk and scared, began to march up and down the dark stairwell making a child's drumming noise in his cheeks. The guerrilla radio announced that all their positions were secure, that they had destroyed twenty-one tanks along the N'Chala road.

"Where's that?" the consultant asked.

"Who knows?"

"North, zer in the desert . . ."

"There's oil in the desert."

"What zis is always all about is oil."

"No, it's not. It's global."

"Global my ass," Adam said.

"I'd like a piece of ass, and a scotch-and-soda," the consultant said.

"You guys got a whole flatbed trailer full of beer kegs out there."

"Ze army machine-gunned zose zis morning."

"They shot the fucking beer!"

"Zey shoot ze sky, zey zink zey are shooting out ze eyes of God, zis is no joke."

The army radio station announced the guerrillas had been driven back into the bush. "Jesus Christ," the consultant cried, "the goddamn bush is only five hundred yards away."

Henri appeared at the head of the stairs, elbowing past the marching German who was making an abrupt right turn on the stair. "Gentlemen," he said, "I have just informed the army that everything is normal in here. Absolutely normal. We will forget them if they will forget us. They have agreed, but I must point out, they cannot forget us if they see us. It is a piquant point, *n'est-ce pas?* It has a logic, *oui? Qui demande pourquoi se figure qu'il a un futur . . .*" Someone began to sing, "Strangers in the night," and then he said, "This war's not going nowhere . . . you watch, we're stuck."

Adam lay on his mattress thinking of trees, lilac trees and weeping birch, red-wing blackbirds and bobolinks and red berries on bushes and a soldier he'd seen on the road sitting under an umbrella surrounded by piles of his grandfather's long underwear and shoes, and he lay thinking of the bare feet and breasts of a woman he'd loved and the pointed breast of a woman he did not love and old Father Zale's blackboard equation $- 2 = 1 -$ which seemed more and more to be about life as it got lived because the equation contained, hidden within its own logic, its own impossibility, a negation even as it remained an affirmation, because all equations by their nature had to be an affirmation, and he heard in the back of his mind's ear a heavy splash from the day when, as a child, he'd fallen off the end of a dock into dark water just like he felt himself falling here, entirely unprepared, into this darkness, hearing Miss Klein's wry drunken singing and laughter down in the dark, *There's no business like show business*, but also the murmuring laughter of Gabrielle as she lay naked, stroking herself in her sleep in the dark in San Juan – dreaming of hummingbirds and delirium – and he had heard her saying on either their fourth or their fifth night together that it was going to rain, that she could feel it on the wind, a promise of rain, and so they had gone to sleep that night enclosed in each other's arms, a ring around the moon, full of promise . . .

Toronto
Father Zale carried a furled umbrella tucked under his arm, even on hot dry days. He had a high forehead, a long thin nose, and smelled of talcum powder. He loved birds and had built a cluster of wooden birdhouses close to the school on the edge of the bluff. In the mornings, he went out with a knapsack full of crusts hanging from his shoulder and he spread crusts on the ground and filled the feeders.

"Sometimes," he said, "in my black skirts I must look like a scarecrow."

One afternoon, while he was spreading crusts across the lawn with great sweeps of his arm, he said, "I was from the farm, you know. See, I've got farmers' hands," and he held out a big fist, thick through the thumb and the heel. "There are puzzles on the farm," he said. "My mother used to spread out a crossword puzzle as big as the kitchen table and work on it for a week, but there are bigger puzzles than that, like why pigs gang up and kill one another. Nobody knows," and he dug his fist into the sack of crusts.

"You always seem to like it when there are things nobody knows," Adam said, his Leica hanging from his neck.

"And why," Father Zale said, throwing out another handful of stale crusts, "do whales beach themselves and commit suicide? Tell me that."

"I don't know."

Without breaking stride, Adam lifted his Leica and shot him, three-quarter profile.

"Nobody does."

"But they will, somebody'll figure it out," Adam said, taking two shots in succession.

"They'll find out," the priest said, paying no attention to the camera, "that the answer is only a bigger question."

He rubbed his hands together as they walked under the tall cedars along the bluff, seagulls swooping and crying behind them.

"Life's divided into two kinds of people," he said, "and it's all a matter of temperament. Those who find questions more interesting than answers, and practical men who want good sensible answers at any cost, even if the cost is self-deception."

Adam stepped in front of Father Zale, snapped a shot, and got back in stride, saying, "So?"

"So, the new deal in physics," he said, "is chaos. Trying to figure out how whatever we thought was order turns into disorder, like when you're watching someone's cigarette burn down in an ashtray, did you ever do that?"

"Yeah, my mother. I used to keep my eye on her smoke rings the whole time."

"I figure we're just like that smoke. We unravel into a million particles in a moment of chaos, and chaos is in the core of the human condition, like someone flicked us on fire and up we went in smoke, it's what they call the inchoate. Maybe that's the evil that's in us, in the universe."

"So long, Satan," Adam said sardonically, "I don't think the Pope is going to like this."

"Gone up in smoke," Father Zale said, smiling, complicit in the joke.

They were standing above the bluff of eelgrass and shale worn by the wind.

"Or maybe things aren't evil," Adam said, putting the cap on his lens. "Maybe they just get tired, get weak. My father says, 'Walk around long enough and you get a hole in your shoe and a hole in your heart.'"

Father Zale laughed and leaned forward on his furled umbrella, the steel tip digging into the earth. "You're going to send this old man copies of those pictures, right?" A maple tree clung to the edge of the bluffs and half its roots fanned into the air, the earth eroded under it. Other trees had fallen down the slope, the bark stripped and the trunks bleached by the sun, balls of upended roots full of seagulls. "You're not going to forget, now," he said, "you're gone so often, who knows, you may never come back." It had grown chilly and he tucked his umbrella under his arm and slipped his hands inside the sleeves of his black soutane. "One of the last delights of life," he said, "is recovering our memories of ourselves as we grow older. Those pictures will do me just fine."

He turned and looked back over the cedar hedge to his bird-feeding houses. "Only seagulls around here and seagulls don't really count as birds at all. They're like bone-pickers. Anyway, memory's got its own mind, and sometimes what we remember most is what we'd like to forget."

"Sometimes," Adam said, "my photos of my mother make me remember what I'd like to forget, like how angry I can be with my father, at least for a while."

"Is that your sadness? You don't favour your father?"

"He was always off somewhere when I was a child."

"I'm sure he shares your sadness."

"He was gone, too tied up with being true to himself. But I'm not sad, Father, life's too extraordinary for me to be sad," Adam said. "It's just that I've inherited his disease. I'm always on the road to somewhere, too."

"You've always been too much alone, that's true, maybe kind of cornering yourself. You've got to watch out. An animal in a corner finally just dies."

"Well, sometimes, like I'm a baby, I wonder why the people I love have to die."

"We never do," the priest said.

"What?"

"Die."

"My grandfather's dead as a doornail."

"Not at all. He's alive in God."

"I'm not sure I believe in God, Father."

"You don't?" he said. "You're sure of that?"

"No, I just don't beat my brains in thinking about it."

"Well, He'll be back in your brain, you'll see, popping up like a memory you'd forgotten you had. We come from God and we always remember Him. I believe that."

"I'm glad you do, Father."

"Why?"

"It'd be awful if no one did."

"Ah well, when all's said and done, so will you."

"Never say die?"

"No, never say die, though we do die, but never say so. That's what my own father told me. Never say the word. It's bad luck."

❧

Gabon

In the morning, Adam watched as oval armoured cars sped down a side street, fired into villas west of a traffic circle, and then sped back, parking in front of the hotel. Tanks and a howitzer opened up: *thrumpfthrumpfthrumpfthrumpfthrumpf.* He had had little sleep, his mind reeling, and he kept breaking into cold sweats. He sat almost rigid as he listened to the clattering racket of gunfire, as if giant children were loose in the bush with huge wooden noisemakers in each fist, whirling clackers, and he sat very still, letting the sound seep into him so that it became normal while any silence seemed arbitrary. Looking out of Henri's office window, he could see that the army was shelling a three-storey block to the east. "It is the insane asylum," Henri said, waving his hand.

"What in the world will they think is going on?"

"Who?"

"The crazies in the asylum?"

"I think," Henri said, "they are probably talking peacefully about their childhood for the first time in years. For the first time the thunder of the world is like the thunder in their heads. They know now they are sane." He laughed, and Adam, crouching by the window curtains, kept taking photographs *click click click click* until Henri said, "If the sun catches the lens, if the army sees the light, they will fire with abandon . . . You will forgive me, but what you are doing is stupid and wherever it is you think you are going you won't get there, they will kill us."

"Sorry," Adam said, "it's a kind of compulsion, maybe even a kind of drug," and he laughed with a sheepish little shrug but he felt a sudden sickening in the pit of his stomach: *Dead.* It struck him with finality, and a pathos that made him want to cry: *And she wouldn't ever know I'd loved her so much that I'd got this far. Only to die.* But then he said out loud: "It's all ridiculous."

"*Mais oui,*" Henri said. "*Mais oui.*"

On the ridge of the far hill, black blossoms of smoke spread and opened against the blue sky, cocks crowed as if the afternoon were the dawn. He heard a loud keening, before he saw the white woman, bare-headed and bare-breasted in the long grass, holding her high heels in her hands, stumbling in wider and wider circles until she walked into a tree trunk and fell down. She began to wave both hands at the sky. He couldn't see her face.

A small black man opened the office door and came in, the baby gorilla bounding along beside him. The man had a hunch in his left shoulder and a jutting hip. He carried a large galvanized washtub, with two inches of water in it. Henri slumped into a chair under oval photographs of nameless stockholders in the old colonial company. He took off his shoes and socks and rolled up his tan trouser cuffs. "You do the same," he said to Adam. The black man set the tub down on the floor.

"But we've no drinking water," Adam said. "I haven't had a drink of water for three days."

"We've whiskey, Pernod . . ."

"Where's the water come from?"

"The roof. Over this room. A cistern on the roof . . ."

The black man dragged a wooden chair to the other side of the tub. Henri settled his bony feet into the water and spread his legs; his knees began to flap. Adam slipped off his sandals, sat down, and put his feet into the water. He felt instantly soothed. The hunchback gave him a whiskey and then lit the front burner of a propane stove, slid a chipped enamel pot over the flame, and put two dirty glasses on a packing-case table. He served hot syrupy tea, and then crouched beside Henri, who closed his eyes and rested his big hand on the man's hump. The whiskey and hot tea drew the blood to Adam's empty stomach, making him drowsy. Drained by sleeplessness and the relentless reverberation of gunfire, he went to sleep in the chair.

Toronto

In his darkroom, Adam opened a box filled with negatives and held one up to the light; shadow figures caught in a stillness, each a transparent tissue of time, like a cell tissue, that's what he'd told an editor, holding the cell in the air to the light, *see*, he'd said, a negative that confirmed a fact, an objective fact confirmed in time . . . *but what is an objective fact?* That was a question his editors shied away from, *because they knew, intuitively or not, that to be objective,* as Adam had insisted, *was to have no cultural identity. It was to exist in such an existential solitude as to have, in fact, no place in the world,* and always, after a shoot, he spread six or seven prints on his table and constructed a scene, a situation, *pretty much the way it was,* and then he reconstructed the scene *into what it might be, or might have been, but then,* he said, *maybe all that matters is that somehow I come out of this with a detail I can attest to, a glimpse of how it was and maybe a glimpse is the best we get if we learn to trust our own eyes and ears.*

He telephoned Father Zale. "I just wanted you to know, you're not only there, which you are, but you're in an envelope, too, you're in the mail." He went back into his darkroom where he liked to sit with new prints hanging on a wire line. He'd leaned into the dark, he said, to listen to the sound of the stillness between images, between an empty shoe and an empty shoe, the stillness that sometimes, if he sat in the dark for a long enough time, became a kind of dread, a dread that threatened, more and more each year, to take on the face of the man in his recurring dream, the face that would not only appear to him in his sleep but would give him give the kiss of death, becoming one with him in a complicity in death.

It was this sense of complicity that had come to him one windless hour in Jerusalem when he'd found himself in the ancient stone city with a writer named Amichai whose wife was the only person from her large family left alive after the death camps. Amichai had told him that he lived in "a household of ghosts." He had spoken of these ghosts as they had walked together toward a Palestinian refugee camp, and then he'd said, "We have helped to create a people of ghosts. We have done it the way we do everything. We collapse, yet everything is normal. It's a kind of ordered chaos. We collapse into ourselves every time we stand up to the world. We've had to change our attitude so many times – the Germans, in all their evil, tried to exterminate us. Now, they are our friends because they've paid us reparations – so many shekels per dead soul – so that now every yes has its no, so that our big problems are now empty. We've ended up with questions that have no weight, and solutions that only weigh us down. We are caught up in endless negotiation with complicity, certain that we are right." Adam, photographing him at noon in the deep shadows of Solomon's Stables, had watched him emerge in a print as a dark, almost silken shadow etched against dark shimmering rubble, and then the next day he shot him in the falling light of dusk outside Dung Gate, his round open face flattened as a cold moon.

Adam said: "See, you and yourself, there you are, your two faces together, each of you alone, so I hardly know who you are, but no one can say you're not there." They laughed and embraced, and for the rest of the week Adam walked through the lean stone alleys, his Leica around his neck, photographing beggars and holy men at the base of a white stone wall, a young soldier with a red beard slumped above a rain gutter, cradling his Uzi as pilgrims genuflected at one of Christ's Stations below him; and, at the old temple wall, as evening darkness fell, his last series of shots was of rows of young soft-faced paratroopers who stood at attention in battle dress, adult boys being inducted into the army as the paratrooper insignia, writ large in the night sky, was set on fire and a man let out a whining nasal cry, a prayer . . .

Adam sent those negatives, those rapt faces, their rifle barrels beside their cheeks, staring at the lone bearded man in khaki reaching into the darkness under the arc of fire, to his magazine with a note: "You collapse, yet everything is normal. *Man kann sich totsiegen!*" They were never printed, and coming back home several months later, asking why, he had an argument about those pictures with his editor, a stern woman with broad shoulders and small breasts:

"Why not?"

"We'd get crucified," she said.

"What the hell are you talking about?"

"You wouldn't want to take a picture like that unless you wanted to make a point."

"The point was right there in front of my eyes, like it always is. I trust my eyes."

"The whole world's in front of your eyes. You're gonna give me Jewish soldiers and burning letters in the sky in front of the Wailing Wall and not expect me to get the point?"

"I didn't light up the sky."

"The trouble with guys like you," she said, "is you don't love. You just look, and that lets you think you can be cynical about people who deserve to be loved."

"So now I'm a lousy lover. Next thing you'll tell me I'm a bad photographer."

"You're a great photographer, one of the best, but you've got more balls than brains. And," she said, picking up a photograph, "what is this *man kann sich totsiegen* shit?"

"It's true . . ."

"Don't fuck my mind, I had it translated. *'One can drive oneself victoriously into death,'*" and she laughed, then said, scowling, "Look, we know you're one of the best in the world, but you know how it is. Gimme a paratrooper helping a refugee girl across the road, maybe we'll run them both. Balance. There's got to be balance, you know that."

"What you call balance, objectivity, is a lie."

"Nonsense, we've all got our responsibilities . . ."

"I just try to shoot what I see. That's my responsibility. What else can I do?"

They stood apart, Adam staring out the window through metallic slat blinds. Then he turned, smiling, as if they had not had a dispute.

"I hear you've got all kinds of shoes, racks of them, fifty pairs of shoes."

"I got a lot of shoes," she said. "I like shoes, it's not a crime."

"I hear every Saturday morning, you vacuum the insides of your shoes."

"So, maybe I do," she said, drawing back after he'd put his hands on her shoulders, and kissed her lightly on the cheek.

"I'd like to photograph you vacuuming your shoes. I would. I once did a whole series on empty shoes. It's how I'd like to remember you. Doing that to your shoes."

PART SIX

Puerto Rico

On their fifth morning in Ponce, Gabrielle woke saying that she had had a broken sleep, bad dreams, anxiety, and holding on to Adam's arm she asked, "You hear the coqui? In the middle of the night?"

"Night birds?"

"They're not birds."

"It sounded like the trees were full of chirping birds."

"They're frogs, tiny little frogs."

"They sound like birds."

Her cheek was hot, even feverish, against his shoulder.

"Weren't you feeling good last night?"

"Of course."

"But you feel feverish."

"I've never been happier," she said. "Never. It's like I'm a girl again."

"What I know is," he said, getting up from the bed and folding open the wooden shutters to the bedroom window, "it's morning, and there's nothing like the morning air coming off the sea. And the hummingbird's back."

"Okay," she said.

"The bird's been coming every day, like it's a blessing."

"Birds scare me," she said.

"Why in the world would birds scare you?"

"They just do. Harry, when he was upset, he always walked like a bird, bobbing his head. I always thought birds came from the place of the dead. Like grief."

"I got news for you, they live in the trees."

"Yeah, but when I was a kid, the men on the street, after all the leaves had fallen, they'd rake the leaves into great big piles at the curb and they'd burn them and sometimes the leaves would smoulder for days, and there'd be these great big clouds of billowing smoke, it smelled so wonderful I can smell it now, it used to make me dizzy standing in the smoke, it was better than the smell of incense in church, and whenever there was a lot of smoke, particularly at the end of the day, there'd always be birds that I never saw anywhere else but in the smoke . . ."

"Maybe they weren't real."

"Maybe. It was always around Hallowe'en, when there were these monster pumpkin faces, and bats and skeletons. That's how I won my first CYO dance competition. I put on a black body stocking and I painted a glowing white skeleton on it so that I could be a dancing skeleton and I danced all the Fred Astaire steps to "Tea For Two" like I was Mister Bones at five in the afternoon in the movies at the Ritz. It was hilarious. It brought down the house, I was Harry's little girl skeleton, and they lifted me up and took me off stage, I disappeared wrapped up in a black satin bedsheet."

She leapt off the bed and stood with her hands on her hips, a dancer with her shoulders back in open admiration of her naked self. He whispered, "My God, you *are* beautiful." She turned, and turned again, and then asked, "Have you had a woman in your life that really counted, that you actually lived with?"

"Once, for nearly a year," he said, "and don't ask me about her. I can remember things she said. I can't remember her body at all. Can't even smell her. But she had this voice, this high-pitched nasal edge. I don't know how I stood it."

"Oh, American women," she said with a shrug. "They have voices that could cut glass."

"She wasn't American. She was French."

"Worse. They all sound as if their sinuses are shot," and when he laughed she said, "And Frenchmen all walk like they were born to be waiters."

"After we'd stopped seeing each other she wrote me an astonishing note, like she was telling me, a little vengefully now that we were done and I was gone, how little I really knew about her, how mysterious and independent she was from me."

Gabrielle rose on her toes and with an arched of tone, as if she were miffed to hear about another woman, said, "It's not the leg that really does it . . . it's the dip in the small of the back." She touched the little hollow above her buttocks. "Without the dip," she said with an aloof little shake of her head, "you really don't have it for a dancer." She picked up a heavy terrycloth towel, saying, "No hips, no dips; no dips, no luck."

"Well, God knows I can't dip," he said.

"And what did she say?"

"Who?"

"Your friend with her note."

"It wasn't really a note. It was just these statements . . ."

"Like what?"

"Like her son was illegitimate."

"She had a son?"

"Not that I knew. But I guess so."

"And . . . ?"

"She said that for a year she was a high-class call girl with only one client."

"That's pretty darn exclusive," Gabrielle said, laughing.

"You shouldn't take that tone."

"Sorry."

"She was actually quite refined, very beautiful."

"I'm sure she was."

"But then, she also said she'd given her mother an overdose so the woman could die with dignity. Then she was convicted of shoplifting after her mother died, and she still had a criminal record when we were living together, so that's why she never travelled with me."

"Do you believe that about her mother?"

"Maybe. But what I didn't know, a few years ago – when we were all the same age in the same town, you and me, too – she was a Sunshine Girl in the *Toronto Sun*."

"You're kidding."

"Maybe she was kidding. Maybe the whole thing's a fantasy. A lie. How can I know?"

"You lived with her."

"Right."

"Did you love her?"

"Not enough I guess. Not like I love you."

"We haven't seen each other for nine years."

"And I still love you," he said.

Her eyes welled up with tears.

"I'm going to take a shower," she said.

As he stepped into the shower stall, after her, her eyes widened as if she were startled to find him coming to her there, and for Adam that startled widening of her eyes had always been a part of her mystery: no matter how self-assured she was, she seemed to be taken completely by surprise by the freshness of any given moment, even staring at him sometimes as if she'd never seen him before which, particularly after they had made love, he found a little unnerving. But though she sometimes shrank back, surprised, she was never shy or reluctant. "No matter what," she said, "I love my body. So why shouldn't I love yours?" Slowly, caressing herself to arouse him, she soaped her breasts as the water poured down over her shoulders, and then she reached out and soaped his chest, as if to make sure he was actually there in the steam before he took her in his arms, cradling her . . ."Give me your mouth," she said . . ."Give me your mouth . . ." They tried to keep their eyes open in the rush of water but they blinked and laughed and she said, "It's like we're those two wonderful kids that we were, I mean, aren't we, I hope, we're back like we were, at least a little," and they kissed, and he kissed her breasts and her nipples and then slid down her body, holding her waist and then her buttocks, his head in the hollow of her thighs, shower water tumbling down her belly and into his mouth, streams of water rushing in his ears until she began to shudder, rising up on her toes, and then she sank down into the shower well with him where they held each other, water coursing over their faces, making them hide in each other's necks. "Yes," he said, "we're back, yes we are," soothed under the force of water, "and bigger, better."

When they got dressed, she put on one of his shirts, saying, "I don't care how big this shirt is. It's you, it's like being inside you, I want to smell you."

"Most of the time we smell like the ocean," he said. "I've never spent so much time in the water."

"Or in bed," she laughed.

"That doesn't count."

"As what?"

"As time. That's somewhere else. That's hummingbird country."

They went out into their courtyard and drank *maccioti* from small porcelain cups in the shade of the red clay walls that were covered by alamanda vines. The *patron* brought them two glasses of Prosecco in ice-cold orange juice. He was wearing a black arm band.

"I am sorry," Adam said.

"What for?" the *patron* asked.

"You are in mourning."

"No, no, it is over," the *patron* said, slapping his hands to his chest and laughing. "It is over, the seven nights of *floron* are over and so now I know the child who died last week is truly dead and there will be playing today by the other children on the little hill."

"What hill?"

"You must have your drink and come to the hill."

A bell struck ten in the church tower in the town. They walked along a narrow sandy road under a pale blue sky, a poised gull in the sky. Passing half-cleared fields and cactus farms and a row of dead trees, they heard voices from over the rise of the hill. They crossed over the hill. Then on a small flatland facing out to the sea they saw twenty boys and girls dressed in white blouses scampering in circles, flying kites off the cliff and holding fistfuls of coloured balloons by long strings and two girls with long black braids curtsied to each other and began to dance in the long grass, and Gabrielle said, "It's like a dream. They are like dream children."

"No, they are our village children," the *patron* said.

"What's your name?" Adam asked.

"Trigueño. The weather is good for you. Some rain. But it is always good at this time of year."

"But it'll be hot and then rain. I heard cicadas."

"The cicadas are wrong. There is no reason why cicadas should always be right." He handed flowers and balloons to Gabrielle and Adam.

"Would you like to go first?" Trigueño asked.

"Where?"

"To throw flowers."

The children had crowded close to the cliff. A strong breeze had come up, pulling their kites and balloons, so that some children while trying to hold on to their balloons dropped their flowers and then, as they knelt to pick up the flowers, they lost their grip on the strings of the balloons. Yellow and blue and green balloons were caught on the wind and carried out over the sea, disappearing into the sun as Trigueño, his hand on a child's shoulder, chanted:

> *Y Dios sobresaltado, nos oprime*
> *El pulso, grave, mudo,*
> *Y como padre a su pequeña,*
> *Apenas,*
> *Pero apenas, entreabre los sangrientos algodones*
> *Y entre sus dedos toma a la esperanza*

The children threw their flowers into the wind and watched them fall to the sea. Two boys who had lost their balloons began to cry and point at the balloons and then they wrestled with the children beside them, trying to take their balloons, and the balloons broke *pop pop pop* as a little girl ran to a tree and threw her arms around the trunk as if she were reaching for her mother's apron strings. As the other children scattered over the hill, going home, running through cactus farms, Trigueño pointed across the water to the yellow, green, and blue balloons that were specks in the far light.

"Souls gone forever," Gabrielle said, holding on to their own two balloons.

Adam took her hand. "Maybe," he said, "but that's not what Miss Klein said."

"Miss Klein?"

"Yeah."

"How come you remember her?" she asked.

"I always remember her."

"So what did she say about what?"

"She told me one day when she was sober that if you heard balloons breaking, then that, in their very own private language, was balloon laughter."

"Maybe they were laughing because some balloons got away."

Here lies
John Plewes Waters
Who came to this city
And died
For the benefit

Of his health
1898–1932

Toronto

"I like to sing at funerals," Father Zale said. He was not wearing a soutane but a tailored black suit and a black shirt. He did not wear his soutane any more. He always dressed in black, carrying his furled umbrella under his arm. Sometimes he wore a white panama hat against the sun. If it was blazing hot he would open his umbrella. "I think graveyards should be places of play. We should picnic on the heads of the dead, let them know we're not afraid of growing old. You know what's strange about growing old? Not just the smell, because age has its own smell, an almost acrid marigold smell that comes out of the pores, but for the first time I can feel the weight of my hand as it hangs at the end of my wrist, the weight of my lower lip. We grow older and get more fragile, yet all I feel is weight, everything gets heavier."

"How about your heart?" Adam laughed.

"Ah yes, the heaviness of the heart. What would life be without the heaviness of our heart?"

The priest was sitting on a white wooden lawn bench under the bird feeders with a Thermos by his feet, the silver cup-top in his hand filled with chilled white wine. His skin was pink and he was flushed because he was pleased; he hadn't seen Adam for almost four years, not since Adam had left photo-journalism school and gone to work abroad. He fussed with a fistful of forgotten notes he'd found in his pocket and then he handed the cup to Adam. Adam sipped the wine. The priest opened a book that had been beside him on the bench. "What do you think of this?" he asked, reading aloud: *"Nearly everything great comes into being in spite of something – in spite of sorrow or suffering, poverty, destitution, physical weakness, depravity, passion or a thousand other handicaps . . . and to be poised against fatality, to meet adverse conditions gracefully, is more than simple endurance; it is an act of aggression, a positive triumph."* Father Zale rubbed his big hand across the white stubble of his unshaven cheek and said, "What do you think of that in these times?"

"These are wild times," Adam said. "God knows I know that."

"More woolly than wild."

"How so?"

"I'm old, I just sit watching TV after supper. That's what old folks do."

"That's what kids do, too."

"Then they're old before their time. Anyway, sometimes life seems like one great big talk show. Never had so many yappers and snarlers pumping information at me in my life but nobody seems to know anything."

"We know their names."

"Who?"

"Everybody who's doing the talking."

"Well, that's just it. It's all name-dropping."

He poured more white wine into the silver cup. They both drank from the same cup, looking up and listening to the drone of an old passing single-prop plane. The tall pine trees were full of starlings. The plane disappeared.

"I know all about droppings," Father Zale said, laughing. "First it was seagulls and now it's starlings, scavengers and noisy twirps," and he took hold of Adam's forearm. "You've been all over the world since we last talked, and now you're going back to Africa, remember how we used to have regular collections for the Missions in Africa – where man began – now it seems to be a regular hell hole, so tell me, what's the most moving thing you've seen?"

"Moving?"

"What touched you, what left you motionless, and ashamed?"

Adam hunched forward, his elbows on his knees.

"A shoe," he said.

"A shoe?"

"Yes."

"What do you mean a shoe?"

"An empty shoe by the side of the road."

"Where?"

"Doesn't matter. Somewhere near Sidon. It was a canvas shoe, maybe a small woman's shoe, like it was just stepped out of by the side of the road, and I stood there staring into the empty shoe, and I thought of all the shoes that have ended up nowhere, just stepped out of by somebody on the road to nowhere. It suddenly seemed to me that the whole of life in our lifetime was in the empty shoe, like it was an open wound along the way to where we all want to go, to wherever we're going, but we don't get there, we just leave our shoes behind."

"Yes," the old priest said. "Yes, I can see that."

"I began to see it all over the place. Even in my own life. Shoes by the side of the road."

They both turned toward the *scree scree* of seagulls settling on the mansard roof. Adam said, "We forget how important our feet are, because the nerves to every place in our bodies are in our feet. A woman taught me that. Her voice was like cut glass but her feet were good. She showed me these little spots that are on your feet, there's a map to your feet, and you can rub and massage those spots to ease your liver, your spleen, your heart. That's why when torturers burn the soles of a man's feet he can feel it everywhere, fire inside the whole of his body. The worst thing I saw was a huge pile of children's shoes. Somehow it was worse than seeing stacked bodies. It was like all those lives had been sucked out of the world, vacuumed out . . . leaving only pain behind, an absence filled with pain, the loss of any potential for love."

"You'd better be careful," the old priest said. Though the ground was already covered with crusts, he took a fistful from his knapsack and cast more broken bread across the lawn.

"Why's that?"

The seagulls lifted off the roof, circled, and then settled around the bench, spearing crusts with their beaks.

"I'm just saying, pain's something a priest knows something about, that what a priest carries inside himself is all the possibilities of pain, the five wounds."

"Is that where you think God's hiding out?"

"In our wounds? Yes."

"Maybe," Adam said, "God is really old Mother Hubbard, living in a shoe."

"Why would He want to live in a shoe?"

"Maybe because He knows that it's only love that mitigates the emptiness of an empty shoe."

"You know," Father Zale said, laughing, "old Shakespeare had it all wrong."

"What?"

"His line – he jests at scars that never felt a wound."

"So?"

"It's those who've been wounded who jest at wounds. The rest are busy looking under their beds for terrorists."

"You mean there's a jesting God who's sitting in his shoe laughing?"

"Yes."

"Why?"

"That's the only defence a victim has."

"And He's a victim?"

"Of all our sins. I heard a man the other night on TV who said he'd lost his whole family in Poland, in the concentration camps, and now he's a minister of defence or minister of public order or something like that. He was standing beside a tank explaining that the world had better understand that there's a new and terrible terrorism loose, and he said that it was made up of guys like you, Adam, out there taking your pictures of kids throwing stones at soldiers and the soldiers who then shoot the kids, they're the victims of guys like you showing soldiers in a bad light, you are all part of this new media terrorism, a terrorism by the victim. That's what he said. This terrorism that can only be exploited by the victim. And just behind him there was this kid with a stone in his hand, smiling, like he had the whole world in his hand, and I thought to myself, there is God in that smile."

Puerto Rico

Flaccid yellow, green and blue balloons lay on the floor beside their bed. The shutters were closed, the room dark, and the floor tiles cold. They could smell jasmine on the humid air.

"I don't want to sleep," he said. "I don't like to sleep in the late afternoon."

"Neither do I."

"Do you want a cold beer?"

"No."

"Neither do I."

"It's funny you should remember Miss Klein."

"Why's it funny?"

"I knew her."

"We all knew her."

"No, I ran into her later, in New York," she said, sitting down in a white wicker chair, closing her eyes and slipping off her shoes.

"When was the old girl ever in New York?"

"Right after I got there."

"After your mother died?"

"After she jumped." They allowed a silence. "I knew she would."

"How the hell could you know that?"

"I did."

"You couldn't stop her?"

"How could I stop her?"

Gabrielle opened her eyes, holding very still.

"So where did you see Miss Klein?" he asked.

"Muriel," she said.

"Really, Muriel?"

"She came to a theatre club. I was a kid in the chorus line."

"And she just dropped in and said hello."

"She didn't see me at all."

"You saw her?"

"She was with her brother."

"What brother?"

"I sat down and said who I was. She stood up. We shook hands and she told her brother that we were friends. He said, 'If you're friends then I guess we're all friends.'"

"I can't believe it," he said, flopping down on the bed so heavily that the balloons tottered on the tile floor.

"She was a lonely lady on the bottle."

"You sound like she's dead."

"Her brother owned a hotel," she said.

"In New York?"

"No, nowhere you've ever been."

"I've been a lot of places."

"Gabon?"

"Cut it out," he said.

"I'm not kidding," she said, laughing. "I worked there, Libreville. I worked for her brother, Danilo, in the casino. Danilo and Muriel got out of Warsaw when they were young."

"During the war?"

"They got to Tangiers where there were these Orthodox Jewish families dealing in currencies, anybody's money, even Vichy francs, and Danilo got in on that and made a lot of money. But what he really made his money on was chocolate."

"Who was making chocolate?"

"He said it was like gold during the war, better than gold. You could trade it with the Nazis for prisoners, if you can believe that. There was a whole yeshiva in Tangiers dealing in chocolate. And when the war was over, Danilo looked on a map for where to go and he went with most of the money to Libreville. He sent Muriel to New York and then to Toronto, and then he built a hotel and got richer and richer. He and Muriel met every three years in New York."

"And you just took off with him? You were Danilo's girl?"

"No. He just liked me. I was hired on as a croupier."

"I thought you were a dancer."

"Not there. A lady croupier, a lady dealer makes a ton of money. You sign a contract for a year, and they were mostly English girls with wonky lower-class accents working to get money to buy into a boutique back home so they could slip through the class system. These girls give the hotels by the ocean a little tone because they seem so stern and thin-lipped. They're not supposed to mingle with the blacks but that's no problem because they're all pretty prejudiced any-way and they stick to themselves but they like being cooed at like little duchesses. Then when their year's over, most of them go home except I didn't go. I met Mio and I didn't go home."

"To Toronto?"

"To New York."

"What about Harry?"

"Harry's where he is and I'm where I am."

"What was Mio doing?"

"Managing the Libreville casino. He and Danilo got into the arms business. They're the only straight shooters in casi-nos, the guys with the guns. And after that I took off back into the bush in Gabon. I worked at a hospital. One of the little duchesses had come down with leprosy, a sweet girl, a friend, so I took her there and I went to look after her."

"You mean, like a nurse?"

"Yeah. She was very very beautiful. The open wound was almost the whole of her ear, but she had beautiful long hair. Her hair helped cover it."

"Hell, I didn't know anybody got leprosy any more."

"These things never go away. Tuberculosis, it was supposed to be gone . . ."

"And you? You were a real nurse?"

"Kind of . . ."

"And what happened to the little duchess?"

"She got better. In a few months. I found out that leprosy's neurological, it's really a disease of the mind. She'd never had a serious thought in her life. That was her charm. Maybe that's why it went away, no place to call home."

She gave a little toss of her head, amused by her own joke.

"I got to know the lepers. Unbelievable, maybe, but we laughed a lot. They laughed. I laughed. At nothing. The way kids sometimes do. Laughter can be infectious, too."

"But that's exactly what happened to me the first night I saw you in San Juan, I was on my balcony staring at all that dark water out there and I was thinking back about you and me, and I just laughed."

"At what?"

"At nothing. That's what was so great about it, I was cutting loose, just laughing, free, like I hadn't laughed since I was a kid. That's how I knew I still loved you."

She blew him a kiss.

"My little duchess never laughed, she giggled. She got better and giggled and now runs her own hat shop in Hampstead."

"And Harry knows nothing about any of this?"

"I don't want him to."

"Why not?"

"Because I don't."

"You treat him like maybe he's dead."

"No, no, he's alive, alive in me all the time."

Gabon

It was raining. A shell burst near the riverbank. Soldiers in grey helmets and grey uniforms, carrying machine pistols and grenades clipped to their belts, slid down a red mud embankment and climbed up into the back of a troop truck, the canvas flapping in the rain and wind. The truck ground its gears, drove onto a short bridge, and – booby-trapped – blew up. Wounded men crawled out into the long grass. One had his hands in the air, waving a map. He was shot dead by a sniper. The map fell into a rut full of slimy water. "Sneak attack, sneak attack," a soldier yelled and fired flares, silver-red blooms in the dark rain, flares that suddenly went out. Henri stepped out of the tub of water, swept up a worn blanket from an old horsehair settee, and hung it across the window. He unchained the baby gorilla and held him in his arms as another shell exploded close to the hotel. A stench seeped into the room.

"They have hit the garbage dump," Henri said.

The gorilla whimpered.

"Seems like it's goddamn dead on," Adam said.

"I wonder where Esmelda is."

"You worried?"

"No, except she has no resilience any more, the heat here draws all your nerves to their ends . . ."

The gorilla curled his lips back from his big yellow teeth.

"Why do you think we met?" Henri asked, putting his bare feet back into the tub of water.

"I don't know."

"No one knows, but even if we do not know we should try to say why."

"Why?"

Henri rested his head against the gorilla's neck. His eyes were hooded, absorbed, serious, his legs trembling.

"I wish we had cigars," he said.

"You want a cigar?"

"*Mais oui. Le chemin par oùù je suis venu je l'ai oublié.* So I close my eyes and dream I'm on a beach in Cuba."

"You ever been to Cuba?"

"*Non. Mes lèvres bégayent un je ne sais quoi.*"

"Why do you want to know why we met?"

"Because this is *une existence sans contour ni désir, stupide.*"

"Who said life had to have a shape?"

"Our only revenge is to laugh, and to insist that there was a point, *un peu de pudeur*, that we met for a reason," and Henri, with a sad smile, reached for his revolver. "Do you think I care what is done by those morons out there, when they are shooting each other in the back?" Henri tossed his head, his hooded eyes half-open. "It is only the brutalizing of their own children that bothers me." Adam stared at him, feeling a stirring of kinship that lifted him out of his lassitude; he had a vague sense of disintegration, of danger in Henri's eyes.

"They are forced to kill their own mothers, rape their own sisters."

"When I was a kid my father told me the world was alive with boils about to burst."

"So they've broken? Here! All over the place."

"Looks like it."

"Have you ever drunk river water?" Henri asked.

"No."

"Maybe that is why we are here together. *La tantouze tient le fin bout*, to get the taste of slime."

"We may never get back down to the river."

Henri nestled against the gorilla's neck. "We'll get back. Just like that, people run out of breath, it'll stop." And then the shelling did stop and so did the rain. A strong breeze came up, belling the blanket in the window. The man with the hunch took down the blanket and asked if they wanted more tea.

Adam tried to get control of a sudden rage that he felt welling up in his chest, his throat, a rage that astonished him, a blind desire to beat the hunchback, to beat someone, anyone, his nerve ends suddenly on fire, and he sighed and started to shake, almost as if he had a fever, a fever fed by his own exhaustion. He slumped in his chair, overcome and sickened by the heavy acrid reek of sour garbage rot and blossoms and he fell asleep to the sound of the hunchback wheezing, fell asleep half-dreaming of a pre-dawn morning in the hotel room above the sea as *the coqui had drilled their two notes into the dark scent of jasmine all through the dawn night, and Gabrielle had wakened him with her moaning, a moaning in her sleep that sounded almost like keening, the sound of a grief that had taken root in her, and the more open, and at moments, even delirious they had become in their happiness – she sometimes threw her arms open to him in her sleep – the more she seemed when she was half-awake to have sunk into herself, lying in their rumpled sheets half-awake in some kind of pain, sweating, saying, "Our mothers are so strange," that's what she said, "sweating it out"...*

"What?"

"Nothing."

"You said that we're sweating it out," Henri said.

"No, no."

"That's what you said."

"I did?"

"Yes. We are to sweat it out."

"I guess we are," Adam said, still feverish, hearing Gabrielle cry, saying she could hear her soul drawing out of her body through her bones, that's how she said it sounded, the high droning note of her soul fleeing . . .

"Jesus, I can't believe it . . ."

"My mother let him . . ."

"Let him what?" Adam yelled.

Incoming shells seemed to be exploding just behind the hotel.

Henri leapt up, and the baby gorilla, flailing in mid-air, bounded to the hunchback huddled in a corner.

"You goddamn better believe," Henri cried. *"Que la tantouze tient le fin bout, et que c'est en quoi que nous sommes à la coule . . ."*

Howitzer rockets were firing *thrumpf thrumpf thrumpf thrumpf thrumpf* followed by the heavy clacking of 50-calibre machine guns and the whine of shells. Explosions blew bits of branches through the window. They sat staring into smoke and fire-filled trees, each leaf on fire, and Henri, saying, "If you're gonna kill somebody you'll need this," as he handed Adam a revolver. They heard a trombone call from the floor below, a low mournful call, then a shot, and running on the stairs. Henri reached under the settee for a machine pistol and as he stood up the door was stomped open by two guerrillas. Henri wheeled around but one of the gunmen shot him, two short bursts, and Henri jack-knifed, landing on his buttocks in the galvanized tub of water, the machine pistol still in his grip, pointing straight up as he stared, firing into the ceiling, tearing holes in the white plaster. The baby gorilla swung away from the hunchback, leaping onto the shoulder of the gunman who had shot Henri, sinking his yellow teeth into his throat, the man reeling back, his gurgling howl smothered in the arms of the gorilla, his jugular blood swooshing like a fan over Henri's head. The other gunman, giggling hysterically, had spun toward the baby gorilla, toward Adam, starting to run at Adam who, aghast at the eruption of blood, the roars of pain, had been unable to say anything or do anything but aim and fire. The gunman tottered backwards, slumped, and rolled down the stairs to the landing between floors. Adam went down the stairwell, the blood-drenched baby gorilla leaping up and down behind him, his eyes crazed, curling his lips. The gunman's running shoes had holes in the soles. Adam couldn't bear the gorilla's screeching. He thought of shooting the gorilla. He went back upstairs. Dead Henri had emptied his machine pistol. Water was pouring through holes in the ceiling, silver streams of water drenching Henri's face and chest, washing the blood from his wounds into the tub.

"Fuck, you shot out the cistern," Adam said.

The hunchback was moaning and weeping in the corner. The baby gorilla sat on the dead guerrilla's face, blood still drooling from his jaws. Then he leapt across the room and crawled like a child into the hunchback's arms. Adam sat down, the pistol loose in his hand.

He waited. The reverberating *thrumpf thrumpf* from the hills stopped, the dry clattering of gunfire stopped. He felt worn out and raw as if his skin had been scraped from his bones. The sun had come out and a strong wind came up, blowing away the haze and smoke. But the trees were still smouldering in this fresh silence. Tanks pulled away from the hotel and parked beyond the traffic circle. Someone turned on a short-wave radio, the music pulsing through the trees. He waited. And then, in a clipped accent, he heard the BBC news. "Fighting has apparently broken out in several parts of the continent, yet the president of the World Bank, speaking in Zurich, said he is optimistic . . ." Adam had never before thought of killing anyone. And he still hadn't thought about it. He had just fired. But now he shook his head and wanted to weep for himself. He knew some deep sorrow had got into his bones. He had prided himself on being a participating witness, free of causes and rabid loyalties, but now he could never again say sardonically, "Why me? I'm just passing through." He stared at Henri awash in his own blood, waiting for someone to charge up the stairs to shoot him or to arrest him, but there was no sound, no one came up the stairs, no one called.

Adam got up, the water from the roof cistern overflowing the tub. Henri was sitting in the pink water, eyes staring into the drip, drip, drip, the floor slimy with his blood. Adam saw the baby gorilla and the hunchback holding each other: "I'm sure you are innocent," he said and aimed at them, surprised by his own cackling laughter. He thought that maybe he'd come unstrung, maybe he was delirious. But he didn't pull the trigger. *I am the king of the condom shoot-outs,* he thought, almost snickering self-deprecatingly as he shoved the revolver down into his belt, took up his camera, and went down the dark stairs to where the dead guerrilla lay, arms bent back, reaching for his pain. He looked down at the face of the man. He turned away, then looked down. Blood pulsed into his head, he could feel it behind his eyes. "You," he said, incredulous, "you fucker you," believing as he blinked and then blinked again, that he was looking into the face that had refused to reveal itself to him in his dream, his nightmare. There were the eyes of the man who had haunted him, driven him to panic, dead. By his hand. He had actually shot him dead. He leaned over the guerrilla, focused his camera on the eyes, the staring eyes that seemed to be turning to mud, turning to swamp, to ooze, and *click* he took one shot.

Carrying his garment bag and his camera bag, he hurried down to the dark elbow-shaped lobby where a bandsman lay dead, curled around his trombone. He was wearing leather short pants and blue-and-white striped knee socks. The other bandsmen were sitting by their luggage, crying. "School's out," Adam heard himself cry. There were no soldiers in the street and Adam waited in the doorway, not moving, waiting for a sign. There were only lone bleary-eyed men in brown great-coats, wearing woollen caps, who stood in the doorways of blown-out stores. He realized what he had been missing: there had been no helicopters, no swarming air-sucking thwacking of the silence . . .

The soldiers seemed to have moved south. A man in a brown greatcoat began to snicker and giggle and move out of a doorway toward him, a hulking man. *That fucker's gonna eat me raw.* Adam got to his car – the windows shot out – and drove to the other side of the traffic circle and across the canal bridge to the north.

There were no tanks on the north road. He leaned forward over the steering wheel into the empty window. There were birds, big black birds flying low. He inadvertently ducked, afraid they might dive and pluck out his eyes, but when he looked up going around a bend he saw a grey tank with a black star on the turret sitting by the side of the road between tall trees. A fist closed in his bowels and he was about to brake but instead he held his foot to the gas, his forearms aching with the weakness that comes with panic as he held the wheel steady on the rough road, watching the tank cannon swivel toward him, picking him up, following him, as he held harder to the gas, screaming at the tank, "You fucker, fuck, go fuck yourself!"

He passed around a knoll, out of the tank's sighting, chin against the wheel. He braked to a stop on the empty road, letting out a whining moan, remembering the dying thief outside the church, pain tearing at his lungs: "You ain't nothing." He closed his eyes and didn't move for a long time.

At last, he looked down the road, down the hollow through the dense green, and then he heard birds. Looking to the side, he saw two barefoot soldiers in tattered fatigues hanging by the neck from a branch. After a moment's silence he began to sing – more of a cry than singing:

> *Oh we ain't got a barrel of money*
> *Maybe we're ragged and funny*
> *But we travel along*
> *Singing our song,*
> *Side by side*

PART SEVEN

Toronto

It was two in the afternoon. Web was on the road, on tour.
He found his mother at her dressing table. Though it was very
hot, she had on a heavy old felt cloche hat and she was staring
at herself in the mirror. She touched the corner of her eye,
the corner of her mouth. Then she said to Adam in the mirror, "You left all the lights on last night."

"No, I didn't," he said.

"Who did then?"

"You did, Mom."

"It couldn't have been me," she said.

"Why not?"

"I undress in the dark now."

Sometimes he heard her pacing in the dark and he would
get up and look for her. Sometimes she broke into weeping in
her sleep. One morning, as she bit into her dry toast, she said,
"When I was a little girl I had a round glass ball. It was very
heavy and full of falling snow and if I turned it, and I turned
it all the time, I thought I had hold of the world. Now everything gets whiter and whiter and I spin and spin inside my
sleep."

On a clear night in early August, after an evening of dry thunder and heat, he found her out behind the house, walking in slow circles, staring up at the stars.

"You always loved the stars."

"Yes," he said.

"They told me in my convent school that there were angels on all the stars and now the angels are gone."

"Are you sure?"

"They were there when I was a child."

"But how do you know they're gone?"

"Because men have walked all over the moon, you can't have angels there now, so I've got no angels any more, and you can't be a little girl without an angel."

In a heavily treed downtown park, there was a plain yellow brick church tower, one of the oldest towers in the city; the gutted walls of the church had been pulled down after a fire that had started on a cold day in a wood stove but the lean tower had been left standing and chemically cleaned. Now it was surrounded by rose gardens and weeping willows across the road from a small squat steam bath, the Grange Health Baths. Adam and his father sat beside each other on an upper cedar bench in one of the white-tiled steam rooms, white towels wrapped around their waists. The steam was dense and they were sweating heavily. There was a man across the room on another bench, a thickset shadow in the steam except for his spindly calves and bony feet that seemed to hang out of the cloud of steam.

"How's it going, gentlemen?" the man said. He had a quiet husky voice. He spoke slowly, deliberately.

"Okay," his father said after a pause.

"Me, too."

"Good."

The man crossed his ankles. "I see you sitting there, Web."

"You do," Web said, surprised, squinting into the steam.

"Sure I do. I sat in a lot of steam in my time. You learn how to see."

"So what do you see?"

"What else? I see you and your son. It's some years since I seen him, now he's a grown man, but he seems like your son. Still, a gent in his own right. How you doing, son?"

"Okay."

"We should all do okay."

"Who are you?"

"You can't see?"

"I can't see."

"You don't know me, my voice?"

"I don't know you."

"I could take offence."

"Maybe you could."

"Except I don't take cheap offence. That's for showboats and dumb heads," he said, stepping down to the next bench, and then to the floor where he stood before them, naked in the dim light, square-shouldered and smiling. He was scratching his scrotum. "Who needs a towel?" the man said, shrugging and laughing. "What's to hide, we're men among men. I got nothing to hide."

"Jesus, Tonton O'Leary," Web said.

"Right," the man said, holding out his pudgy hand. "Right, we passed some time together, you and me."

"That's right," Web said, turning to Adam. "This is Harry's brother, Harry's little brother."

"Some little," Tonton said, smirking and folding his arms across his barrel chest.

"No, you're not little," Web said.

"We do some big things around town," Tonton said, nodding his head to Adam. "Some big things."

Tonton's skin was not pink and flushed from the steam. His skin, Adam thought, had the grey-whitish sheen of the floor tiles.

"Heat don't bother me," Tonton said.

"Except when the heat's on," Web said sardonically.

"Haw. That's good. I like that. I never was quick with words. I like quick words. Among friends."

"How long's it been, Tonton?"

"How long's long? A long time."

"Not among friends."

"That's right. Friendship's short, too short."

"So's life."

"Yeah, but you can take a steam, take a holiday. It pro-longs."

"You can look after your friends, too, Tonton."

"It's easier to look after your enemies."

"How's Harry?"

"Harry's Harry. He looks after himself."

"I guess nothing changes."

"Harry's changed, but he's still Harry. He don't fool me, or what's a brother for?"

"How's he changed?"

"You see him, you'll think he's changed."

"How about you, Tonton?"

"Me? I give change. I'm a businessman."

"So how's business?"

"Terrific. Can't complain, not about life."

He moved closer to them. He had a round face, thin-ning hair, and pale blue eyes, so pale they seemed colourless.

"We should see each other more often. Keep up acquain-tances."

"My son and I both travel," Web said, and Adam felt that there was menace in Tonton's tight little smile.

"You don't say. I hear that your son's some kinda war photographer, but at your age, Web, you're still doing your tours?"

"Yeah."

"They say it broadens the mind."

"Yeah."

"I don't like to travel. I like to keep my eye on the ball," he said, putting out his hand again. "It was nice, a nice touch in the day."

"What?" Web asked, shaking his hand.

"Meeting you, your son, like this."

"Sure."

"Nice to know some things never change," he said, shaking Adam's hand.

"Sure."

"Like you don't like me, Web, and I don't like you."

"If you say so, Tonton."

"I say so. I'm glad to say so. I'm a conservative guy, I get nervous when things aren't the way they were. So Harry makes me nervous, but with you, Web, I'm very easy. Very much at ease."

"That's nice."

"It's terrific. It's terrific to see you," he said, turning away and then stopping at the door. "I'll take a shower, it's very refreshing to take a cold shower after a steam." He closed the door behind him.

"Holy shit," Adam said.

"The guy's a complete shit," Web said.

"And he's Harry's brother?"

"He's a hood. He's Harry's brother and he's a hustler, a bad piece of business. He's always given Harry a little money, to help him out."

"Really."

"Sure, Harry's the family oddball, the odd-guy-out, because the whole family was always in the rackets. Tonton had his hoods, Harry had his choir. It was Tonton who probably gave Gabrielle the money to go to New York."

"You're kidding."

"Why should I kid? It was a close family. But Harry was strange. Nothing gave Harry more pleasure than the two of us getting drunk together and playing a little boogie-woogie on the church organ until the priests came and kicked us out."

"But his wife seemed so straight."

"Ah, his wife. There was a beauty."

"She didn't seem so good-looking to me."

"She was this plain little skinny woman who collected things. That's what she did, old glass, little antique tables. She felt superior to everybody. She turned shopping into an art form, but what was fascinating about her was, she had no charm, no charm at all. She had this smile like she was smiling in helpless disapproval, and it used to kill Harry, it used to leave him absolutely limp."

"Why'd Harry stay with her?"

"She never interfered. He was free as a bird. She'd just smile that smile at him until sometimes he hit her."

"He hit her?"

"He beat her up a couple of times."

"That's awful. Gabrielle never let on."

"What was funny, Gabrielle always seemed closer to Harry, like she resented her mother, but then when her mother jumped she took off like a bat out of hell, leaving Harry all to himself. A long time later, she sent Harry a postcard once from somewhere. I remember him showing it to me, this white jungle mask staring out at him and on the other side she'd drawn a little round balloon head smiling. He said it was all some kind of joke, it had to be a prank. Maybe it was."

"You know what's strange? I've got this thing about her, this little dream, sometimes we're making love again in the most peculiar places. It's almost seven years since I've seen her. I'd love to see her."

"You slept with her? With Gabrielle?"

"We were in love like kids are in love from the beginning."

"Did Harry know?"

"I dunno, I think maybe he did, but I'll tell you this. One day when I was standing in Dachau, of all places, staring at this steel hook in the ceiling in front of the ovens where they used to hang men up so they twisted in the air, I suddenly had this strange feeling that she was there beside me. I could almost see her face – it was really weird. It was like I was turning on a hook and she could see me but I couldn't quite see her, and I've got no idea what she looks like now."

"Jesus, what the hell were you doing in Dachau?"

"Taking pictures of shoes."

"You know I played in Munich, with Klaus Doldinger at the Domicile. It's a great club. Me and Fatha Hines, we were playing at the same time, and one day he said, 'Let's go see

Dachau,' so we went. The mayor of the town heard about us so we were invited to lunch and after the lunch the mayor gave us these beautiful old hand-painted china plates, painted with flowers, telling us, like the concentration camp didn't exist, that what Dachau was famous for was their china."

Puerto Rico

She was sleeping soundly in the breaking morning light. He lifted her short nightgown, drawing it above her breasts. Her legs were slightly parted. He eased his hand along the inside of her thigh into the hollow so that she did not waken but stirred and shifted. He put his mouth on hers, and when she opened her lips and murmured, he then touched her nipple with his mouth and nestled against her belly, drawing his tongue into the crook of her thigh and then back across her belly, resting his head against her breasts. She held his head. She seemed hardly to breathe as she pulled her knees up and opened her legs. He touched her, touched her wetness.

She straddled him, taking hold of him with two fingers, easing down so that he was up in her, her long hair falling across his face as she moved her buttocks slowly. She sat up straight on him, eyes wide open, smiling impishly as she swept her hair back from her face, her breasts lifting, the skin translucent with turquoise-blue veins. He licked his fingers and reached and touched her nipples with the wetness, seeing her sitting framed in the window, the banana tree behind her shoulder, and he said, "The hummingbird is back." She turned and looked, blocking the window from him. She stayed turned away for so long that he asked her if anything was wrong, but falling forward on him again, she said, "Oh no, no. It is all too wonderful. It's unbearably wonderful." She came, crying out, a cry close to laughter, and her thigh muscles contracted, the arteries sinking into the skin as if her blood had stopped. "Each time I come with you I feel like I've been hanged. I mean what hanging must be like. A burning light just jams up in me, in my throat."

"Is that why you laugh?"

"It's like sucking ice when you've got a fever, cold stinging pain in all my veins . . . I can't help but laugh . . ."

"I wish I could make you laugh forever."

"That'd hurt too much," she said and kissed his eyes.

"I was wondering about your guy Mio? Whether he's laughing?"

"Never mind him," she said.

"I've got to mind him."

"What's done's done. He'll do whatever he'll do, and if he does anything you'll never know, he's too anonymous."

"Any guy who struts into a casino with his good hand in an ice bucket is not trying to hide himself."

"Believe me, he's anonymous. He doesn't want anyone to know how he feels about anything."

"You lived with him."

"I was with him but I didn't live with him, and I don't really know what he'll do."

"It sounds like he's capable of anything. Maybe I should fix him up with my Sunshine Girl."

"Don't be ridiculous."

"I like being ridiculous. It gets me through the night."

"Look, he was a man who fascinated me. It was like there was a ghost in him. He was the keeper of his own ghost, his own childhood, I guess. You know how many people there are wandering around with dead children in them? But he never had any self-pity, and I liked that. I liked it a lot. Just like I like it about you. You're not looking for excuses or running scared though there's something in you on the run, there's some kinda screw loose."

"You're the one with the screw loose," he said, gripping her arm, "living with a guy like Mio."

"What d'you mean – like Mio?"

"A gun runner."

"You're jealous."

"Why should I be jealous? You've run off with me. He's the one who should be jealous."

"Not a chance. Aggravated, maybe, but never jealous. Besides, I haven't run off. When I run, you'll know."

They lay very still. Somewhere, children were calling to each other, and to hide how grim he suddenly felt, he whispered, "Nothing else matters, not if we're together!"

"You didn't come," she said. "You held back."

"Well, that's what happens," he said, smacking her buttock hard, "when you put me on my back."

"I want to make love again."

"You do, do you?"

"Yes I do."

She took him in her mouth, and then rolled over so that he made love to her, her legs up in the air, and he rode her higher and higher till she was up on her shoulders, arms spread, clutching the sheet as if she were tearing up roots, pulling him down into her with her legs until he pitched forward, reaching for her hands, locking his fingers into hers as they strained and then slumped and separated, breathing heavily, eyes closed, the light wind from the open window beginning to dry their sweat.

They lay in silence for a long time.

When he opened his eyes, Adam saw a single thread of spider web hanging from the ceiling.

"Do you see that?" he said, pointing. "Do you think the spider just gave up, decided it was going nowhere and quit and went somewhere else?"

"Maybe he just had a passing thought."

"Like pissing in the dark."

"I envy men being able to piss anywhere, it's so free. We've got to squat, get our feet wet in our own piss. We can't write our names in the snow."

"I feel wonderful," he blurted out.

"Me too. I haven't felt so wonderful for years."

"I can still remember the first time I touched your breast. This swollen rise of softness. I loved how you let me touch you."

"One night, you took my shoes off and kissed my feet."

"I did?"

"You kissed my feet and told me I would be a great dancer. I'm a good dancer but I'm not a great dancer."

"I didn't kiss you hard enough. Maybe I've never loved you hard enough till now."

"Hard had nothing to do with it," she said, bending over him so that he could feel the weight of her breasts on his chest as she looked into his eyes. "This is a little crazy, isn't it, what we're doing, it's like we're trying to remember how we were as kids so we can know what to do now."

"Maybe. A little."

"I think I should tell you about Harry."

"What about Harry?"

"About Harry and me."

He drew his forefinger down along her backbone.

"Your backbone's kind of like a flute," he said, humming *when you go out in the woods today . . .*

She said nothing, waiting for him to stop humming the baby-song words, and when he did she said, "No one ever knew how Harry really was but me."

"My father thought he did."

"Your father knew that they were two guys who played the piano, two guys who made music."

She heard the shuffle of footsteps in the hall, then silence, then a light cough, and then the footsteps went away.

"Who was that?"

"Who knows?" he said. "Somebody's ghost. Somebody's passing thought."

She tilted her head to the side, as if she were considering the possibility.

Then: "Harry used to touch me before you touched me, when we were kids, and then he stopped."

"Jesus," he said, sitting up, "you mean Harry molested you?"

"He touched me. He'd always touch me and wash and bathe me and, like I told you, he braided my hair. Then one night when he was soaping me and I already had breasts, he told me to dry myself."

"He stopped?"

"Yes."

"Thank God."

"But then, a couple of years later, my mother saw the blood on our sheet, the sheet you and I made love on, and somehow she knew it wasn't my period or anything, it was us, you and me, and I think I saw this souring look of resentment in her eyes. A few days later, right when we were eating dinner, real casual-like, she told him I wasn't a virgin."

"So?"

"He started again. He more than touched me."

"Did your mother know?"

"Of course. Mothers always know."

"Why didn't she stop him?"

"She wasn't like that."

"Like what?"

"What can I tell you? She did nothing. She hid out inside her own head. It's a family habit. She closed the door and watched *Jeopardy*. She watched *Wheel of Fortune*. How do I know what she thought? She told me she was an orphan, she'd been put away in an orphanage by her own parents. Maybe that was it? Maybe not? There's no explanation. If there was something that made sense, it'd be insane. She just had this hang-dog look in her eyes, like no pain could ever surprise her, she just got thinner and thinner in front of our eyes, wearing these box suits, looking hang-dog scared but stern, but she never stopped him from doing anything. Her way of holding on to who she was to cling, to sit still."

"And did you? Did you try to stop him?"

"No."

"You mean you liked it?"

"No."

"What did you do?"

"I don't remember."

"How could you forget?"

"I didn't forget. I told you once, the night when you were going to the Conqueroo, I was ill. The whole house was ill. There were whole parts of a day, sometimes a week, I'd refuse to remember I was even alive. My pal the mailman had delivered the mail. I knew I was alive but I refused to believe it. How was I supposed to believe what was happening? I hardly believe it now, except I know it's true. I tell you true, it's always true."

Her lower lip began to tremble. She bit her lip, took a deep breath, went to speak, but she had to close her eyes, trying for calm. Then, shaking her head, she said, "I just refuse to remember what he did, what we did. But I remember his smell, his moist eyes, the smell of his hair, the smell of his semen."

She folded her arms across her chest, closing herself in on herself.

"He got me pregnant, that's why my mother killed herself, when she found out I was pregnant."

"Holy fuck, that fucking shit . . . Goddamn, I knew it, even when I was just a kid I goddamn-well knew he was hiding something, always cupping his cigarette. His goddamn dirty little secret. Verdi, my ass. And that's why he liked us screaming together in the choir room, the whole thing was ass-backwards, one long pain. And I loved him, that goddamned . . ."

Adam didn't seem to realize that he was pounding his fist into the bed. She reached out and stopped him.

"Your mother should have killed him . . ."

"She killed herself, and" – she held on to his fist – "I killed the child, in New York . . ."

He put his head in his hands. He gripped his head. He didn't know what else to do. He held on hard. He didn't know how to look at her ... with sorrow, with rage? He loved her, he felt horror for her. He kept his head down and said quietly, "I actually loved him."

"Yeah, well, me too."

"Jesus fucking Christ."

Gabrielle lifted his head and kissed him on the mouth, and then on the neck.

"Now, for me," she said, "you've gotta understand, there's always a dead child ... his dead little hand, reaching. I don't want to die, I just want to escape him, and myself, too, to disappear ..."

"You can't disappear. I won't let you ..."

Kissing him, she dug her nails into his neck, and began to bite him until he was hurt, and aroused by her bite. He said, "Maybe we should make love. If we don't, maybe we won't ever make love again," and he tumbled her on to her back.

"Lick me," she said. "Till I disappear ..."

"There's nowhere to go."

"Lick me ..."

He knelt, putting his mouth to her. She closed her thighs around his head and let out a guttural wavering cry, a wail as she arced into the air, wrenching his head between her thighs. His blood had begun to pound in his ears, an enormous swelling had entered his skull behind his eyes. And then she collapsed and spread her legs and he lay curled up by her thigh, his upper lip swollen.

They lay still, breathing hard, bodies rigid.

"That terrified me," she whispered. "It felt like my soul tore itself out of me . . ."

"Your soul?"

"Something that had roots."

"You think I swallowed your soul?"

"I hope not," she said, and touched his hair. "Does it taste like ashes to you?"

"No, you taste sweet."

"I mean my soul."

Toronto

The big parade through Chinatown passed the memorial to the dead airmen of all the wars, a parade of crimson dragon heads hoisted on poles, and Chinese boys on stilts wearing butterfly wings, hoe-down dancers and seven prancing dwarfs, Snow White in an ice cave, a corps of the Salvation Army marching crisply, and a small stage on wheels covered by spangled blue notes, and a portly brown woman singing:

> *Man's got his woman*
> *To take his seed*
> *He's got the power,*
> *She's got the need,*
> *Only women bleed, only women bleed*

She went out of Adam's hearing, but was followed by a Shriners drill team on miniature motorbikes and Hellenic soldiers in white knee socks and white pleated skirts, and then there was a piercing trumpet blast as two boys carrying a banner – DE LA SALLE TRUMPET AND DRUM CORPS – led a big marching band of fifty silver trumpets and drummers to the memorial, trim in their black uniforms and silver capes. Adam stood on the curb and raised his hand but he realized that Harry would never see him in the crowd, Harry at the head of the boys' marching band, stern-faced and stiff, dressed all in black with beautiful black braiding around his shoulders, carrying a silver-headed staff, jamming it up and down in the air to the military drum beat, *one two one two one two*, staring straight ahead, and then snapping his head to the left in a salute to the dead.

Puerto Rico
They walked along the beach road toward the town of Ponce, past broken lobster cradles and torn nets, rusted oil drums and a disused stone boathouse. There were cats slumped in the roof gutter of the boathouse.

"Those cats make me nervous," she said. "I don't know why."

They passed through a narrow opening in a high sandstone wall and turned into a street of blue-grey cobblestones.

A life-sized carved icon of a naked body was bolted to a corner wall – Sebastian the Martyr bristling with arrows. He had been given a gold halo for a hat.

"That poor guy's been target practice ever since I was in school," he said.

"As a kid, I used to have nightmares about the saints. The nuns had a whole library of mutilations. I'd wake up sopping wet and shaking."

"You're kidding."

"It's no joke. They knew baby Saint Agnes was going to be a saint because a wasp flew into her open mouth when she was snoring and sat on her tongue and didn't sting her. Like I thought I saw Mio sitting in the shadows of my sleep. Waiting to sting me."

"Don't be ridiculous. Mio's not in your sleep."

"He's in my life."

"I'm in your life."

"It beats me how you ever made love to a guy with killer eyes like that."

"I looked him right in the eye," she said, pulling away, offended. "Mio's been through things you'll never know about. They stuck his hand in a fire trying to get him to tell them where his parents were and he refused because he said if anyone was going to kill his parents he was going to kill them. So believe you me, he doesn't fool around over nothing."

"Thanks a lot."

"So let's pretend," she said, taking his hand, "that you didn't say what you just said, this cockeyed connection between whatever night sweats you've got and who your saints are and a man who lived through a real nightmare."

"That's what I can't figure out. Why you wanted to live with a nightmare?"

"Because I always live with a nightmare," she said grimly.

"I didn't mean that," he said.

"But I do. I mean it. Mio understood. I killed my child, my own father's child. I could have killed myself. That would have been easier but I didn't, and Mio lives with a dead child, his own childhood buried alive. You think Mio wants into your life? Not likely. Anyway, who've you got in your life now? Who's your new Sunshine Girl."

"You."

"Listen, with Mio I had a certain kind of freedom. Nothing more to lose. But I love these days with you, attached to you. I love feeling like there's a little girl alive in me again, a little girl I'd forgotten all about, a little girl who tells me that there is another life like this, only it's beautiful, on the other side of the horizon, but there are wounds and these wounds Mio and I never had to talk about, and that's a kind of love, too, when you don't have to talk."

"You mean I should shut up."

"Yes, you should shut up. Like, I don't care if your girlfriend killed her mother. Or if she was warning you that you got off lucky."

As they came into a street crowded with cafés and stuccoed walls, a dusky boy with long braided black hair, hooded black eyes and wearing a coat down to his ankles, rose up out of a doorway where he'd been sitting cross-legged and began to follow them. Filthy, he was carrying an empty beer can and a wire coat hanger. When he came close, Adam offered him some coins but he shook his head. He kept following them, and then he jammed the hanger wire into the can and dragged it up and down against the open mouth of the tin can, making a flat scraping sound, a raw screech, keeping a ragged rhythm, falling into step behind them, shadowing them down the street and around the corner. Adam turned and waved him away but the boy kept sawing his jagged music, shaking his braided hair, staring at them, his black eyes mournful and menacing.

"What the hell does he want?"

"Who knows?"

"It sounds like strangled birds."

"Maybe he's got a knife?"

They passed an empty baby carriage abandoned by the curb. It was missing one wheel. The wind was flapping in the boy's long coat, and then the boy, working the hanger like a rasp against the tin, circled ahead and waited beside a high stone wall, the veins standing out on his neck. There was a doorway in the wall.

"Let's lose this kid."

They pushed their way through heavy creaking wooden doors and found themselves standing beside an empty porter's gatehouse in the town cemetery, looking down long narrow avenues of tiny stone and marble houses, obese little cherubs with stubby wings who cradldled each other on wrought-iron porches, and two effete angels holding avenging swords alongside a relief carving of a young socialite in her dressage jacket and cap as she stood over the open sunken room of her family's tomb, the bunks for six caskets inexplicably empty.

They looked back. The boy had not followed them.

"Maybe he thought he was serenading us?"

"Jesus, no! He wanted to hurt us." Then she laughed. "Imagine, a boy like that giving us the willies. Scaring us like we were kids. Sometimes when I was a kid I got so scared I'd say the same little prayer over and over again."

Walking between two stately tombs, she said, "These are the houses of beheaded prayer."

"The what?"

"That's what Mio calls cemeteries."

It had begun to drizzle.

"I think you got that guy in your bones."

"No. I just know how to sit silently with him, between his rages, though they're not really rages. They are astonished laments that sound like rages against God, but then, he does not believe in God either. Would you believe in God if you had been buried alive by your own family because your hair was black?"

"Why'd they do that?"

"Because everybody was blond, blue-eyed and blond. And when the other peasants dug him up his hair was white. He dyes it black now. The most intimate moment he ever shared with me was when he let me see his white hair. He washed all the black out, and there he was, like a ghost of himself. And I didn't have to love him, or want to love him, and I never knew if he wanted to love me."

"Well, nothing says you've got to love me either. Or God. Nothing says you've got to love this God who let His own choirmaster get his daughter with child."

"Is that what nothing says? Are you sure? You are far too dark, too melancholy, Adam, for a man who insists that he's happy."

"I am happy."

"And so am I. I'm happy happy. These days have been like a long-lost dance." She stepped away from him and held out her arms. "We've made love, beautiful love, but we've never danced together . . ."

"Here?"

"Why not?"

She was wearing low-heeled sandals and with her hands on her hips she beat her heels against the gravel, then bent her knees, pivoted, and shook her hair. Her blouse came undone as she spun and she held her body straight. She took his hands and together they danced slowly, in a kind of waltz, between the tombs, erect but separate in each other's arms. He led her as they turned, but only as she allowed him to lead. "I hardly know what I'm doing," he said as they rocked to a standstill and he enclosed her in his arms and sang quietly in her ear, now pressing his body against hers.

> There's a line between love and fascination,
> It's hard to tell them apart,
> For they give the very same sensation,
> Take care my foolish heart.

They stood holding each other in silence for a long time.

"Look," she said, "you don't need to know this, but I'll tell you how it was the day I knew I didn't love Mio. He was holding my hand and he told me he saw a grave in my open palm. A grave. Okay. And maybe I live with death in me but when I touch the world I want to touch the world with love. For me and Mio, it was always a dead-end. So here we are, you and me, and where are we? We're in a graveyard. But you see my hands? No Mio. Only love. Straight from the heart."

They walked to the end of an avenue of small, narrow houses. Then he rubbed his shoe against his ankle. Suddenly, his ankles were itchy and he bent down and scratched inside his sock. He thought he could smell urine in the gravel. She bent down, too.

"Jesus, it's fleas."

"You're kidding."

"It's goddamned fleas," he said, scratching his ankles.

"The graveyard's full of fleas."

"The kisses of the dead," she said and laughed.

"The dead, my ass," he said. "This is living. Come on," and he took her hand and broke into a loping run to the other side of the burial yard, away from the gate where they'd left the boy with the coat hanger and tin can. The evening sky seemed swollen, seemed ready to rain. "Come on, maybe we'll be lucky and maybe it will pour while we go for a swim in the sea."

PART EIGHT

Gabon

As he drove deeper and deeper into the dense enclosing bush, his face scalded by the rush of wind through the empty windshield, the narrow road flared onto a slope of trees that had been burned by a flash fire, the slope stippled by thin bare grey trunks. He drove off the slope down to the river, docks and sheds, and at the foot of a wide mud road he found pirogues drawn up on the shore. Adam tucked the Glock into his belt under his jacket and stepped out of the car carrying his garment bag and his cameras. He walked across a narrow bridge, past an old blind man wearing a wool cap who sat in the shade of the bridge cradling a harp made of charred wood covered with iguana skin. There was a carved white mask on the bald end of the harp. The blind man was not singing, he was hissing at Adam, a snake's hiss. Two mahogany-skinned women, their lips tinted with papyrus juice, wearing white face powder and long skirts, were given four ritual kisses by their husbands who then went into a prayer house where they hunched forward on rugs in the rose-coloured dust.

Adam caught a whiff of gunpowder and iodine on the stagnant air. A child said, "It's going to spill," but no one was carrying anything, not that Adam could see. A black girl, whose beaded pigtails were tied into a crown on top of her head, stamped her bare foot in the dust. She had raced another, taller girl to a board fence. There were posters plastered to the fence: militiamen aiming Uzis at the sky.

"My shadow mek it first," the tall girl yelled.

"It did not, Dainty."

"It did. It mek de fence first."

"Show me your shadow," she cried. "There's no shadow."

"I tank you stupid."

"De sun fled away, when we are running de sun fled away."

"I saw it," the braided girl screamed.

"It didn't get to there, I tank you got no shadow."

Two leper boatmen, one wearing a bowler hat, were sitting on their haunches on a concrete jetty at the end of the board fence. Adam got into their dugout canoe and sat very straight and still, turning only when the boatmen pointed to a peaked blue roof through the trees but he didn't hear what they said. He could see across the broad water a cleared sand beach under tall okoumes and long narrow sheds with peaked roofs of corrugated iron raised on piles to let rain water run downhill freely, built from east to west so that the sun would not beat down on the roofs directly except at noon. The boatman wearing a bowler hat asked: "You mek mercenary?"

"No."

"No mek mercenary here?"

"No."

The other boatman wet his lips from his water bottle.

"What are the sheds?" Adam asked.

"Old hospital."

"Old?"

"All mek rotten. White ants."

A hill angled up behind the sheds, a hill that looked like it had been skinned alive, like it was the underside of animal pelts sewn together, the dried black veins and tendons and patches of flesh left on the skin.

"What happened here?" Adam asked, pointing.

"Farms. Doctors mek farms. Big machines, now nothing."

The boatman wearing the bowler hat had been cracking small nuts between his teeth and spitting out the shells.

"I born there, bass," he said.

A heron with long yellow legs lifted off the water. It flew in a swooping circle, dragging its legs in the air, and then settled in the papyrus as Adam shifted his bags on his shoulders and got out of the pirogue. He started up the grassy road, alert because the trees and long grass were so still.

When he looked back at the two leper boatmen, they were sitting on a concrete abutment, their legs dangling over the water, staring after him. One tipped his bowler hat as Adam crossed in front of the ruined hospital sheds, the siding rotted or torn away by the winds. Rows of wooden bunk beds stood empty in the falling light. He didn't know if Gabrielle had got any of the letters he'd written to this place because he'd received no replies. As he got to a bend in the road, to a stretch of broken paving, he heard a bell, the same four notes over and over again ... CDEF ... EDCF ... CDEF ... EDCF ... a dead clanging followed by DDDDDDDDD and several minutes of silence as he walked on, and then the clanging began again.

He passed two squat concrete-block buildings. There were ornate burglar bars in the windows. Security men wearing mushroom-coloured trench coats, khaki short pants, and patent leather shin guards laced to their boots were standing in the doorways. Farther along, there was the beginning of a cement sidewalk, but only a short block later it came to an end where a square-shouldered white woman wrapped in a cape with a silver comb in her hair suddenly hurried out of a long low ochre brick building. Fallen roof tiles lay in the rough grass. The woman passed him. She looked angry and she curled her lip as she said, "Ev'ning." She was wearing a corsage of wilted red flowers on a plastic wristband. He went to speak but a tall white man with flat cheekbones hurried after her, glancing at Adam. He was carrying a gun. "Nice night," the man said to Adam. "Leek's the name, don't forget the *boules* tomorrow."

There were high barbed wire fences along the street, fences that went back into the bush behind the houses, each house set back from the street, all the houses surrounded by flowering bushes threaded by barbed wire to enclose the compound, and there were little white wooden frame doorways in the barbed wire fencing. No lights were on in the houses. Adam looked for the woman with the corsage. She and the man with the gun were gone but an elderly black man and boy had come out of the shadows between the compounds, the man carrying a big canvas suitcase and the boy wearing a cardboard sailor's hat.

"Where can I find somewhere to rest?" Adam asked.

The boy scurried on ahead, pointed past a corner tobacco shop and turned and waited, touching his hand to his lips. Adam looked down a short street. The boy held out his cardboard sailor's hat. Adam dropped a handful of coins into the hat and walked toward a low grey building that had a small bell tower, a clock, and a tilted cross. It was a mission dispensary. Black women were seated on the benches, waiting on the veranda of the dispensary, and as Adam came up the stairs a white nursing sister hurried from a room crowded with battered young women – women who, he was sure, had been raped, probably by young soldiers – into a front room maternity ward, a room of six or seven camp cots. Young mothers were nursing in the occluded light. In the far corner, where a mother was settled under heavy blankets against the dampness, the sister reached into the conical tent of white mosquito netting and lifted out a tiny reddish-black child, the head smaller than her hand, and she held it aloft and said, "See, only fifteen minutes old – look, life, isn't it wonderful?"

Adam leaned into a small front office, the windows also protected by rococo wrought-iron burglar bars. An older white man, a priest, wearing a freshly washed but worn white soutane too short at the ankles, stood up and faced him. Walleyed, he folded his left hand into his soutane, keeping a long deliberate silence as he held the bridge of his nose between his right thumb and forefinger, as if he were in pain, waiting for Adam to speak.

"Could I talk to you?" Adam asked, not quite sure if the priest was looking at him. He seemed tired and drawn, a bristle of white whiskers on his cheeks, his left eye looking away as he sat down in his corner chair. "I just wanted some advice."

"Yes, yes, of course."

"Before the sun goes down."

"Would you like a glass of water?"

"I suppose I would," Adam said.

"The glass of water freely given is still the most convincing proof for the existence of God, Who is always present in the fevered face of the poor man," the priest said, pouring water from a jug into a glass and handing it to Adam. "What is your name?"

"Adam Waters. And yours?"

"Father Chamane."

Adam shuffled his feet in the stillness.

"I was wondering where I might go."

"Well, surely there's the town hotel."

"I didn't know there was a hotel this far back in the bush."

The sun had gone down. The surrounding elephant grass gave off an acrid musty smell. The priest gestured toward the door. "Just go to the centre, you'll see." Adam, as he left, thought he heard the old priest's muffled laughter. The women on the veranda bench were very quiet. No one was on the street and three streetlamps were broken, but he found the small three-storey hotel. The lobby was brightly lit by two chandeliers, two clusters of dewdrop crystal, and the whitewashed walls were reflected in the polished gumwood floors. The front desk had tiny niches, roll-top drawers, and folding shelves. There were two signs on the counter: one, elegantly etched in black glass – VALET PARKING IN THE REAR; and the other, on pulpy cardboard – MAKE MONEY – over grainy photographs of landmines, machine guns, grenades, and pistols, promising that cash would be paid at the police station to anyone who found weapons and turned them in.

The dispensary bell began to ring again but then stopped abruptly, as if someone had got the time wrong.

He signed the register for a white woman who wore a cameo of carved jet at her throat. *A death's head,* he thought, bemused, wondering why there always had to be a frazzled white woman running the lone hotel in these towns deep in the middle of nowhere. "Anyone looking for you?" she asked.

"No," he said. "Why?"

"No reason. I just always ask. I worry about a man no one's looking for. That's a man all alone."

"I am," he whispered, leaning across the counter, "the *adelantando.*"

"You don't say now," she said, drawing close. "And who might that be?"

"A man who's at home on the front porch of the dead," he said. "But no one's looking for me. And they've moved the porch. I'm looking for a woman."

"What else?" she said, sniffing, losing interest in him.

He went up the stairs to his room with his camera bag and his two shoulder bags. For no reason, he opened the drawer to the bedside table. He lifted out a small black leather-bound book, a bible. Inside, pasted to the flyleaf, was an old yellow strip of folded newsprint. Lying down on the bed, he read: "WORDS FROM DOCTOR LIEBIG – WORDS TO ALL IN DESPAIR: 'The reason thousands cannot get cured is easily explained. There are so many causes of Seminal Weakness, Impotency, Loss of Vitality, Memory, Sight, Hearing, Feelings, Imbecility, etc. Onanism, self-abuse, may cause the above diseases and symptoms which require a certain treatment; men whose strength is gradually wasting away, before all hope of restoration, should examine their urine: if any ropy sediment or brick dust appears, that is the warning stage of Seminal Weakness. Be of Stout Heart. Do not indulge yourself. We guarantee permanent cures in curable cases. No miracles performed.'"

Gone Home

MOHR

Adopted

WATERS

Henrietta   Susanna

```
S V W E T B S A 15 S T M O R E
E I R T E 2 Y D & H N S 10 H E
M A A D 17 & S H T N O A R M T
N A Y D H D R O F S M Y E H E
E N S O W M H M E O 2 D 26 T T
E V & E I R O M I F S G E E E
H R S 27 D I I E T W R 7 A O M
D A U H T A N M I S A 8 9 M T
H T S E S M E R E T E L I E S
Y E A 1 P H N I T A Y R I P M
E W N 8 9 5 A G E D 23 A P E L
E R N H S N W F W O I D T D H
I G A I 2 D I E H D E 27 H G O
T F R M O A D R N W N E V N A
F S O G D N A E O I H A E M Y
```

Readers Meet Us in Heaven

Toronto

The weather changed. Late in the winter, with deep snow on
the ground, high winds out of the south swept across Lake

Ontario breaking branches and shutters, blowing powdered ice off the crusted snow. The winds turned warm. It was hard to breathe, hard to sleep. People sat in the slush at tables outside the cafés. They smiled, soaking wet. Snow houses, the children's dark tunnelled world, collapsed. Old socks and shoes appeared afloat in the street gutters. Where the snow melted down to the flowerbeds, the earth reeked, giving off an acrid smell of decaying roots and stems. Adam came home from his work at The Telegram, where he had begun not only to report internationally but to conduct apprenticeships, and found his mom standing in the bathroom doorway. She was wearing only panties and was in her bare feet, her thighs white and loose. "Sometimes it hurts, sitting inside your own head. When I was a girl," she said, "they brushed my hair over and over, stroke by stroke by stroke, and taught me to sing and arrange flowers . . . to arrange . . ." Then, sternly, accusingly: "Look at you, what are you? Twenty? You look more and more like your father."

"I do?"

"Yes," she said.

"Does that mean you love me more or less?"

"Wouldn't you like to know?" she said.

Pale, thin, her hair cropped, she locked herself in her bedroom. "There'll be fire next time," she called out. He stayed home from the newspaper and knocked on her door for three days. She did not eat. She refused to speak. Then, when she came out, she spent hour after hour washing the leaded front windows, breathing on the glass, polishing the panes. "So that the whole world," she said, "will seem to be shining." She went to the bedroom closet and took out one of Web's long-ago scissored suit coats that she had hidden among her dresses and she put it on. Swamped by the shoulders, and with half a sleeve missing, she looked mutilated and desolate. "I don't think I'm anybody's anybody any more," she said reaching out to Adam. "I'm just your mom gone wrong."

"You've never been wrong, Mom, not once."

"Now isn't that a seductive thing to say."

She began to go out at night by herself, three or four or five nights a week, coming home at midnight.

Finally, he asked her: "Mom, where have you been going?"

"Bowling," she said, with an impish little toss of her head.

"For Chrissake! What're you doing bowling?"

"I just decided to find out what it was like to go completely wrong."

She took out a small ad in the community newspaper, announcing that she was going to sponsor bowling every Wednesday night:

BOWLING: TWO LANES
FREE FOR THE HOMELESS
AND FREE SHOES TOO
7 PM – 11 PM
WEB "SWEET" WATERS
WILL NOT ATTEND

The owners of Monarch Superior Bowling Twenty Lanes, two Korean brothers, were upset when six or seven homeless people answered the ad and asked for lane time and bowling shoes.

Adam, who had come with his camera to see who would respond to the ad, took a dozen or more photographs of a homeless man who liked to take out his false teeth and smile a lot, peeling back his lips, baring his gums, and then Adam took over the organization of the two lanes for his mother and for four hours he paid for shoes and for the lanes. Only one woman fell down with a big black ball in her arms into a gutter, and two men had to be told they were too filthy to be loaned bowling shoes.

At the end of the evening the owners spoke softly to his mother: "Please, Mrs. Waters, never again."

"Never say never," she called out gaily, taking Adam's arm at the door. "You might get what you wish for."

"I wish Web had seen this," Adam said. "This was so wrong, it was absolutely right. Right beyond belief."

"You tell your father. You tell him what his Florence did. He'll believe you and he'll be sorry."

One week later, after a working studio session with the photojournalist Paul Rockett, Adam came home and found her slumped against the front window, her eyes wide open, dead. "Her heart just seems to have stopped," the doctor said.

Adam offended the doctor by taking several close-ups of her face, her eyes still open.

"I'll shoot her, and then I'll put pennies on her eyes," he said to the doctor who said sternly, "I believe that's what they used to do, so the dead would no longer have to look upon this world."

"You would have loved her," Adam said as the paramedics wheeled her away. "She saw angels, she talked to the angels."

Two days later, the snow, wind-blown, was deep. Web had not been found. He was said to be somewhere on the road with Buddy Tate, perhaps in Bavaria, heading for Copenhagen, where, Adam was told by an agent in New York, Tate lived and played.

"He's got a beautiful house on a canal."

Somehow, two of the homeless bowlers had heard of her death and they attended a short funeral mass, along with Dorothy Alt, the singer, widowed, who now walked with a cane, and Father Zale, Harry O'Leary and Miss Klein.

"Is there a family plot?" Miss Klein asked.

"She won't be buried," Adam said.

She had written a note saying she wanted to be cremated, turned to ashes. He showed her the note: "Closest thing to the real thing, burn me, like I was a Jew."

Miss Klein broke into tears and fled.

Father Zale shook his head. He said cremation was not necessarily a good thing, "And the note's all wrong. The horror of the concentration camps has got into the bones of people in terrible sinister ways."

"Right," Harry said, "we're all supposed to believe that we carry a little concentration camp in our hearts? Whatever happened to the lightness of love, to Mozart, to the music of angels?"

Father Zale went back to the house with Adam, who made the priest a cup of tea, and then he went in to his parents' bedroom and he sat alone on their bed, wondering how a cozy cluttered room could seem so abandoned. He called his mother's name and he thought he could hear an echo out of the corners of the room: *Florence.* He opened her dresser drawers, looking for anything, for nothing, looking in the bottom drawers for his childhood drawing books, and his books about the stars. They were not there. Nothing that had been his as a child was there. He found dozens of colourful empty matchbooks from bars and clubs where his father had played, and amid her underwear, a chrome-plated handgun. It lay gleaming in the half-light. As he picked it up he saw himself in her big oval dresser mirror. "You're more and more like your father," she'd said. He pointed the gun. "Are you looking at me?" He pulled the trigger. A cap popped open at the heel of the barrel. There was a small flame, it was a fancy old cigarette lighter, and he stared for a long time into the eye of the flame, and then he said, "Well, goddamn," and laughed and went into the kitchen to tell the waiting priest, "Believe it or not, I just saw the end of the world."

In the summer of that year, there were high winds and no rains. Long hanging veils of white dust rose off the bluffs along the lakeshore, whitening the sun. It was hot and Father Zale was dressed in his good black slacks and a black linen short-sleeved shirt. He and Adam had intended to go downtown to stroll through a music store, but instead they had gone down to the base of the bluffs. It was so quiet they could hear the rustle of dry leaves in the white birches. The sky had a mother-of-pearl sheen, as if it were going to rain, but it was not going to rain.

"It's a mock storm sky," Father Zale said. "God patiently mocks us. My mother always said that and these days I hear the words of my mother and father more and more. I wonder why they're talking to me after all these years, butting into the middle of my prayers."

That's what his parents did as he lay in bed late at night, he said. Or he'd lose track of who was saying what to whom, who the characters were, when he was reading a novel, and he'd turn out the light and hear his father say, *You discover the light in darkness, that's what the darkness is for.*

Standing on the scrub sand along the shore, Father Zale squinted in the glaring white sunlight and wiped the dust from his cheeks and mouth. He turned his back to the wind, clearing his throat and tasting dust, spitting with the wind. "You should always pray toward where the cattle beasts are turned in the morning because that's pure air coming in on the light, my old man told me that." But he hadn't seen a cattle beast in the morning in twenty years. "Now I'm an old man, too, and I've put the beast behind me," he said sardonically. "Though now, what the light reveals is danger and what it demands is faith. Those aren't words from my father, that's an old parish priest friend of mine who died last year as an alcoholic, stiff in the service of the Lord," he said, laughing quietly as he sat on a flat rock between two white birches, staring at the water and seagulls riding a swell. "I remember my old parish pal got drunk one night in a shed behind the church house and he insisted that he had never felt so close to God, he was laughing and chanting:

> *The sexual life of the camel*
> *Is stranger than anyone thinks*
> *One moonlit night on the desert*
> *He attempted to bugger the Sphinx*
> *But the Sphinx's posterior entry*
> *Was clogged with the sands of the Nile*
> *Which accounts for the hump on the camel*
> *And the Sphinx's inscrutable smile."*

And then Father Zale took a searing blow through his throat as if his brain had been bolted shut, the air slamming up into his eyes so that he thought his skull had shattered, and when he tried to howl he felt he had swallowed the iron bolt. The sky folded over his head and he began to seep blood. He had been shot through the throat with an arrow, by a boy out on the beach with a crossbow hunting birds on the bluffs. Adam ran and tackled him, though the boy had not tried to run away. Later, the boy said to the police, "I got no beef with the priest." He insisted that he'd seen a crow in the birch trees and that he had not seen any man wearing a black shirt and black slacks crouched at the base of the white bluffs.

"It is a highly professional stainless steel crossbow and the boy had borrowed it from his father's basement workshop, the father who uses the bow only in survival war games he plays with other professional men, his friends," the detectives said at the inquiry. It was concluded that there was no quarrel between the boy and the priest and there had been no intent to kill (the boy explained that there had been a strange light that day and that he had intended to walk the other way on the beach, but what he had intended had turned out back- wards, and he hoped this wouldn't be held against him because his secret dream was to represent the country and his fellow citizens on the national archery team), and the inquiry recommended that bows and arrows, especially crossbows, be banned for bird hunting within twenty miles of the city lim- its.

Father Zale recovered at a nunnery north of the city. "I can still pray," he wrote on a mass card for one of the nuns. "I can't speak, but it doesn't matter. I've nothing more to say except what my mother said – God patiently mocks us." The nun became upset and told Adam, "No, no, he mustn't believe that." So Father Zale wrote: "Don't worry, I am full of light, it's just that it's a light that demands a faith in darkness." After six months he stopped shaking and clutching his throat. Adam took him home by taxi to his room at the school, to his bird feeders, where two young priests he didn't know were assigned to look after him. When he wasn't sitting in silence on his bench casting crusts from his knapsack, he sat for hours in the small lookout room on the mansard roof, or stood outside on the widow's walk staring out over the water.

From time to time he would write notes to Adam: "I have decided that the inchoate is how evil exhausts itself. Evil feeds off itself – it is a corruption inherent in growth, in life itself, but when it becomes only the feeding – hatred at the throat of hatred – as with the Irish Protestants and Catholics, as with the Serbs and Croatians, as with the Israelis and Palestinians – all we can really do is let that evil exhaust itself, wear itself down, burn itself out as a brush fire burns itself off the land and becomes smoke. Then, seizing the moment, like birds coming out of the smoke, that is then the time for the peace-makers, blessed be they, stinking of that smoke, which is the chaos at the very centre of the human condition."

One afternoon as Adam walked away from the school, he turned and looked up to see the priest standing with his arms flung wide open – in an embrace, he wondered, or an act of surrender? – to the wind.

Gabon

As he left the hotel, the woman behind the desk rested her elbows on the Valet Parking sign and said with a sly laugh, "Off you go now, sonny. Off you go."

He walked to the centre of town where there were tall trees in a small park and instead of grass under the trees, there was finely raked gravel and several men – white and black – were playing *boules* on the gravel, Mr. Leek and the old priest in his frayed white soutane standing among them.

"Well now," the old priest said, palming the brushed steel ball in his surprisingly big hand, "watch this." He closed his left eye, aimed, and looped it toward a small white ball, hitting and driving the white ball between two bare tree roots.

Leek called out for two beers and clapped Adam on the shoulder.

"Where's this place you're off to?"

"*Village lumière . . .*"

"Why in the world would you want to go there?"

"A woman I know."

"It's lepers," he said and drew away a little. "It's a jeezly leper camp off by the hospital."

"She's a white woman, Gabrielle . . ."

"Hell. I've had a gander at her."

"You have?"

"Crazy as a bedbug. But terribly good-looking, give her that." He took a long swallow of beer. "Terrible shame really. Good-looking, but lost in a daisy chain with the lepers. This whole fucking world is leprous enough without going to the heart of it – pardon my language, Father Chamane. But have you ever seen lepers, Mr. Waters, real lepers? It's in the wounds, that's the *lumière* business, it looks like there's this glistening light. The light's in the rot . . ."

Toronto
On a cloudless afternoon of sunlit-crusted snow in the yard, Adam and Father Zale sat on the back porch. The priest wore a heavy woollen muffler around his throat. He had grown paler and thinner, as if his silences were slowly starving him, yet he smiled continuously, his eyes sparkling. Several years ago, Adam had seen him walking down the street with Harry, who had been dapper in a double-breasted suit and straight-last shoes, carrying a silver conductor's baton under his arm. Excited in his conversation, Harry had stopped to make a point, standing on the sidewalk in front of the nodding priest, crossing the air with his baton, and Adam had heard him say firmly, ". . . the seventh angel sounded the trumpet . . ." They had walked on, Father Zale still nodding, taking Harry by the arm, just as he now reached out on the back porch, trying to comfort Adam as Adam said, "I can't somehow get it out of my mind, always seeing Mom's body slip out of the coffin into the fire, and I know it doesn't make much sense because the fire's probably better than rotting away in the scummy earth,

but I kind of see her like a cocoon of skin and bone, exploding into ashes. It's hard for me to see that she really wanted it that way, though she wouldn't have said so if she didn't want it. That was the thing about her, honest as the day is long, too honest. I remember sitting here a couple of months before she died, with her looking out over the roofs, because sometimes she saw her angel moving over there, and I don't think she was really crazy or anything like that. It just amused her to think she was getting a visitation from wherever her family of ghosts were coming from, but then she turned to me, solemn, with this pleased kind of glint in her eye, and she reminded me that when I was a boy she'd told me that the less I knew about her and Web the better it was for me. Knowing next to nothing, I'd be free to love them longer, she'd said, except now she was going to tell me something so I would understand them as well as love them."

Adam pulled the lapels of his coat across his chest against the chill wind. The sun flared off the snow, cutting his eyes. He stepped down a stair, tucking his head out of the glare, and turned back to the priest, who had edged forward in his chair.

"And Mom said that if I looked back I'd know that she and Dad had always treated each other the same way, accepting who they were, accepting themselves just the way they'd found each other. Dad, Mom said, was a driven lonely man – like I didn't already know that – who loved her as long as he could continue to be alone and feed off his own loneliness. That's where – and she had closed her eyes and was absolutely firm saying this – that's where any greatness Dad had as a musician came from, his own loneliness which he tried to fill with more loneliness, a loneliness that, of course, left her more and more alone, too. She said she could have told him, right there and then, that if he really loved her he would have absolutely had to stop being who he was, that he would have had to become who she wished him to be, but to do that, he'd have had to betray himself. Which is what Mom said most everybody mistakes for love. Your lover has to betray himself, he has to accommodate and compromise, he has to be anybody but who he is."

Adam turned away, stepping down the stairs into the snow, through the crust, and Father Zale came down the stairs after him. "Since Mom was a woman with her own loneliness, her own darkness, she told me that as it had worked out she had given Dad no real gaiety, the blind gaiety he needed to lift himself out of his own gloom, and so I guess – looking back – I can see how they disappointed each other. But at least they never made each other betray themselves. She thought they loved each other better that way, better than anybody else she knew."

Adam stood out in the deep snow in the sunlight with the old priest beside him. They stood with their arms around each other, the priest weeping because he could not say a word.

1842 – 1896
To the memory of Annie Waters
Who was the water in everyone's wine.
She punished the earth upwards of 40 years
To say nothing of her relations.

One night, not long after his mother died, he walked around the empty house humming mournfully to himself, drinking whiskey straight from the bottle. Drunk, he decided to walk over to Harry's because he felt sorry for Harry who lived alone, and he was going to stand and sing on Harry's porch, sing to his old choirmaster. But when he got there and before he could start singing, Harry opened the door and said, "Come on in," and Adam said, "I didn't come alone, I brought you a bottle."

They sat at the dining-room table. Harry lit a cigarette. He cupped the cigarette in his hand, hiding it. Adam had always believed that Harry hid his cigarette in his hand because he was smoking in church behind the altar, but here he was in his home, hiding.

Adam sat hunched forward, his head down, troubled by how rumpled Harry looked, his clothes unclean. A full choir with brass and strings now boomed from the living room corner speakers – "*Kyrie, Kyrie eleison*" – and Adam, puzzled – but also because he was quite drunk – rubbed his face with both hands – thinking, *Harry's your doomed gentleman song-*

ster. But Harry was sitting very straight in his chair, eyes closed, listening, with his hands folded on the table, *except he doesn't sing*, and though the cuffs of his coat were frayed and his wrists looked bony and thin, he had beautiful hands . . . long tapered fingers, and the skin was pinkish-white, scrubbed clean, the nails carefully clipped, the cuticles cut back.

"It's all in the touch," Harry said, "the laying on of the hands." He lifted one arm with an elegant gesture, the hand hanging bent from the wrist in the air for a moment as if it were a flower that had just died on the stem. He began to conduct, the hand caressing the air as voices of surpassing sweetness rose, saying, "Now this, this is the real trumpet stuff, this is it, *Dies Irae*, and you gotta listen to this, and if you're drunk and you're a lucky drunk who knows how to hear, you'll hear it . . . all of Verdi's easy equilibrium, what your father would call good-rocking, every note, every syllable as precise as a raindrop . . ."

He lifted both hands, seeming to hold a moment's silence between them, ". . . it's bold, right out front, the boldest thing . . ." Harry stopped conducting and filled their glasses, hearing deep in the corners of the room a bass voice, *Mors stupebit et natura, cum resurgit creatura . . ."*And the boldest thing," he said, pointing his finger at Adam, "is what Verdi called the *parola scenica*. He sculpts the situation, makes it clean, he takes you into neutral zones where there's no clear word, just a blur of voices, and sometimes the voices hiss at you . . . it's wild, you sit in there in those zones, the hissing . . ."

They sat across from each other at the table until the bottle was empty. Then Adam got up and Harry, with his arm around Adam's shoulder, walked with him outside.

"I really came over to sing on your porch," Adam said.

"So sing . . . to your whole life that's ahead of you."

"I was going to sing you a song old Edmund taught me up at the Moon River . . ."

"Sing . . ."

Adam hollered with a nasal twang, to the tune of "What a Friend We Have in Jesus":

> *Life presents a dismal aspect,*
> *Full of darkness and of gloom,*
> *Father has a strictured penis,*
> *Mother has a fallen womb.*
> *Brother Bill has been deported*
> *For a homosexual crime,*
> *Sister Bette has just aborted*
> *For the forty-second time*
> *Cousin Sue has chronic menstruation.*
> *Never laughs and seldom smiles,*
> *Oh, life presents a dismal aspect,*
> *Cracking ice for father's piles.*
> *Amen*

They stood together on the top step, laughing and howling Amens into the night, and then Adam went down the walk. Harry lit a cigarette and when Adam turned to look back he saw the red tip of fire disappear in Harry's cupped hand as Harry called out, "Come to mass tomorrow, you'll really hear something . . ."

The next morning, when Adam crossed the cobblestone square and entered the church, he found it was the feast of Corpus Christi and the pews were crowded, but the first three rows on both sides of the centre aisle had been cordoned off with white tasselled ropes. A priest in a black surplice and white mitre was sprinkling holy water over the altar. The choir filed onto the altar, but the choir was much smaller than it used to be, only seven boys and seven men, and Adam realized that there was a wooden music stand in front of the choir stall. The choir, dressed in red robes, waited.

Then, outside the church, there was a drum roll, followed by a steady drumbeat. The central doors opened and the De La Salle Drum and Trumpet Corps, in their black uniforms and silver capes, marched in single file up the aisle to the front rows. As the last drummer turned into his pew, Harry, robed in red, came onto the altar, to the music stand, and as he lifted his baton the priest appeared, his chasuble scarlet red with a white cross. Someone hidden was playing Harry's organ, the choir began to sing.

Harry conducted the *Kyrie*, and the small choir sang with precision, each syllable clipped and as clear as Harry's flicks and turns of the baton. During the sermon, he did not leave the altar but stepped back to sit in the chair set aside from the stall. He sat very straight in the chair, his legs crossed beneath the red robe.

At the moment of consecration, when the people in their pews all knelt, the drum and trumpet corps stood as the priest lifted the Host over his head for the first time and Harry slashed the air with his baton. There was a rising drum roll and then trumpets blared, a piercing, rending note that startled and threw those kneeling back against their seats. The choir joyfully sang *Sanctus* into the echo and as the Host – the Word made Flesh – was lifted again, and Harry lifted his arms, too, drums rolled, the trumpeters blew the silence open, the note resounding and hanging in the air. *Sanctus.* Harry stood with his arms raised, waiting, at the moment before the wine becomes blood and the blood becomes wine, with a little lopsided grin on his face. As the priest lifted the Host for the last time, Harry hunched his shoulders and slowly swept the air with his arms, urging a heavier and deeper drum roll, and then he almost leapt as he stabbed the baton toward the front pews of forty silver trumpets. *Sanctus. Sanctus. Sanctus.* The triumphal crescendo caromed through the church. Adam stood astonished. Harry, in rapt concentration, stood with his arms thrown back, turned away from the choir to face the crowd as the priest walked down to the altar rail, to the people slowly coming forward to take Communion. Harry, staring, his teeth clenched in an ecstatic pain, reached up, as if he were trying to leap out of his shoes.

Puerto Rico

"I'm always afraid that things like fleas get right into your blood," she said, as they drove through the black and tan hills and saw the cove of mangrove below them, each tree like a huge water spider poised on the water.

"Ponce, my crazy old Ponce," Adam said, as he drove toward the docks in the cove, "when he came along and set up his sundial to keep track of the hour of the dead, the old Indian hunters thought he was crazy." She had her hand on the inside of his thigh. She began to sing, "It's three o'clock in the morning," but he said, "With his face the colour of dead fires, they worried that he was some kind of god, but he knew no matter how many times he called himself the *adelantando*, you know what the *adelantando* is . . . ?"

"No."

"The front runner. Old Ponce, the plunger, thought he was the front runner . . ."

"What's a plunger?"

"A guy who bets every dollar like it's his last dollar and never bets against himself, not even in his own mind."

"So he thinks he can get all the tattooed ladies, too?"

"Exactly, because he's out front and on the road. Most people live like they're renting their lives but not me and Ponce, we're trying to find some joy up in the hills of our illusions. But the young Indians stood inside their stag skins and they shot him with an arrow. And old Ponce, delectable, irrepressible, impeccable, and sensational, said, 'God helps those who help themselves and I couldn't help myself,' and he wept because he only wanted to be young again, to be loved, to be the *adelantando* . . ."

"He did not."

"What?"

"He didn't say 'God helps those that help themselves.' That's you, you're making it up."

"Okay, he didn't, but he should have because he got himself killed and he didn't come back."

"Maybe he had no one to come back to?"

"Maybe."

"Or maybe he forgot to leave behind some shoes?"

At the docks, a man hunched up under a wide-brimmed floppy straw hat agreed to rent them a light aluminum boat that had a small outboard motor. The rains had backed off. The water was calm in the cove. The boat eased by the first mangrove trees, stragglers on the edge of the dark web-work of root branches looped and hooked in the air, their leaves blocking out more and more of the sun the deeper they went into the grove, the oily water the colour of the leaded side of a mirror, only broken by sudden mirror-like flashes of light through gaps in the foliage as they snaked through the tunnel channels, hundreds of water striders leaving swollen silver lines on the surface.

"Why did you want to come out here?" she asked.

"I don't know. Because it's here, I've never been in a mangrove before."

"Do you always go where you've never been before, just because it's there?"

"Maybe. Maybe most of the time."

"Strange."

"Why?"

"Because you're so attached to your home, it's in your head all the time, your memories."

"I used to think that that's what immortality is."

"What?"

"Being alive in someone else's memory."

"And now?"

"I'm not so sure. I know now that everything begins in the memory and I love you like no one else, I love you so very deeply. I don't want us to be a memory. I want us to be a never-ending now."

"We are," she said, the overhead roots shadowing her face as she sat upright in the bow.

"I woke up this morning," he said, "and I could actually remember us doing what we did when we were young but then I could hardly remember what we'd done yesterday, or the day before. I just felt this quiet sureness about where we'd come from. It's the one thing I'm sure about. It's something my father told me years ago, you don't know who you are until you know who your ghosts are. And at the same time there's this sudden forgetfulness of mine, like a complete loss of memory. I couldn't even remember the names of some people we just met. There was just us. It made me want to lock up all my cameras. It was as close as I've ever come to bliss, or what bliss must be, or suicide."

"Suicide?"

"It crossed my mind, maybe love is something like suicide. You just leave off from yourself so you can't remember yourself, and you don't need to, you just are. Like this mangrove or a flower at the back of a garden . . ."

"It's spooky in here."

"Maybe love's spooky?"

"No, no. I couldn't be happier," she said.

"Sure you could."

"No, I couldn't, I'm not prone to happiness."

"Why not?"

She reached to touch the roots.

"I can't ever really forget."

"But you told me you don't remember."

"That's right, I can hardly remember what I did with Harry but it's like what died in me is still alive. Every day that dead thing is more and more alive. That's what I can't forget."

"But we've been happy like mad here."

"And I'll always remember everything. You're immortal already, see."

They came out of the channel, out of the grove into the late sunlight, pale pink and mauve through layered clouds, the sun sinking. There were hundreds of black and white frigate birds with long tails that looked like open shears (*Edmund's shears, yes, for scissoring ducks!*), and though the frigates fed on flying fish farther out to sea, the wind was wrong for feeding, so they were hovering overhead, over the boat, low-flying, and the males had a flash of startling scarlet red. Lying back in the boat, Adam cut the motor dead so they could watch the drift of the birds in the air currents, their undulation, funnelling into line for a moment and then flattening out into a huge sickle shape, and the only other movement was from floppy-winged pelicans suddenly lifting out of the trees, their throats of heavy loose flesh like old bags. "Like the old Gladstone travelling bag my grandfather used to carry," he said.

"I remember something your grandfather said."

"What?"

"'Don't eat the red berries or you'll die.' I just remembered it now looking at the red on the black wings of the birds."

The light was going down in the hour before the moon rises. He started the motor and swung the boat around toward the bay beyond the docks, the gently heaving water in the shadow light of dusk like ebony glass, except after a while, as they entered the mouth of the bay, an effervescent foaming began to appear in their wake and waves rippled away from the boat's bow like ribbons of glowing confetti.

Suddenly a fish leapt in the dark. It was luminescent, an arc of inexplicable light, and as the boat moved, small schools of fish skittered away, leaving faint trails of glowing handstitching under the water. He trailed his hand, a foam of light churned around his wrist, and as she began to laugh gleefully he scooped up handfuls of light-loaded water and poured it back into the blackness and then, dipping his arm up to his elbow in the water, he held it up open-handed, and light, like illuminated balls of mercury, rolled through his fingers over his palm and down his forearm.

"Stop," she said, "stop."

The boat rocked, as he shut off the motor.

"I've never seen anything like this," she whispered.

"Me neither."

They sat watching for fish, for beaded trails of light.

"Let's take our clothes off, let's go swimming," she said. "It'll be wonderful."

"We don't know what's in these waters."

"And you," she said, pulling her blouse free of her skirt, "you're the man who always goes where he's never been."

She dove in and he dove after her, cutting swaths of light down through the water, their bodies rising to the surface, shouting. They thrashed the water, smacking their palms against the water, driving sprays of light into their faces, light streaming over their shoulders as they kissed, kissing droplets from their cheeks, trying to touch the bursts of light all over their bodies. He lifted her so that her breasts were against his face, and then he fell back with the current of the water, covering her with quick kisses on her eyelids, her throat. They sank under, hanging in the water, and she locked her legs around his waist, each kiss tasting of salt. He kept his mouth on hers.

They were locked, straining, fondling and spinning as they fell under a wave, and then they broke apart and dove under again, seeking to go as deep in the darkness as they could so that they could make a turbulence of light as they came back up. She arced into the air, a necklace sparkling and breaking apart over her breasts. Turning and swimming on their backs, they lost sight of land and saw only stars and then, suddenly, the moon came up over the hills and the sky brightened, the stars dimmed. With the brightening sky the beads of phosphorous light in the water disappeared. All traces disappeared, leaving them swimming in the black water, reaching for the boat.

PART NINE

Toronto

He lay in his boyhood bed, eyes closed, but with the bedside light on. *A house,* he thought, *even more than a woman, should not be left alone.* He could hear his father snoring in the next room. He fell into a half-sleep, dreaming that he was still awake, walking in the shallows of the Moon River with Gabrielle, except the river was leaking through a huge iron pipe into Christie Pits where the tattooed man lay spread-eagled on his back across second base, alive and trying to embrace flying fish circling overhead, and when Adam turned, Gabrielle was standing naked at home plate, her body stencilled by blue dots, and he joined them together, drawing his finger across her collarbone and breast, her belly and hips, and with each joining, snowflakes took off from her body like winged stars, the ceiling in his room covered by stars, creaking under a huge weight until the ceiling of stars broke open and a Southern Cross fell through and his mother said, "You'll see, we all carry one of those things," the cross falling at the feet of Father Zale as he stretched out in a lawn chair snoring.

But it was his father's snoring that woke him. He pulled his covers close to his chin, glad of the otherwise quiet of his room, the stillness inside the silences of his home, though he'd always slept well wherever he was, unafraid of sleep, only afraid of that one terrifying dream that had made him break out in remorse-stricken sweats, but then the snoring stopped and he heard a woman weeping. He sat up, quickening but confused, wondering if he'd really heard weeping . . . as his father appeared in the doorway. Adam said, "Did you hear her weeping?"

"What weeping?"

"I heard it."

"I didn't hear anything. I woke up and I didn't hear a thing."

His father was carrying a furry little bear in the crook of his arm.

"What in the world is that?"

"Your teddy bear. When I woke up I suddenly remembered it's been up with the hats in the closet all these years."

"I never had a teddy bear."

"You played with it in your crib."

"That doesn't count, I don't remember anything from my crib."

"Exactly. So how many fathers give their sons back their childhood in the middle of the night?"

Adam laughed, taking the bear, and looked into its face, its amber eyes, its slightly torn red felt tongue flapping beneath a battered snout, and he tossed it into the air.

"That's what you did as a kid. I spent half my life picking up that bear. You'd fire it out of the crib like you couldn't wait to get rid of it and I'd pick it up and bring it back to you and then one day I just picked it up and put it away. You howled and howled, and since then I've never known what to do with you as a kid."

His father sat on the end of the bed, bent forward, his elbows on his knees. His forearms and wrists were still muscular, powerful.

"You know," he said, "I've got friends who've got sons all over the world, and they talk about this one and that one, saying that having a lot of sons is a kind of protection against bad luck, against one of them dying on you, against all the evil out there in the air. But you're it, you're all I've got."

In the kitchen, Adam gave his dad a glass of freshly squeezed orange juice. "It's a habit I got into in Cairo," he said. "Sunlight on the tongue to start the day."

His father studied the glass. "If you say so," he said, but he did not drink the juice.

They sat across from each other in the living room, facing the leaded windows.

"Kinda nice, being together again."

"Yeah."

"It's strange," Adam said, "the room doesn't seem smaller, there just doesn't seem to be as much light."

"It's the ghosts," Web said. "That's what ghosts do. They become a crowd and they suck up all the light. They swallow so much light that they disappear during the day and glow at night."

"What crazy man told you that?"

"My father, when I was a kid. You're sitting in his chair, the chair he always sat in. He was a frightened man, your grandfather. Scared of his wife at first, but she died young. So, like most people, he kept on being afraid without having anything to be afraid of. He was such a nice quiet man no one ever wanted to do him any hurt. That's why he had those off-in-the-distance-looking eyes, like he was always waiting for someone he knew would be afraid of to show up . . ."

His father sat with his chin in his hand, staring out the window into the bare black branches of the sugar maple tree by the front hedge. In their silence, they heard the old wood scantling snap in the walls and the hot water pipes clank with the cold wind blowing against the east wall. Adam saw little linings of frost along the inside of the leaded windows.

"I keep thinking I should hear Mom's step in the hall," Adam said.

"Yeah."

"Except I don't. I mean, I think I should hear her but I don't. I don't know whether to be disappointed in myself or her."

"For what?"

"For not showing up."

"Oh, she's here."

"I guess she is. She said she'd always be my shadow. But there's a stillness in the house I never knew was here."

"There's probably all kinds of things we don't know are here."

"I think we need a drink, except there's nothing to drink. No one's been here for months."

"How little you know," his father said, standing up.

"You've got drink?"

"You think if I can find your teddy bear I can't find a drink?"

"I looked everywhere."

"You only looked where you looked and that isn't everywhere."

Web went down the hall. Adam slumped in his chair and found himself seeing things as if for the first time: the frayed hem of the window drapes and a dead begonia stem in the big blue porcelain bowl on the radiator lid, the face of a Renoir woman his mom had cut from a magazine and glued to a board and varnished so that it looked like an old canvas in the soft light from the beaded lampshade above the piano, where Web, carrying a bottle, put two glasses.

"Single malt, boy, and so," he said, handing him a glass, "you haven't got your ass shot off yet? It scares me all to hell, you trying to get yourself killed."

"That's not what it's about. You know that."

"Sure, but I've still got an aggravation on my mind about you getting shot up in someone else's war."

"I kind of make it my own war."

"How's that?"

"Not too many people can actually see what they see. I see what I see. My editors think it's a gift."

"We all see what we see."

"No, I figure, maybe it's by temperament, or maybe I got it from you, that somehow I'm always prepared to see what is actually there, not what I'm supposed to see, like when Grandpa told me as a kid not to eat these red berries, I can still see the detail of those berries. So the way I work through a shoot, a sequence of stills – it becomes not just what it is, but also it's probably a pretty detailed reflection of me, almost like a kind of confession of how I've lived through what I've seen. It's like you used to say about the silences between notes – that's where all the music is. That's my music. It may be a silent music, it may even be an elegiac silence, a lament, but whatever it is it comes from working through the details to get to my own point of view, and if that leaves me with a kind of loneliness, like I've got this peripheral point of view, it's no lonelier than you knowing that what people hear and love when you play is not what you hear and love, and what's worse is, you've got to love your fans for loving you for all the wrong reasons, or at least not the reasons you'd like to be loved for . . ."

"It's what drives musicians crazy."

They sat in silence for a long time. Though Adam could see that his father was thinner, his skin drawn, his body bent, there was something eager, intense, in the way he leaned forward, coiled in his stillness, brooding on what his son had said. Then: "See, what I think you're talking about is what I was talking to Buddy Tait about in Copenhagen last year, the whole question of melody. Like, I'm playing 'Stardust' and each note, is maybe like one of your photographs, distinct, it's honest, clean, but still it's a melody, and the question is, how do I hear what I remember of the first three notes of the melody when I'm playing the last three. Do I hear the melody differently at the beginning than I do at the end? There's a real thing here worth thinking about. How I play the melody I hear and how I put it into chords that are those notes, and then improvise around them, that is not only a reflection of who I am, but like you say, it's kind of my confession, too . . . a confession of how I've heard the world," and then his father said casually, "You got your legs on?"

"Where you want to go?"

"I thought we might go up by the graveyard."

He stood with his father at the entrance to the old cemetery. The street frontage had been sold so that the burial yard was like a park enclosed inside a city block, and there were shops along the street. Aviva's Adventures in Bamboo, Christen Birger Unisex Creations, Tehran Fine Carpets, Harvey Adelman's Quick Quiche Cuisine . . . and between two tombstone shops, a laneway leading into the burial yard, family plots, with the domed crematorium in the centre of the yard. There was no one else walking in the snowbound yard.

"I used to like coming here with you as a kid. Nobody else's father took them to a graveyard."

"No, I guess not."

"Sitting out here under the trees eating hot dogs for lunch."

"We're sure not sitting in this snow."

"We could lie down and make angel wings like when we were kids."

They turned down a walk between bare weeping willows.

"We're not going to see much in this snow."

"Maybe not."

His father walked ahead, past the cluster of Waters tombstones to an oak that stood away from the path, broad dead leaves clinging to the branches. The snow under the tree was unbroken, the crust glittering in the sunlight.

"So what's up?" Adam asked.

"Come on," Web said, and broke through the snow crust till he stopped by a lean slab. He brushed the blown snow away from the face of the stone and stepped back a pace, to stand beside Adam.

BABY
Still
Waters
Run
Deep

"Here," Web said, with his arms folded across his chest, "lies your twin brother."

"My what?"

"Your twin brother, stillborn. We never really named him, but we had to have a name on the papers so we called him Still. There's no date, man, because he was never alive."

"Jesus Christ . . . you mean I've got a brother?"

"No, you never had a brother. He was dead in the womb."

"And you tell me now . . ."

"We thought it was better . . ."

"Better than what?"

Adam grabbed his dad by the shoulders.

"Better not to carry around a dead brother all your life," Web said, "man, nobody needs to live with a dead twin who was never alive. Nobody."

"You did."

"And so did your mother. Always cutting her hair, like she did. It was no fun for her giving birth to a child dead. Her sweet little angel, she called him."

"You're out of your skull," and he shoved Web, who stumbled, falling backwards, his arms wide open as he fell into the soft deep snow under the oak tree. He lay flat on his back, staring straight up into the clear cold sky. He seemed strangely at rest, open to the whole sky, and Adam put his hands on his hips and began to laugh. "You're an old son-of-a-bitch," he said.

"Well," his dad said, smiling, "we all got our songs that ain't never been sung."

"You got more to tell me?"

Web began to wag his arms and legs in the snow, making an angel.

"I'm going back to Copenhagen, for good I think."

"Whose good?"

"I got me a new woman, a young woman . . ."

"Holy, sweet Jesus," Adam cried, throwing up his hands and spinning so that he, too, fell into the snow, close to his brother's lean stone slab. "Here I lie beside Still Waters," he said, and began sweeping his arms.

"They never let us see him. His face."

"It's crazy. All these years, one way or another I've had this feeling in my bones that someone dead was with me. That death was always with me. For a while, I even thought it was God. That's what Mom told me when I was a kid. That God had died for me."

"Man, you don't want to mess your mind with God."

"Meanwhile, you've gone and messed your mind with a woman."

"She's beautiful, she loves me."

"Where'd you run into her?"

"She's a painter, Anna-Maria, she was having a show in a gallery in Amsterdam by the canal and I heard this guy say to her, 'Your new paintings, they look like fields of pollen, bursting flowers, they make me happy,' and she said with her sweetest accommodating smile, 'They're faces, faces who were shot, my family, explosions of blood,' and I thought right then and there, there's a woman I want to know, so now I know her . . ."

Adam kept wagging his arms back and forth. "I'm gonna goddamn-well make a good snow angel." Then they both lay still.

"Fucking peaceful, eh?"

"Yeah."

"So you're in love."

"I guess so. Old guys like me don't cross-examine their emotions too much. I'm excited, I'm happy, I'm flattered, I can't wait to get back."

"And here we are lying in this graveyard."

"It's nice. And besides, I got to straighten up with you and also to say so long to your mother."

"It's awful in there, that damn crematorium, playing that endless elevator music."

"I'd like to get her out. I'd like to sprinkle her ashes on the snow all over our family graves, let her melt down into us . . ."

"She might like that."

"When I die . . ."

"Yeah?"

"You bring me home," his dad said. "There's two empty plots here, one for me . . ."

"Okay."

"So just drop me in, and if you want . . . since she went out the way she wanted to, you could plan on using the other plot for yourself, end up beside Still, beside your old dad, if you still love your old dad, what with all he's done all these past years . . ."

They lay quietly for a long while and then got up and brushed the snow off their coats and stood staring down at the two angels in the snow, the sun shining on them through the black branches, and then Adam put his arms around his dad and held him close and whispered, "Maybe that boy child has been beside me all my life, dead, but by God I was born to sweet waters . . ."

Gabon

Down a narrow logging road, a sign staked in the long grass said CAFÉ LUMIÈRE, but there was no café, only a winding dirt track through high brush, and at the end of the track, rows of small plastered one-room white shanties tinted by red dust so that it seemed to be a village shaded in gentle ochre and russet and sienna, the doors and windows shuttered, and close to a communal water tap, there was a sheltered wall with long benches in front of it. There was no sound. Then, as if a signal had been given, the doors opened and staves and poles angled out into the light. Stumps of arms, feet in cloth bags, old men and women lepers, heads down, poling themselves forward as if the air were water, saying nothing, poling through the deep slow corruption of the body, not a secretive corruption, like a cancer, but an open prefiguration of death, dry yet glistening white wounds eating away the softest parts, fingers, toes, the disfigurement of a whole hand that is coming off, a foot, hobbling in the sun, alive in a disease, in the living rot. A man draped in a worn grey shawl hunched toward Adam, his eyes wide open, his hand held out, the hand one man extends to another, thumb, forefinger, and little finger gone, a creamy white scar in the black flesh where his thumb had been, a stub hand, almost a club, and in the still, hot silence of the afternoon, before Adam could recoil, before he could say, "This is not what I came here for," the leper had left him no choice: a refusal to take his hand would be a recognition only of his rot, his corruption, his death. As the man's two hard fingers went into the palm of Adam's hand he felt a shudder, a bond with the leper, with an inevitability, but the man was smiling, his eyes filled with laughter and an enormous satisfaction that seemed simple, and open.

Adam looked over the leper's shoulder and saw Gabrielle: surprisingly pale, with cropped hair, wearing a plain white skirt, a short white smock, and white sneakers. He knew it was her – still lithe but somehow years older: her beauty deeper, more elusive – so unassuming as she spooned mealy-mealy into a child's mouth, spooning, scooping, spooning. She took four or five steps sideways away from the child and then stopped at a water tap and stared at Adam, stared hard at him, looking puzzled, alarmed. "It's me," he said in a big friendly voice. "Is this your town? Well, here I am." She closed her eyes and said, "So I can see. My God, how . . ." tap water overflowing her pail, soaking her running shoes. She turned off the tap and jammed her fists into the pockets of her smock, saying, "God help us, it looks like you've really come ..."

"Yes ..."

"Yes, there you are ..."

She called to the leper women and men and they called back, laughing, throwing open their arms, embracing her. He put down his travelling bag and cameras, his arms open, too, expectant, eager to embrace her, but one woman, her cheek pinched by creeping leprosy of the eye, hobbled up to Gabrielle, giggling coquettishly, letting out a low moaning cry and Gabrielle kissed the woman and they draped their arms around each other. Then, Gabrielle, breaking free, walked straight down the incline to Adam, saying, "Well, I can't leave my lover standing here all alone, can I?" She took his hand. She kissed him on the cheek, paused, and then said, kissing him lightly on the mouth, "What can I do, I don't know what to say, how can you possibly be here?"

"How can *you* possibly be *here*?"

She kissed him again on the cheek, but then turned on her heel and took several steps toward the shanties, graceful in her effortless stride, waving, smiling, while men and women kept wobbling toward her out of the shadows. She beckoned to Adam, almost as if she were at play back in their childhood, telling Adam to follow. He picked up his bags. He had the sudden unsettling thought that he'd come to the wrong town, that this was all a game of hide-and-seek, a demonic game begun a long time ago when he'd first started trying to find a

Southern Cross in his own world, and what will I do, he wondered, if she's the wrong Gabrielle, a decoy.

Bending forward to an old grey-headed man wrapped in a frayed brown blanket, Gabrielle touched his cheek with delicate care, an intimacy so entirely open that Adam, incredulous as the old man crossed his arm over her arm and rested his head against her hand, almost as if he were an old dying lover, stopped and cried, "What the hell's going on?" He had expected a *whoop* of happiness. He had counted on her being overjoyed or so surprised at his coming that she would want to collapse into his arms, perhaps uttering a playful "Holy fuck." Instead, she was rewrapping loose bandages, squatting in the doorways to fondle watery-eyed children, glancing back, until she paused and waited for him to come close to her, where he complained, "Jesus Christ, it's me."

"Of course it's you, you think I've lost my mind?"

"I was beginning to think I'd lost mine."

"Finders keepers," she warned him, gathering bandages into a string bag.

"Don't be silly," he said.

"Losers weepers . . ."

"Nobody's lost."

"But everybody's weeping . . ."

"Look," he said, growing exasperated, "for Christ's sake, I'm lucky to be alive."

"Yes . . ." – frowning – "yes, unbelievable. Yes, you are . . ."

"I like to think so."

"Yes, here, you are here, and these people, I'm lucky, too, they give me so much joy."

He stared at her, at a loss for words. She closed her eyes, and then let out a helpless little laugh.

"For God's sake," she said, "it's like you just fell out of the sky. What do you expect from me?"

"Nothing, I don't know, maybe everything. Last time I looked, you were my little Gabrielle . . ."

"Well, your little Gabrielle will do what she can," she said, taking a deep breath, suddenly laughing easily.

He saw at the end of the alley of mud-plastered shanties, a shaded clearing under tall palm trees, "That's where I live," she said, pointing beyond the palms to a cinder-block cottage painted white with a pink tiled roof.

"In the little house?"

"Yes."

"That's it? Pink and white?"

"Yes, I painted it."

"By yourself?"

"Yes."

"And you're by yourself?"

"You mean do I have a man?"

"Maybe."

"You're preposterous."

"What do I know? I just got here."

A little bell, like a child's dinner bell, tinkled when she opened the door.

"No place like home," she said. "Welcome to my three rooms." But she took him by the arm and stopped him, she stood in front of him, and she began to laugh, a puzzled laugh. "How wild is this," she said, "I mean you're actually here like your being here is normal, like I should think nothing of it."

He took her in his arms. She clung to him. She shook her head and then sighed and said, "Oh Lord," and rose up on her toes and kissed him eagerly.

"Incredible," she said, opening the door to the bedroom. It was dimly lit by five tiny windows in the east wall and under the windows, there was a table covered with a white cloth, a water basin on the table, beside the basin the silver pocket watch he'd given her when they were young, and beside the watch an electrified old kerosene lamp with a tin shade, the shade set so that it would cast reading light on one of the pillows on a graceful iron bedstead that was painted white, the bed draped in a cone of white mosquito netting.

"I must look different," she said, putting her hands on her hips.

"Your hair. How about me?"

"Different, a little," she said, touching his hair, "in the eyes. Darker, maybe."

"You've still got the pocket watch."

"I don't lose things like that," she said.

"Except things get lost, lives get lost."

"That's why we need things from when we were kids."

"I need to lie down."

"That's how I last saw you," she said, "you were lying down, sleeping."

"The last time I saw you, you were naked and getting into our bed, and when I woke up . . . you were long gone."

"That was the only way I knew how to go."

"To disappear?"

She put his two garment bag on the floor by the bed.

"You sure do travel light."

He folded his arms, putting his head down, forcing them into a pause, a silence.

"I only need to know," he said, "right away, though this is a little crazy, me showing up like this, that you still love me."

"I do. I do. Of course I love you. When I think of you, the cow jumps over the moon and the moon is blue. How's that?"

"So pack your bags," he said, trying to sound confident and hearty, "come on home."

"I am home," she said.

He took a deep breath, so that he could hold back a surge of angry frustration – and at the same time he felt a wearying heaviness through the shoulders, as if a weight of inevitability was presseing on his throat. He blurted out, "I want you and I want you to be where my heart is." And then, embarrassed by his own earnestness, he laughed, and put out his hands to her as if he were about to explain everything, and he said, "I'm here, and I'm not quite sure how I got here, but goddamn – among other things, it cost me the killing of a man two days ago."

She covered her mouth: "My God."

"Otherwise," he said, with a jaunty sourness, "I'm the same old me, famous in hotels, and famous among long-distance operators, and I'm alive because the guy I killed didn't get to kill me first."

But he was not seeing in his mind's eye the guerrilla dead on the stairs or Henri dead in the tub. They were in his shadow thoughts, but he was seeing the little mole beside Gabrielle's nipple.

"I want to talk about your beauty mark. I've stood at three o'clock in the morning in several cities singing the praises of your breasts."

"To an audience of mangy cats," she said, with a coquettish little shrug.

"That's who I am, that's where I've been," he said. "Just another stray among the cats."

"Don't talk silliness."

"Listen to her! There I was in Cairo last week, sitting beside a swimming pool as blue as Blue Sapphire gin and now here I am, somehow, lying down in the heart of the world, a world that looks pretty much like a bedsore, a goddamn leper camp. Silliness! Me! Here! Not on your life. Not on my mother's life."

"Your mother."

"Yes."

"How is your mother?" she said, eager to change the subject.

"Dead. Six months ago."

"Oh, God. I'm sorry."

"Burned. Cremated."

"Really."

"She'd warned me plenty of times. It's what she wanted. The fire. The fire next time. She only told me what she'd already told her mirror," he said, "burn me," reaching out to touch Gabrielle's hair. "Listen. Maybe I'm completely out of my mind, my coming here. But maybe being crazy is all that counts. Me and old Ponce."

"Some white people," she said, taking his hands in hers, as if she were about to console him, "they stay out in the sun too long, they go crazy here."

"Maybe that's it, I stepped on sunlight."

"What . . . ?"

"Something else my mother warned me about."

"My mother never warned me about anything. Not that I remember. No. She had that studied air of gloom that people mistake for dignity. But she could swallow anything. She didn't have any dignity at all."

Gabrielle helped him to stretch out on the bed, shoeless but fully clothed, putting a pillow under his head. He closed his eyes, but kept talking, as if trying to keep himself awake in his exhaustion, telling her with a quiet intensity how hurt and humiliated he'd been, waking to find her gone from their hotel room. How – giving up any dignity – he had looked for her in the casinos and made a fool of himself with Mio, who had smiled pityingly at him and said, "I feel for you, but if she's gone, she's gone." He told her how Mio had taken the rose from his lapel and given it to him, like a flower for the dead. "And I was," he said, "going to crush the rose in my fist, but instead I played his game, so I took the chance, I plucked the petals . . . *she loves me, she loves me not . . . She loves me*, and I kept the last petal as proof that you love me and gave him the stripped-down head but he only shrugged and put the dead head in his suit coat pocket, and told me that I had to speak to the nighttime concierge in the San Juan hotel, this plump brown woman – you'd know who she is – she told me, 'Gabrielle, she say she going to where she ain't going to weep no more. And she say she going to the village of light where it's light all night long.'"

"I'm sorry," Gabrielle said to him, stroking his hand, "I'm sorry you had to go through all that, especially with Mio, but yes, here I am and I'm very happy here."

"You are?"

"Yes."

"You're sure?"

She touched two fingers to his lips, stepped outside the cone of mosquito netting and took off her white sneakers and smock, wearing only panties.

"You've still got the legs," he said.

"And I always liked the way you looked at my legs."

"I looked because you always made me feel free to look."

"It's true," she said, "that's how it is, I guess, no matter how long we're away from each other, I'm never shy with you."

She began to sponge herself down with water from the basin on the side table, her shoulders, her arms, under her outstretched arms – he saw that she had stopped shaving: he was surprised, the tufts of underarm hair aroused him – her thighs, as the sun going down became a lurid, early evening streak of lemon in the five small windows.

She lit the lamp, asking, "Who'd you kill?"

"This guerrilla, he was coming right at me," he said, "and all around the hotel I was in, there was gunfire and he was this crazed face lunging at me out of a stairwell, and I just pulled the trigger. Like, it was simple. Nothing I could think about. BAM. But afterwards, the whole time I was getting out of there, it was like I was zeroed in on him, not just his face but his eyes – his eyes were the colour that black looks like when it's been burned, a black rage in his wide-open eyes, that's what I saw when I looked down into them. He was going to kill me so I killed him and I don't feel what I think I'm supposed to feel at all . . . because the way it happened, it was like I was there watching myself in my goddamn dream, I was watching me, myself, kill that man, this guy that's been driving me crazy all this time in my dreams. I'd finally found his eyes. I've been trying to look him in the eye for years. And now that I've really killed him, now that I know I really did it, I know I'm never going to see that dream again."

"No one saw you?"

"He saw me."

"I don't mean him."

"The militia was shelling the hotel from downriver. It was quick, too quick for anyone to stick around, and I got out quicker."

"God, what a catastrophe – you must be so unhappy?"

"What?"

"All this way here. To see me. Crazy. Absolutely crazy. In your own way, you're terrifying. Miraculous. And I love you for it. Because it's terrifying out there. In some parts of the country, toward the Congo, it's even worse than you can believe."

"You know what W.C. Fields said? They asked him what he believed and he said 'I believe I'll have another drink,' so what've you got to drink?"

"Palm wine."

"Jesus."

"No, that's Palm Sunday," she said, giggling. "Besides, it's very good."

She reached under the bed, and then sat beside him, a jug in her lap. "I sip a little at night. When I get bored with the doctors. Doctors can be very boring when they think they're cynics. And worse when they're idealists. They're one or the other out here. So, I need a drink. There's always a chill at night, and the noise, all the awful birds, all the screaming, animals, vermin. I don't think I'll ever get used to the noise of the night."

She helped him tilt the jug to his lips.

"Do you think your village friends are outside the door listening?" he asked.

"Oh no, not at all. You're the first white man they've seen in my house, they'll assume we're in bed."

"This is nuts, you're out here lost in the middle of nowhere and maybe you're glad to see me and maybe you're not and maybe you love me and maybe you don't, but right away we're carrying on talking just like it's yesterday between us . . ."

"Because," she said soothingly, "before everything else, no matter what, we're friends."

". . . like you didn't pack up and disappear on me."

"You're too tired. I'll get you undressed."

"Anyway, who wants to be friends . . . ?"

"A friend in need is a friend . . ."

"Cut it out."

She brought a bucket of water to the bed. He took the Glock .9 out of his jacket pocket and put it on the bedside table under the lamp. He said, "Aren't you afraid the fighting will move here?"

"Not particularly."

"Why not?"

"To a hospital that's mostly a madhouse and a leper camp?"

"It's already a madhouse out there. They wouldn't know the difference."

"They know the difference." She picked up the gun, said, "Holy fuck," and put it under the mattress at the foot of the bed.

Together, they took his clothes off. He sank back on the bed. She began to sponge his body, at first finger by finger, then his forearms, his armpits and shoulders up into his neck, his stomach, thighs, and feet. "You're so tired you can't keep your eyes open," she said, prodding around his ribs. "You know, it's almost a year since I washed a body that wasn't sick with a wound somewhere." He was drifting deeper and deeper into sleep. She was washing his cock. He thought he had an erection. He wasn't sure if it was an erection. "Your body is very strange," she said. "It's so long since I've touched a healthy body."

Eugene Euclid Waters
1901 – 1967
He died
In
Public Relations.

A ragged early morning fog lay in the air between the leper houses. He had parted the beaded window curtains and stood listening to whistling parrots. She said they were parrots. He had never heard parrots whistle. Maybe they weren't parrots. She made coffee, boiling water in a small pot, pouring it through a filter into two cups.

"So, who runs this place?"

"There's a small hospital between here and town, a couple of doctors and nurses living in chalet houses that look like Switzerland."

"Why not live near them?"

"I want to live here," she said, "not in some fake Switzerland. I came back, I didn't know exactly why. I live here in this house in the same way. It's right for me and I don't know why."

She smiled.

Her teeth seemed more even, whiter.

Her broad smile unnerved him, a smiling aggressiveness. *That is it,* he thought, as she got ready to go out into the village, *she's got that goddamn exuberant air of conviction, that air of inner satisfaction that Jesus converts have. But,* he thought, watching her stand very erect with her arms folded across her chest, folded in on herself, *there's also something absent in her,* and with sudden dread as he sipped his morning coffee he wondered if he hadn't got a glimpse of his own absence in her life, if he hadn't made a terrible mistake, a terrible assumption. She had given him a strong kiss and a hug in bed but there'd been no craving between them at first light; in the hotel outside Ponce, they had always made love in the morning but they had not made love this morning, nor, as he'd listened to her shower, had he thought of joining her. And to his own surprise, when she'd come out of the shower, a towel wrapped around her hips, and stood in front of him as he sat on the bed, her breasts close to his face, instead of kissing her breasts, he'd said, as if he, perversely, wanted her to know that his mind, too, could be elsewhere, "You know the damnedest thing I ever saw, it was outside the hotel where all the shooting was, and down by the river, a dead soldier who'd been stripped down naked of everything he owned, he was lying there stretched out and his dead body had an erection and I thought goddamn it, that man wants to live, and I took a couple of shots of his cock up in the air, the old rooster still wanting to crow, not that anyone will ever want to print that."

She had sat on his lap and he'd got an erection and she had said, "Umm," but they had not made love. They'd held each other in a deep silence, a stillness, that they'd agreed – by saying nothing – was soothing, comforting.

After they had dressed, he'd put his Leica in his jacket pocket.

As they walked out into an alley, the sun inching down the shanty walls, she said, "By the way, that gun, it's still under the mattress, leave it there till you go."

"Who said I'm going?"

"Adam, don't be ridiculous."

"But I am ridiculous. I just figured it out, it just hit me this morning."

"You've never been ridiculous. I'd never love a ridiculous man."

"You love me?"

"Of course. Of course I love you. Which is why I'm ridiculous."

"No beautiful woman can be ridiculous."

"What do you know about ridiculous women? In New York I was ridiculous. All the time. I'd sometimes start crying. I'd just stop and stand in the street weeping, overwhelmed by sorrow and fear. Now I think fear's like a virus, it spreads, like they say consumption used to be spread by breathing on each other, by a kiss, but I don't have that fear any more, not since I'm here. And I don't weep."

Along the alley, a young man with copper-coloured hair was weaving a sleeping mat from thin papyrus strips, working on a raised platform in front of several cells that had heavy wooden lattice bars on the doors. Solitary men and women sat inside in the dark on litters. "They're bound hand and foot and dragged out of the bush by their families," Gabrielle said. "Whatever's inside their brain is too mad, too evil and too deep for any drugs we have. We keep them in there, otherwise they'd be thrown into the river, or poisoned. Even the lepers won't go near them." She moved from cell to cell, peering in, talking quietly, and she unbolted one of the doors although the weaver warned her: "He want to kill . . ."

The man was about twenty-two, naked, except for trousers sheared at the thighs. There was a bowl of uneaten mealy-mealy beside him. He was very black and thick through the shoulders and stared out into the light, a shrouded gleam in his eyes, the whites a greasy brown. Each dart of his eyes was a warning of an impending lunge out into the light, but she lifted the bowl and told him to eat. He didn't move. He stared at her, kneading his knuckles, and then cupping his hand and blowing into it, as if he were trying to cool whatever was in his hand. She leaned forward within his reach and quietly said, "Yes, yes . . ." They stayed that way, silent, staring, and the man hid his face behind his cupped hand, ducking and furtive, but then he began to laugh, a playful clucking at the back of his throat. When Adam, standing behind her, began to laugh, too, because he remembered Harry and the way he cupped his cigarette in his hand to his face, the man scowled, grabbed the bowl, and turned it upside down. The mealy-mealy spread across the floor. She backed out of the cell and closed the door and the man, glaring, lay down.

"You have to be very careful what you let them see," she said. "And I should have warned you. We must never laugh."

"So I see!"

"We don't understand their minds," she said, going down another alley toward a small square. "We don't understand how they can concentrate the total darkness that seems to be in them in their minds, and whether it's the same darkness that's in all our minds, just bigger, we don't know. Nor do we understand their purity and power. I've been in the forest with them, you'll believe this if you've ever had a vision . . . they initiated me, you see, they have such feeling for trees, they were all singing and this old man concentrated so hard for so long that a tree bent its branches toward him . . ."

"You're sure?"

"Sure I'm sure."

Adam, smiling indulgently – and he could tell that she didn't like him smiling at her that way – put a comforting hand on her shoulder. "Remember our tree," he said, "the tree in the backyard, Dad's Dead Dick?" She burst out laughing, as if glad to remember being a little girl, and put her arms around him and then looked into his eyes with such intensity that he thought she was trying to see back through his eyes to the time, the actual days, when they were young, back to that country where they had been children. "And my mother," he said, leaning away, confused by and wary of her sudden intensity, "she used to see her little angel out on the garage roofs, and she'd talk to her angel. Given half a chance my mother could have ended up here with you living as an angel instead of being ashes in a jar at home. Maybe she'd have been right at home here? The two of you together."

She startled him by stepping closer, almost as if she wanted to crowd against him, as if something had come unhinged in her because she said a little too loudly, too forcefully, too gaily, "I remember your mother, I can still see her. The way she watched me . . . she knew you and I were lovers before my own mother did . . . she had a way of knowing a lot of things that she kept to herself, but I still remember what you taught me, that little song she taught you,

> *Two Irishmen, two Irishmen, sitting in a ditch,*
> *one called the other a dirty son of a Peter Murphy*
> *had a dog, a dirty dog had he,*

sold it to a lady to keep her company . . .
she fed it, she fed the little runt,

and suddenly Gabrielle held her hand against his crotch, arousing him, *and slipped up her petticoat and grabbed her by the country boys* and then she said, "No dead dick here," making him remember how, on the night before she had left him in the hotel outside Ponce, she had moaned and scissored her legs around his hips, crying, "Yes," and *if you get hit with a bucket of shit be sure to close your eyes,* but she had said nothing more and he had said *Harry Harry's the shit* and then there, in the room, she giggled like a girl and let go of him, saying, "I love it when we make love, but we forgot this morning. I could kiss you to death. Eat you up."

"Tell that to your travel agent," he said wryly, feeling again the humiliation he'd suffered as he'd listened to the *patron* tell him that she'd ordered a car and had warned the *patron* not to wake him.

"I'm sorry."

"I don't need to hear you're sorry."

"Sorry."

"Haw. Smart ass. I need to hear how my little girl loves me."

After a pause, she said, "I was almost never a girl, you know, not a girly girl, I never had a chance to really be a girl. You're the only man who's ever given me back a bit of the girl I was."

"And you're the only girl I've kept loving long after I got to be a man."

She gave him a darting kiss. Her lips were dry.

"I'm sure they'll find the cure," she said.

"For love?"

"No, never for love. For this," she said, sweeping her arm toward the *village*. "It'll be in the mind, this disease comes from the mind, some unbearable stress. These people are so spiritually alive in a way we don't know about. It's all in the mind . . ."

She put on her smock and closed her fists in the pocket.

He wanted to say that this sounded too close to what they had grown up with as children, the ecstasies of the mutilated and the martyred, but instead, he got dressed in silence and together they went out and entered a courtyard of plastered houses. He whispered playfully, "We could always go right back and take the morning cure in our bed."

The plaster on the house walls had been painted coral, the benches by the door turquoise. "Why not?" she said, but kept walking across the courtyard. The yard was empty except for several large enamel, aluminum, and plastic bowls on the ground and a machete between two of the bowls. But then, doors opened and men and women came out, timorous yet fearless, and they sat down on the benches, and she threw open her arms, and to his astonishment and their delight, she did a little dance like a jig. Some of the men and women seated on the benches crossed their scarred legs, pulling pieces of coloured cloth across their throats, resting a forearm stump under a chin, a head tilted with haughtiness.

"Do you have your camera?"

"No."

"You'll need your camera."

She kissed him on the cheek. One of the lepers applauded, beaming.

"This is awful," Adam said, pulling away. "Terrifying. Two minutes ago I was ready to make love to you."

"These are not the worst off," she said, coming close to him again and kissing him again on the cheek. "These people are here with their families, they can do a little work. It's not even all the raped women in the forest, or the mobs of boy soldiers who are the worst. It's all the handicapped . . . children born with withered legs, or arms coming out of their shoulder blades, or no colon. They're the abandoned ones, they're like reptile children dragging themselves through the forest . . ."

Facing the leper men and women, Adam said, "How does a thing like this happen?"

"I told you. It's in the mind . . ."

"No, no, no. In your mind. Your own. How did you ever end up here?"

"I had to leave you."

"But why? All I did was love you."

"Because suddenly, I was afraid, I didn't want to quarrel with you. I had to get out before the thing that was so good between us could go wrong. It was going wrong in me, so I had to go to the place I'd already decided I was supposed to be, and that was here."

"You're talking like it was do or die."

She took his face between her hands, as if they were all alone in the courtyard, pleading, her voice faint. A clucking pigeon flapped toward the forest and a flock of queleas hovered over the tree line, then scattered in all directions.

"Sometimes," she said, "there are things love can't do anything about. The bell just goes *bong*, it tolls."

"The bell tolls?"

"Sure."

"You've got to be kidding. We've had moments that were blessed, that were nothing short of mystical and you're telling me *bong*."

"Beneath every blessing, there's a boil about to burst. Your own father said that."

"No he didn't. Not for a second. He never said anything about the blessing."

"Maybe it was Harry, then."

It was stinging hot under the noon sun, but they heard a man who was wearing a heavy cloak bang his staff, complaining that he was cold. A wizened old woman with weary, expressionless eyes, limped toward Adam, blinking dully.

"Get out your camera?"

"Nonsense."

"Take their pictures."

"They won't want to."

"That's why they've come out, so you can see them."

"I'm not sure I want to."

"This is their vanity, they want you to see them, how they are . . ."

As he circled around the benches, focusing, he could feel them yield to his presence, preening, but he also saw in them – to his utter surprise – an audacity (maybe it wasn't, he thought, a smiling aggressive exuberance that he'd seen in her in the morning; maybe it was this force he was suddenly aware of in the lepers, an awareness of themselves that she seemed to have, too, beyond doubt and temerity, men and women who knew in their very nerve endings what condition their condition was in), openly assessing him in what they understood was his uncertainty among them as he moved in a stutter-step, trying to focus. And as he tried, a young woman with a pinkish-white open wound inching into her eye looked at him with an amused lascivious glint, and he thought, taken aback, *I could never make love to her*, but then he was ashamed – not because he felt he should be able to make love to her, but because he heard Father Zale admonishing him: "No shame, having no shame is when, in the locale of your own head, you are able to be all alone and still be happy," or was it Father Zale? He couldn't remember, and he turned suddenly from the men and women on the benches to find himself stricken by the sight of Gabrielle standing in her smock as a dark outline against the sky, so alone, he thought – there on a knoll in her shabby canvasback sneakers, so all alone, and then she confounded him by bowing, and, like a playful young woman, she arced her back and performed a perfect turn, *en pointe*, stopping to angle her leg out against the sky.

"This is lunacy," he thought, and then, "totally crazy." He realized that the woman with the open wound, the woman with the lascivious eye, was covered from chin to toe in a loose grey sack dress, while it was her wound, the open wetness of the pink under-flesh close to her feverish eye, that was sensual, that was alive. It was this rot, yes, it suddenly occurred to him, this sensual rot that was a sign of the creeping, all-pervasive evil that he had come to believe was inherent in the inevitable sensual increment of decay, the dying upon which all life necessarily fed, the betrayal in which all that was beautiful was begun – evil feeding itself, just as he believed that envy or self-deception could feed like a consumption on someone's soul – a shadow like a shadow on a lung – a viral consumption that could leave a man alive while he hacked for air, lost and desperate while looking for a point of view, wanting to be able to cry "I am" while surrounded by people who were capable of justifying the doing of anything, people who had no shame. And these were not just mindless thugs on the loose, not just the mobs of militia men and children trained to gut their mothers and decapitate and rape their sisters, but worse, all those middle-rank officers in their mix-and-match battle fatigues, righteous, driven by their God-derived destiny, their shameless idealism.

"You tek picture," one of the lepers called out, "you mek me be forever." Adam aimed the camera eye. Then he remembered the voice of the naked black girl: "You tek me when I sleep, you steal me." He couldn't focus. There were tears in his eyes, he felt overwhelmed by sorrow, something worse than sorrow; seepage, a seepage of the spirit (for a moment, looking around wildly, he could not find Gabrielle), but then he found that, by his body's habit, he had started shooting, as if suddenly he was Henri in Henri's room with the gorilla, lying on his back, firing into the ceiling. Blam. Blam. Blam. *Click. Click. Click,* awash in his own blood, *in the blood of the Lamb* he heard Father Zale say. *Dying. And in his arms, his twin brother, Still.* He felt that he was going to weep and so he stopped shooting and hurried to Gabrielle, taking her arm.

"I have this sick feeling," he said.

"So don't look at them."

"No, no, when I turned around I didn't see you there. You'd stopped dancing. I didn't think I'd see anything I knew here. This awful loss. It'd all be gone, the whole future would be gone, the past would be one long illness. A wheezing lung. How can you live here, how can you dance alone here in this wheezing lung?"

It rained steadily for days, torrents of rain. The alleyways between the leper houses turned to deep mud and pieces of plaster fell away from the house walls into the muck, revealing the rib work of the walls. Clothes were clammy, the bedsheets damp. Gabrielle held on to him in the house, most often seated on the bed, enclosed in the cone of mosquito netting, speaking brokenly, as if she were distracted, her nerves taut. "I miss my mailman, I loved my mailman, remember him . . . ?"

She said she often wished that she could read a real book – in New York, she had come to love reading Jane Austen – she thought Austen's women were so elegantly surreal – "Kafka only makes sense if you believe in Jane Austen's world," she said – but there were only magazines around the village and the hospital, stacked here, scattered there, and some of the magazines were almost a year old. It was disconcerting, she said, almost too indicative of what it was to be human – didn't he think? – reading and re-reading stories as if they were the sudden astounding news of the day, knowing that the news was already so old that no one could remember it. She kissed him hard on the mouth. She knelt to make love to him, then suddenly laughed and said, "No, there's no future in that either . . ."

She insisted that in such dampness his muscles had to be massaged – the blood made to move – and she stood behind him for an hour kneading his shoulders and neck, saying nothing, shushing him when he spoke, as if he were a child, but suddenly covering his neck with little kisses, "little flea bites" – she called them – and then – "Why shouldn't I bite you, into every girl's life a little blood must fall."

The rain poured. "Dreary," she said. "The world has gone bleary-eyed. Harry, when he was drunk, used to come home bleary-eyed." He told her that he hadn't thought while he was there about Harry. Instead, he'd had this peculiar little moment, it had come on him out of nowhere like a flash, like light that had leaked for a split second through an aperture, "of Harry's brother Tonton sitting naked like a white bag of suet in a steam room, and Tonton was laughing at me." She bit him and said, "I hope you laughed right back at him."

"I wanted to kill him."

"Well, now you know how," she said.

White-faced, drawn, her eyes shining, weary from her restless nights, she went to bed in the afternoon and slept. She said she was sorry she had become so difficult, that she had become distracted during the day and troubled in her sleep. Through the night she lay in his arms, but always on the edge of waking, and then he felt her body break into a cold sweat as she made a low, almost growling moan, tucking her legs under her body, sweat pouring off her, her body shuddering. She'd drawn herself into a fetal huddle on her side as she lay calmly for an hour, and then, for a few minutes – as he had seen her do once before – she lay stroking herself until she woke and he, sleepless, exhausted, asked what in the world was going on in her sleep and she said, "Little creepy-crawly dreams . . ."

"What dreams?"

"Hard happy dreams."

"Yeah, but about what?"

"You can dream that you're in my heart," she said, smiling wanly, her eye on the little windows, on the grey rain falling in wind-blown sheets, "but you don't want to dream in my head."

"Those are absolutely useless little windows," he said, touching her forehead, finding her a little feverish. "They don't give any light."

"I told you. It's dreary and bleary. And Dancer and Prancer are dead. There is no light out there now."

"This house should have been built up on high ground. If this keeps up, the floor'll flood."

"A missionary built the house."

"Perfect," he said.

"The windows face east, he thought he was looking into the five wounds of Christ in the morning light."

"And what do you see?"

"Rain."

"Rain, rain go away . . ."

". . . come again another day."

She giggled.

"The rain in Spain . . ."

". . . falls mainly on the plain."

"There was a young man from White Rock," he called out, "who tied harpsichord strings to his cock; when he had an erection he played a selection from Johann Sebastian Bach."

"Bravo."

She clapped her hands, she was gleeful.

"I've come all this way . . ."

"Yes . . ."

". . . all this way to sing children's songs and discover that your eyes are not full of joy but rain."

"Listen! You think I don't know how happy we were, how much joy I felt? Of course I was happy. Sometimes even during the day I dream it. I was happy happy happy," her voice rising until, to his shock, she was screaming *Happy*, her whole body shaking.

He held her until she calmed down.

"I'm so tired I feel like screaming myself," he said.

"So scream. Scream. I wanted to scream in our little sunshine hotel. Every time we made love I wanted to scream, I was so happy. People scream all the time here. Go ahead. Nobody'll notice."

"EEEEEEEaaaa!"

"No, no, no. Like this," and she threw her head back: "yeeeAAAAAAAA!"

"Jesus," he said, taken aback as she then stood up with her mouth open, making no sound, "it's a wonder everybody around here isn't nuts."

"Everybody is, a little."

"Don't you want to get out of here, don't you want to know anything about back home?"

"Not much . . ."

"Why not?"

"Well," she said, lying back down on the bed, suddenly listless, closing her eyes, "it wouldn't make a lot of difference."

"To what?"

"To the future." She held out her open hands to him.

He took hold of her hands.

She said nothing.

"Maybe I should read your palm," he said.

"Or you could tell me a bedtime story."

"Like what?"

"I don't know. The mailman meets his girl, make it up, maybe she's got a glass slipper . . ."

"There's the one about the princess, her being locked away from her lover in the tower, and she didn't know what to do so she braided her long long hair into a rope so that her lover could climb up and rescue her . . . except" – and he folded her hands into his – "you've cut your hair."

"Yes," she sighed, freeing her hands and touching her cropped hair, "yes. I did. Didn't I? Yes. With a good pair of scissors. At the hospital."

With her eyes closed again, she reached for his body, reached for an embrace even as he felt that she was drawing farther away from him, away into her own world, whispering *Adam Adam Adam*, rolling on to her side with a deep sigh, falling asleep with one arm hooked behind her head.

Adam Adam Adam.

He recognized it: he heard grief in her sounding of his name.

Shaken, he sat for a long time listening to her breathing and listening to the rain running off the tile roof, staring at her face, thinking, *You'd let me swallow your soul but not your bad dream.*

He got up and shifted the lamps closer to the white cone of mosquito netting, loaded his Leica, and he began slowly and quietly, almost stealthily, to move around her, standing still for long moments – not reflecting, not meditating, but just staring at her, waiting for some idea, some inkling of a precise, telling image to come to him . . . some way of seeing her that would not betray her, that would look entirely right . . . until at last he felt at a loss, and a little bewildered by his feeling of loss – and he found himself quietly singing one of his father's old blues songs – "You cain't lose what you ain't never had."

He decided not to photograph her. He didn't know exactly why, but he sensed that a photograph of her here would be a failure. Maybe he even wanted it to be a failure. He didn't believe she was herself here. He'd felt it from the beginning. Too much around him reeked of failure. In the midst of ferocious growth he felt the inevitability of a dead end.

He wanted to somehow succeed in seeing her as he believed she was in herself, between the *click click,* there in the pauses – to see her not through the camera's eye – but to see her as if he could feel the contours of her face, to feel her in the way a blind man possesses a face with his fingers – not only to remember her features in his fingertips but to know the sculpture of the bones beneath the skin, to know the *her* that had eluded him, and he whispered, as he touched her forehead, "I hardly know you, you've got the face of a saint without God."

Wanting only to comfort her, to shield her, he wrapped her in his arms and held her and as she pressed against his body, murmuring warmly, he said, "Don't worry, the devil ain't going to get you."

"The devil don't believe in me," she whispered, "and I don't believe in the devil. I believe in evil."

"Never mind," he said. "I eat evil like geeks eat the heads of chickens."

"You what?"

He smiled.

He had jolted her, he'd got her attention.

He'd seen, he'd told her, a geek bite off a chicken's head in Mexico City. He and the geek had for a moment locked eyes and the geek had smiled at him before spitting the head out.

Adam made a clearing noise in his throat and said, "See, after you snap off the head, all you've got to do is let that head suck up the evil that's in you and spit out the head," and he pretended to spit.

She shook her head and said, "Oh you poor man," and went back to sleep.

"Oh?" he said.

An hour later, half-asleep himself, he felt on fire, sopping wet and on fire, his eyeballs burning, his sense of where he actually was nothing but a blur as he lay there afraid he was going to choke because his throat was so dry and he couldn't seem to get what felt like tiny feathers out from between his teeth.

The day it stopped raining, brilliant sunlight broke through the high branches, smearing light on the leathery trunks, while rainwater that had been held by broad leaves dripped from the branches. Heat poured down through the trees, the damp earth turned spongy. The shadows were thick with translucent flying insects.

As they walked out of the village toward a grassy rise behind the shanties and block houses, he was struck – not by how frenetic and fragile, and even tormented, she had been – but by how, walking with her face tilted up into the light, she moved within her own stillness – with the confidence of a dancer – smiling and exultant in her own beauty, her own free stride. And, walking up the grassy rise, he was about to tell her that she was beautiful, but he suddenly suffered a wave of something deeper than weariness, something close to acedia – a tiredness in his blood that swept through him – a fear that in the stultifying, oppressive heat, he was losing his voice – losing the tone, the edge to his voice that he knew was the same loss of tone that he had come to sense in the imperceptible monotonous growth all around him, and with a jolt, he thought, *I'm all wrong for this.* He reached out and took hold of Gabrielle's arm, angry because he felt that right under her eye, an acquiescence had already taken hold of him – not quite the air of acquiescence he had seen among the lepers – audacious as they might be, face-to-face – but a deeper yielding to what was to come, so close he could smell it, like smelling a sickness, a sickness that was inherent in everything, a consumptive rot.

He blurted out, "This is all wrong."

"What?" she asked, playfully slapping his hand away from her arm.

She led him along a narrow track that skirted the village, going toward a wide clearing where there were several white wooden buildings.

"I meant that maybe my coming here was wrong," he said, "that it was me trying to pretend we are free to be happy."

"Everybody's free to pretend a little," she said.

He noticed a little skip to her step.

"Maybe," he said.

"No maybe about it. That's how children are. Free to pretend. That's what happiness is. When you're so free you don't know you're pretending. It just is, like nothing else ever was, like we were. Like I am."

They walked between two long clapboard buildings raised on piles, ducking under the morning's wash, ragged colours hung on lines between the tribal wards, and went into a small dispensary and pharmacy where, in a back room, there were plain plank cupboards along one wall, a single steel stool, an old, disused, grey steel operating table, a big broad overhead light, and to the side, a sink and coffee maker. To Adam's surprise, the old walleyed priest, wearing his frayed white soutane that now seemed even shorter at the ankles, was standing behind the operating table.

"No one's working today," he said. There was a pot sitting over a Bunsen burner and he turned up the flame. "Sit, sit," he said to them, "the doctors are in town. When the doctors go there, I come here to cook up a little coffee."

"Do you?"

"Yes, I do. And what're the two of you doing here?"

"Just nosing around," she said.

"Looking for trouble," the priest said, pouring them coffee.

"Trying to figure out how things work," Adam said.

"Work," the old priest said, tugging at his grey eyebrows. "Work, is it? Well, you should know that I cut timbers and dug the postholes here. Trying to construct some order. That's a laugh."

"A laugh?" Adam asked. "What's to laugh at?"

"You can't escape it," the priest said directly to Gabrielle, who sat unsmiling. "What works here is the forest, the bush. Of course, it's all a matter of how we look at it in the midst of our priaprismatic lives, this purging process," and he cocked his head as if contemplating what he had just said, and what he was about to say: "Yes, it's true, learn a reverence for the way the undergrowth always reaches toward the light," he intoned. "Sustaining itself, it must lead us to a compassion for all those who are trapped in pain, trapped in the disease at the heart of life, the rat's hair in the soup . . ."

"Compassion is good," Adam said with a mocking smile, amused by the pleasure the priest took at his own turns of phrase.

". . . the rat in the soup, I like that," the old priest said.

Faintly they heard CDEF . . . DECF . . . the nursing station bell ringing through the forest. "Ah," the priest said, "perhaps yet another child born into this life."

Holding a cup to his lips, he paused, then he swallowed his coffee.

"Oh Roland, for God's sake, cut it out," Gabrielle said.

"Roland?" Adam asked.

"He's no priest," she said, "or maybe he was but he's no priest now, though they all think he is and he says mass for them . . ."

"And of course you are lovers? We all think we are lovers," Roland said with a cynical grin that wounded Adam. He folded Gabrielle in his arms, as if she needed to be taken under his protection. Yet he had become increasingly distressed by what he thought of as her possession of herself, the way she seemed not to need him though she said over and over that she loved him, and in loving him, and in saying so, she was almost tauntingly open to him, especially in their bed where she gave him everything of her body but not what he wanted most – any sense of dependence on him – any sense that she not only needed to be with him, but would also allow him to deliver her from the dark afflictions that haunted her. "You can absorb my sins, you can even absolve me of my sins," she'd said, "but you can't have my darkness, no one can."

"Out of the darkness . . ." he heard himself say to Roland, in Roland's tone, making Gabrielle turn to look up at him, "comes the light . . ."

He laughed: "At least that's the story."

"Yes, but think of it," Roland said, paying no attention to Adam's mocking of him, "that a child was in fact the light – a child who heard a voice tell him that he was the Son of God, a child who somehow knew that in this life of attrition, pain and suffering, he was doomed to be the Messiah, a child-man who would tie his life to death, to the cosmic *catastrophe* that would signal final judgment and deliverance . . ."

He lifted the pot away from the flame and turned up the flame so that it stood as a hissing blue-orange jet in the air.

"I had a mother who looked at fire the way you do," Adam said dryly.

"You see," Roland said with a dismissive shrug, turning the flame down and pouring more coffee into their cups, "yes, you see, in his poor benighted messianic consciousness, so obsessed with pain, affliction, disease . . . Jesus must have seen his miracles as a prefiguration of the kingdom of deliverance to come, and through atonement, through his voluntary sacrifice, his chosen death, he would save those who believed in him . . ."

He handed them cubes of sugar.

"The only trouble is, the great cosmic collapse didn't come after Calvary. Jesus had deluded himself, there was no deliverance, and the affliction remains everywhere . . . but one profound truth emerged, and only St. Paul saw it. . . . In this terrible vale of sickness, a man might lead a life of sacrifice, in this web of darkness such sacrifice might help to bring to pass the final liberating event. We might renovate the future and in the renovated future, death would die and there might at last be the light of joy . . ."

"Joy . . . ?" Adam asked.

"Yes, joy."

"So that's what you're up to," Adam said. "You're in the Yellow Pages, under 'Renovation.'"

"Like it or not, we live burdened by old truths," Roland said.

"No, we live burdened by men who think like you," Adam said as he took Gabrielle by the shoulders, turning her toward the stairs and away from the walleyed old man, and together they went down to the walkway between the wards. The bells rang again, CDEF, and Adam said, "I can't stand that old son-of-a-bitch . . ."

"He's harmless," she said. "The woods are full of old Christian cranks like him."

"He's got no light in those eyes. It's frightening. There's nothing there to trust. Atonement, my ass. His next move always looks like it's going to be a handshake."

Again they heard the bells: CDEF.

"Maybe another child has been born," she said.

"That's how the future gets renovated," he said, angrily. "That's what makes life redeemable. Every time you and I fuck, we're fucking on the side of life."

They went up another set of stairs into a ward, into a dark long room of cots and pallets on a board floor, and as she took down a clip-chart from a wall hook, she said, "The fact is, Roland's afraid, he's afraid of the sun, he's afraid of the light. It makes him ill, he's afraid of sunstroke . . ."

"So why the hell do either of you stay?" he asked at the foot of a bed, staring at a scarred black body in the bed, a black face on the pillow, eyes that were watching him.

"Among other things, I'm happy."

"You're all alone."

"No, I'm not."

"Jesus Christ . . ."

"We just went through that," she laughed.

"This might be the loneliest place on earth."

"I was thinking last night," she said, taking his arm, "lying there awake beside you, about how close we've always been, you and me, and yet we're not always that close. We are so beautiful together and yet you've got your own way of looking at things, for sure, each thing in a special light, the light you see it in and it makes you seem like you're standing apart and very alone, but you're not lonely at all."

"I wouldn't be so sure about that."

"You're the least lonely man I've ever known," she said. He was watching the black man in the bed move his hand across the white sheet, thinking *He's lost his little finger, like I've got no little finger, he's just like me.* "Because you're fascinated," she continued, "fascinated by everything around you, including me, yourself, maybe especially yourself, and perhaps even aroused by your own intense feeling for things, but maybe, you know, maybe that's not love. . . . It's wonderful being amazed, star-struck, I'm amazed at you, but maybe amazement is not love . . ."

"Whatever it is, it only happens to lovers."

"Maybe amazement is really only for kids. Like we were once kids."

"What does that mean?"

"Kids'll be kids, they know what's true," she said, kissing him. "But you've got to watch out for us kids, we can be so happy, so purely happy it makes you want to cry, but kids can be terribly cruel, too, just like us, at the strangest times, so the only thing you can do is laugh."

"I wouldn't know, we used to laugh and I don't have a kid."

"Yes, but I do," she said grimly. "I've got my own kid."

"Don't be like that."

"I have to be like that."

"Why?"

"Because it's the way it is."

"Nothing has to be the way it is."

"Yes, it does. We're here because we're here and tomorrow you won't be here."

"And tomorrow maybe you won't need to be here."

"Not likely."

"Remember those kids we played with on the island, those kids with their balloons, letting the balloons go loose on the wind. When we were there we were so close we were magic, I can't figure out why you let go of all that, why you took off and ran away the way you did."

"You think you'd like to know why I left you . . . but be careful," she said and wagged her finger at him. "You don't want to know."

"I do."

"No, you don't."

"I've had a hint or two."

"A hint!" She sounded almost scornful. "You think you've had a hard time, your dead man showing up in your dreams, you think you've been through some nighttime sweats?"

"I've had a bad time or two," he said defensively, surprised, because she sounded as if she wanted to hurt him, as if he had done something to her and she wanted to retaliate.

"Bad times beget bad times!" she said.

"You sound like you've got the Bone Picker blues," he said.

"If I've got the blues, it's because of you," she said, "because of our good times . . ."

In the stifling heat of the airless ward, with the coffee turning his stomach sour, his eye began to reel, as he stared at the scar where his little finger had been. He started to sing, "*the blues don't like nobody . . .*" He was standing squarely set and flat-footed on the edge of the long row of cots, their crisp white cotton sheets folded and tucked over each black body in each bed, but each bed was becoming in his eye – as he tried to concentrate on Gabrielle, to listen to her – a piano key, he couldn't help it, he saw a long row of black and white piano keys, and there, loose on the last key, doing a tap dance, moving up and down the black notes, calling *Anna-Maria Anna-Maria* and singing *Back snake crawling in my brain*, was Web, just as Adam made himself lean down to listen to Gabrielle who was whispering, "Bad, it was real bad because the more joy I felt – and I did feel joy, an almost inexplicable joy when I was with you – inexplicable since it got worse every night, inexplicable because the happier I was with you, in your arms, there, there in that room, in our bed, the quicker my dead child would come crawling toward me in my sleep, crawling, you understand, my dead child – DEAD CHILD CRAWLING in the penitentiary of my brain – and sometimes deep in my sleep I'd see him coming from a long way off, I was sure it was a boy, 'A boy, it's a boy,' coming from a long long distance, moving on his belly like a turtle moves . . . dead inside his shell but moving deeper than the deep I was in, the sleep of contentment beside you, so deep, but then, I knew he was coming up the sand of a sand beach,

I knew, crawling toward me and there were my legs opening up to him, my child, my own father's child, and though his eyes were closed dead, they're always dead, I could feel how he's thinking – he always keeps his mind as clean as a wound that won't heal – after all, I *am* his mother – I can feel how he's going to hold me and haul himself back up into my womb where he's going to nest in me . . . and the longer I lay there in that room with you, in that happiness with you, in fact, the more that I had come to trust our happiness – and worse, to cherish it – then the closer he got to me . . . inching toward me, leaving me terrified and sopping wet, just like I was sopping wet on the night I aborted him, closed his eyes dead, and on that last night with you, even though I could feel his little shoulders pushing on my thighs, elbowing them open, I somehow suddenly shut my legs, I refused to let my dead child come back to nest in me, I do not have the strength or the courage to allow that. I woke up . . . I woke up horrified, and ashamed . . . like it's always been, except with you it had got worse and worse because I truly love you, I love you love you, but always, whenever I've had any happiness at all in my heart, any, my dead child, he makes sure I understand that out there, on the ready, he's more resilient than any moment of joy that I might have . . . he hunts me down . . . he comes after me in the night . . . except for here, he hasn't come after me here, he never comes here, not to this place whose people fill me with their joy, not once has he come to me . . . but now, over these last few nights, these nights when we're back in each other's arms sleeping so soundly together, when it has been so good to make love again, I got this glimpse of him . . . I could hear his shell dragging through the rain on the sand . . . DEAD CHILD CRAWLING . . ."

"This is insane," Adam whispered.

"No, no, it's not. You don't understand."

"No, you don't understand. You forget, like I'd like to forget, but the fact is when nobody was looking, I actually did kill a man – because he was there and only because he was there, I shot him dead – and what happened? My dead guy's gone out of my dreams. Just like that. I didn't get rid of him. He's just gone. My dead guy's gone like that guerrilla's dead and gone. Tit for tat. Retaliation. Good. Fucking great. Now I know what the unbearable lightness of death is. And now you're telling me that by tying yourself here to the living dead, you've got rid of your dead child, he's not hunting you down, you've got rid of your own nightmare?"

"I've got free, from him."

"That's no freedom, it's some kind of wacky atonement. He's still out there, you're letting him lie there in the reeds, he's just on the other side of the river, that's all. The evil, if that's what you're dealing with, the evil was done to you. Let Harry atone."

"Maybe so, maybe not, but this is the way it is. This is in me. This is the only way I've found that I can keep that dream out of my mind. Being here."

He was so exasperated he realized he'd bitten the inside of his cheek. He could taste his own blood.

As quietly and calmly as he could, he said, "Listen, when we're fucking, when we're making love, I can feel your whole body, that's the light I feel in me, it lifts me right out of myself. You want *lumière*, I'll give you *lumière*, you give me *lumière*, it's the light I get from you, the light that is in me, it's real, I know it's real."

"But that's not what I'm telling you. With me, when there's light there's death. That's it. That's all. Period. I've loved you till my heart breaks. I can live with a broken heart, but I could not live with that child nesting in me, hearing him say with every step I take, '*Dead child crawling*.' Poor old Roland, though he's totally crazy, is right. The rat's hair is alive in us from the day we're born, it's in our cells. Okay. So what. A rat's a rat. I was a dancer so I danced. And there's our poor Christ, still trying to prove that a little healing can be the sign for a great big healing, but when you get right down to it, what we all know is that no matter how many cures come along, no matter how many dances are danced, it's always there, the rat is underneath the floorboards, new plagues break out . . . AIDS, SARS. And never mind leprosy, what about E. coli – our flesh eating itself. That's what we do. Harry is evil – I mean how evil can a father be? But in another way, like I said, he's just a sore, a boil, that broke open. Pus. There are some people who are out there singing their song for all they are worth, but they are the people who leave behind pus. Harry's one of them. That's his snail-trail. There's no cure for where the pus comes from, only clean bandages and a little comfort, like when we washed each other, washing our wounds . . ."

"You're losing your mind here," he said.

"Well, it's a beginning."

⬥

At dawn, though deep in sleep, he heard a light knocking, a *tap tap*, someone at the door? He heard himself say, not to Gabrielle but to someone standing at the foot of the bed, "Answer the door," though he knew there was no one else in the bedroom, and there was no one at the door.

"Still," he said, "that you?" and then he woke up.

"Are you all right?" Gabrielle asked, face into her pillow, half-asleep.

"I'm okay, I guess."

A rooster crowed. She pulled the bedcover close to her chin. Another rooster crowed.

"I'm all comfy," she said, turning her cheek to his.

"I was just thinking," he said, cradling her, "I wish you hadn't cut your hair."

"I don't want to talk about my hair."

"But it reminds me of my mother," he whispered in her ear. "She cut her hair close whenever she was really unhappy."

"I'm not unhappy. I'm not your mother. And don't breathe in my ear . . ."

"You should be unhappy. I'm going home."

"You know that's not what I mean."

"Still, I am going."

"You sounded," she said, sliding her hand along his thigh, taking hold of his cock, "like you were calling out for someone."

"I guess I was," he said.

"Who?"

"Still . . ."

"Still what?"

"Still . . . that's his name."

"It's too early, don't tease me," she said, slowly stroking him.

"I'm not," he said, "it's just that still waters run deep."

"You *are* making fun of me?"

"Not at all. I just want to laugh," he said.

"You do?"

"I told you. After I saw you in San Juan, I broke out into laughter. That's how I knew I still loved you. I laughed and laughed staring out over the dark water. It's hard for me to laugh when your hair's cut so short."

"So what're you trying to tell me?" she asked, hurrying the stroke of her hand on his cock.

"We don't laugh like we used to. I think maybe the laughter's gone."

"Maybe we just know each other better."

"Maybe. But even though my head's so full of everything we've said, maybe there's a thing that's missing, a thing we could look after."

"Like what?" she asked, slowing her hand, sensing that he was about to say something discomfiting.

"I was thinking maybe we should have a child."

"Sure," she said dryly, "why not? Why didn't I think of that?"

"I'm not kidding."

"Look, for the love of God, I mean, when we were kids making love in the little shed, back then I sometimes thought I wanted to have a child with you . . . but now, the way it's turned out, even if you were staying, I couldn't have a child. How the hell could I have a child?"

"I told you, every time we fuck we're fucking on the side of life, defying death."

"Fucking me is not defying death," she said sternly, letting go of his cock.

"A child does," he said, "every time that bell in the dispensary rings . . . BONG . . . that's a child, that's a great big 'fuck you', Roland, and your rat's hair in the soup."

He rolled over and lay on top of her but did not enter her.

She crossed her legs at the ankles, saying, "A child? You *are* serious."

"Our child."

"You want this morning of all mornings to try to get a child?"

"Yeah."

"I can't believe you. You're incredible. And you wonder why we're not laughing!"

"Listen, I believe you, with all my heart I believe what you said about your dead child coming to claim you. How awful that is."

Hunched forward, she said very quietly, almost menacingly, "Don't mess with my mind."

"I'm not."

"Around here, that's where it all starts. In the mind. So don't, I'm asking you, and I'm telling you don't mess up my mind. Please. Don't go there."

"Go where?"

"Where you're going. You're going nowhere good."

"I'm thinking about us."

"And . . . ?"

"There's nothing wrong with that."

"No. But it depends."

"On what?"

"What you're thinking."

"I'm thinking we should do something big, something good."

"We should not," she cried as she leapt to her feet.

"And if I insist, if I insist that we make love and when we make love we try for a child? I mean, between us, we could make that death die . . ."

"No."

"And if I make you say yes?"

"Listen to what you're saying . . . this is hilarious . . . you're threatening me . . . what those thugs out in the bush do . . ."

"What I'm threatening you with is even more love."

"And you think I've lost *my* mind. Listen to you. I can't do that. And even if I wanted to, I don't have that kind of strength. I don't run that deep."

"Still waters," he said getting out of bed, too, "run deep."

"What *are* you going on about? This some kind of lame joke?"

"No, no," he said, reaching for her, taking her in his arms. "It's just something I never told you about. We both carry around our own dead child."

"Like how?"

"Still *was* a child's name."

"What?"

"Still."

"You mean there was a child called Still?" she asked, shaking her head in disbelief.

"Yes."

"Where?"

"My twin brother."

"You had a twin?"

"Yeah, but not really. He was born dead."

"Still-born!"

"Yeah, but I never knew about him till Web told me, maybe about a year ago, just before I saw you in San Juan. They had no name for him so they called him Still and buried him like that. My father showed me him, showed me his grave, buried in the snow, and he got down on top of him and made him into a snow angel. So I got down and made him an angel, too. Twin angels."

"Maybe, at heart," she said, "that makes me and your mother twins, too."

"How so?"

"We both gave birth to death."

"Maybe we are crazy," he said. "Maybe the two of us together are crazy."

"Each of us alone, too."

"That's how we are, I guess. Alone together."

"My God, this is all unbelievable.

"It is," he said, letting go of her, "more like God than you think, unbelievable but I believe it. I have to."

"I need my cold shower," she said.

She turned on the water in the shower stall. Lacking force, it was little more than a drizzle.

He lifted the bottom end of the mattress, taking up the Glock, letting it lie for a moment on his open palm, testing its weight, and then he put it on the pillow.

"Right. I'll be right with you."

"You're incorrigible," she said.

And then he heard her begin to cry. He opened the shower stall door. She was shaking, her hands, her whole body.

He drew her out of the shower and, though sopping wet, into his arms.

"There's no help in crying," he said, stepping back so that he could look into her eyes.

"No help in crying," she repeated.

"No."

"Not now."

"Promise?"

"No."

"Why not?"

"I can't help it. All this talk, as if there was something I could do. I can't, I love you, and I love you even beyond any kind of love I've ever known. There are times when I wake up, and I have my hand on myself like I did when I was a little girl, and I'm all wet and I know I've been dreaming again of that night in the bay . . . it's always with me, it can never be taken from me, from us, and a person's got to be crazy to think you can get that twice in your life . . . spinning and falling like we did in the water, down into the dark, the light like hundreds of little necklaces – whatever we did, then and there, we only made light – and I really felt as close to God then as I'll ever feel, but no matter, we ended up swimming in the black water, and that's where we were then and that's where we are now, that's life, black water, and the more I love you, the more I try to love you like I was free to love when I was a little girl half-asleep, the more I get eaten alive, by whatever it is, my child, my own child of evil. I don't know. But I hate it. It's evil. The more I'm filled with love the more I start to hate, the colder I get. Can't you see that?"

He held her as close, and tightly as he could.

"I see, said the blind man," he said, letting his laughter erupt, so she would feel that he was laughing openly, freely. "That's what the woman in San Juan said you said to her when you told her you were going to the *village lumière*, 'I see, said the blind man' . . ."

"I know," she said, laughing a little with him, knowing that their laughter had always led to their touching, to a fondling that quickly eased any tension, any hurt, a fondling that they had always accepted not only as a forgiveness, but as an affirmation of their belonging together, to each other, but now they both knew that they were trying to laugh, which only made them sad, and sadder still as she looked up into his eyes and said, "I know, said the dumb man . . ."

Dressed, he gathered his loose clothes and his camera equipment, jammed the Glock under his belt, and put on his safari jacket with its several pockets for cameras and film. She had washed the jacket and he felt ill at ease, too clean, too un-rumpled.

"I don't think I look right," he said.

"You look like you," she said. "Like you should look."

The bells at the dispensary were ringing steadily. CDEF, CDEF, CDEF . . .

"Unless they're popping babies by the minute up there," he said, "someone has gone crazy."

"No, no," she said. "They know you're going, they're say-ing goodbye."

"*Bong*," he said, "goodbye."

Before she laced on her white sneakers, he said, "Wait, I've got something," and he unzipped a side pouch to his travelling bag.

He handed her red slingback shoes.

"These are yours. Empty and yours."

Startled, unsure for a moment, she took the shoes to her breasts, holding them close, and sat down, as if suddenly winded, out of breath.

"So," she said, "you knew I could never go back."

"I guess, but I think I thought it'd be a way of telling you that you could still wear those shoes at home. Anyway" – and he picked up his garment bag – "you'd find going home even stranger than I do. Last time, I started looking up names in my telephone book, to see who was still there, and who'd flown the coop..."

"And...?"

"Almost nobody's there. My father's off in Amsterdam with some Anna-Maria I've never met and all those people who've said 'give me a call' are gone. And I look at you and already I feel like you've got an unlisted number."

"Unlisted..." she said, with an approving smile. "That's kind of good, I like that."

"Right," he said, as they closed the door behind them, "I know you – WANTED – in all the post offices of the nation."

She threw her head back and laughed.

"That," he said, "is the first real laugh I've heard from you in days."

"It's just that it gets more and more unbelievable the way things have worked themselves out."

Doors opened down one of the shanty alleys.

"It was all worked out a million years ago," he said.

Lepers came out into the light, leaning on walking sticks and poles, huddling forward, coming close to Adam, smiling, but careful not to crowd him, to interfere.

"They know you are leaving."

"You told them?" he asked, buttoning his jacket, not wanting them to see the Glock.

"They just know. They're going to miss you."

"Why in the world would they?"

"They like the idea of me having a man. They can't imagine a woman without a man. Particularly," she said, taking his arm, "when they find me singing to the trees."

"Remember that kid with the coat hanger and the tin can?"

"Sure," she said.

"Scary."

"Yes, he was."

"Maybe he thought he was playing our song?"

"A lonely crazy song," she said.

"Maybe to him we looked lonely?"

"To me he looked crazy."

"Maybe he was," he said.

"Or maybe he only wanted us to know how lonely he was. And afraid. Maybe that was it. And instead, we were afraid of him, but what if he was afraid of us?"

"Or for us . . ." he said.

"Actually, now that you mention it, I'd like to think that the kid's music is what Harry hears when he's alone and afraid at night."

"The awful truth is, the only music Harry hears is Verdi," he said. "He's out there still singing the *Sanctus* and sneaking a smoke. Still writing VERDI for little boys on his chalkboard wall. Alone, I guess. On his last dance."

They had entered into a small square at the crossing of alleys. He put down his bags and held out his arms to her, an invitation to dance. She took his hand and to a silent music, they made three or four formal waltz turns, and then broke apart . . . to stand, heads down.

"So when I'm gone," he said at last, "when you're alone, are you going to be afraid?"

He was aware that she was now leading him away from the lepers who had gathered in the square and the alleys, leading him to a cove of trees on the edge of a gully beyond the shanties, a gully he'd not been in before.

She folded her arms, as if becoming very serious.

"I'm going to lie down and drink palm wine and look up at the stars."

"Make sure you connect all the dots."

"What dots?"

"Ever since I was a kid I've looked up at the sky like it's been my own great big tattoo parlour. There's a whole lot of fish up there," he said, "who are mermaids and birds who burst into flame at second base. But you know what's funny about the stars?"

"I never found the stars funny."

"What's funny is people try reading them . . ."

"Sure, they want to know what's going to happen."

"But the stars are the past. The light you're looking at has actually been there for a million years. You think you're look-ing into the future, but you're reading the past, the best you can ever do is find out where we've been. We never know where we're going."

"You're going home."

"Yeah, but my daddy told me you only go home when the mortgage is due, and I've got no mortgage."

"Right. So you're free. And that's the way it should be. For you, the whole world is out there, that's your world, you're a photographer, everything's out there for you to see, to show the world, whether the world wants to see it or not, to give the world back to itself."

The light filtering through the leaves in the dark grove of tall palm trees where fetishes had been hung from stakes driven into the soil was soft on her face.

"I thought I should show you where I want to be buried," she said with a mischievous little smile that he found disconcerting because she seemed suddenly to be so at ease with herself and even bemused by being in this place with him. He was about to protest, to say that he didn't want to see where she would be buried, but she said, "You see, you're so attached to the tombstones of your own family graveyard, I thought I should show you what'll be my place. Except here there's no tombstones, here you're sewn into four palm leaves and the hole is very shallow, that's why those mounds are there, and in four days you're gone. The ants get right in and clean you out."

"I've got to have a tombstone," he said.

"None of those here," she said.

"You've got one of those things?" he asked, pointing at a fetish.

"I've got one of those things."

"You do? How come I've never seen it?"

"I couldn't show you everything, not all at once, and Roland's got one, too, and some of the doctors as well. I mean, Roland's crazier than crazy, he takes his with him walking at night. It's his little fear bag with lots of things in it, hairs and two pieces of a skull, dyed red . . ."

"And yours?"

"Well, what I really wish is that I had my school braids."

"Your pigtails?"

"But what I've got is an antelope horn, see," and she took a horn out of her pocket and handed it to him. It fitted into his open fist, the carved figure of a kneeling man, his chin in his hands, mouth open, a little zero, staring wide-eyed.

"I don't know," he said. "He looks like he needs a drink of water."

"He makes me smile," she said. "He looks like Harry blowing smoke rings."

"Look," he said, "I want you to promise me something, and I promise I won't bring it up again, but when you've been here long enough, and if it turns out that you think I'm right about the child, and you're strong enough, you call me . . . we'll finish that little dance . . . promise you'll call me . . ."

He handed her the fetish and she put it in her pocket.

"I promise . . ."

They walked down a river path close to the cement pier and the pirogues.

"There's one thing at least that I'm happy about," she said, "not just that you have given me so much love, but, you know, we haven't quarrelled. We've always been who we are face to face, we've done nothing false to ourselves."

The leper boatman with the bowler hat was waiting.

They sat down past the dock on a rise, an elbow of yellow sand, where the river was wide, a muddy green (slime green along the shore), and slow moving, sluggish.

"Looks mighty dirty, but boys were swimming in there yesterday."

"Of course. But it's a great risk," she said. "Some doctors talk like the river is seething with contagion, infection . . ."

"Ah the doctors," he said quietly. "I always liked that word 'contagion.'"

"Yes."

"Repeat after me," he said with mock seriousness: "Contagion."

Trying hard not to laugh she said, "Contagion."

"Con-ta-gi-on."

"Con-ta-gi-on."

"Contagion, thy name is this river."

She broke into laughter and folded her arm under his arm, nestling against him.

"That's what doctors do," he said, "and priests. They've got their eye on the contagion."

He picked up a stick and drew a big letter C in the sand.

"Con . . . ," he said, and then let the word trail off into a moment of silence between them.

"If it's so infected it sure is deceptively still on the surface," she then said, "except for those swirls you can see out there, it's the undertow, that's what scares me when I go swimming."

"You're scared?"

"I told you how free I've always felt whenever I've been close to the sea. But I've always somehow walked away from the sea. I don't know why."

"So here you are, stuck by this river."

"No. Now I'm free, as free as I've ever been."

"In Ponce," he said, "you were free as a bird. You were free, I was free. But it's all ended up trapped in your dreams."

"In a way, that's true."

"What is?"

"When we were together I did get this quick, sudden look at myself, like I'd never seen myself before. It was after we'd gone swimming in the bay with all the light in the water, I got this fantastic feeling that I had become the exact same dream I'd had when I was a kid, like I really was one of those great amorous women I'd loved in the movies, all the women I'd envied. They had nothing on me when I was in your arms, nothing..."

"We could still be in our own movie."

"Sure. Sure we could. And I could pretend that forever after I was wearing a necklace of light..."

He laughed.

"And then I would find out they were rhinestones."

He had gone on cutting letters in the sand with the stick, almost idly, as if he were paying attention only to her and not to what he was doing, but then she said, "What's that, what're you doing?"

He dropped the stick. "Nothing," he said as she read aloud,

BABY
Still
Waters
Run
Deep

and then drew away from him, saying accusingly, "You are trying very hard to hurt me."

"No. No," he cried, taking her into his arms, "no, not at all. No."

"Then what is it?"

"What it says on Still's tombstone."

He broke into tears, not a shudder of sorrow but a silent weeping. Eyes swollen, he wept. Then he threw his head back, taking a deep breath, and said, "I'm ridiculous."

"Tears are never ridiculous," she said.

Without a word, he took her face in his hands and closed his eyes. He drew his fingertips over her brows, the bridge of her nose, her lips, like a blind man learns a face, and for a moment she was frightened by his silence, by his blind touch, the desperateness in that touch, but then he said, "Yes, you see, I wanted to be sure I knew your face by heart and now I know I know it."

"I must get you something, I'm going to get you a face to take with you."

She loped back up the hill path, disappearing between shanties and the wards. He sat down to wait, feeling helpless, hardly able to hold back more tears that he felt welling behind his eyes, wanting to protest that their separation was wrong while knowing that he had already accepted its inevitability – and this sense of inevitability made him feel the same panic he'd felt as a child when he'd suddenly found himself alone in the dark. Remembering how as a boy he'd stretched out on a pew at the back of the church and pounded his heels *boom boom boom* because his voice was too small to be heard, and how he had wanted to be heard, how he had wanted to sing, and how he had hidden his shoes, afraid they'd be taken from him by Harry, and how he was now wearing what his father had called "loose shoes" – he thought, if this is how it has to be, if this is the beat of how things are, if this is the song that has to be sung, then what he should do – the only thing he could do – was what he was doing, walk on, walk on and perhaps go to wherever his father was, not to say too much to his father nor to ask too much of his father, but to sit down and listen to him play on the black notes and let the black notes be his own song and the silences between the notes be Gabrielle's song, the two together, each alone, as a celebration of their way of love, the way it was, and the way it was to be as he watched her come back down the hill, her eyes full of pleasure, carrying a white-faced mask that had long, loose straw hair and a straw beard, with little lopsided gouged holes for eyes, a pug nose and a pursed mouth. "It took me time to get it," she said. "It was crawling with lizards, chameleons."

"Why the white face?"

"The white keeps off evil."

"To protect me against myself."

She kissed him on both cheeks and on the mouth. And again on the mouth. "Make sure you sit very still in the pirogue. The water is dangerous, especially with a wind."

She, and then Adam, hesitated as they stepped out on to the pier – smiling awkwardly – knowing they had not been false to each other, and yet – by embracing their separation they knew they were also betraying a promise, the promise of their childhood.

The boatman helped him into the pirogue, his leper hand streaked pink by the wound in the dark flesh. Adam's throat was dry, he wanted fresh, cold water. They pulled out into the river, clouds coming with the falling sun. "I do love you," she cried. "You know I do." There was an Uzi on the bottom of the pirogue between the boatman's feet. Instinctively, he felt for the Glock under his jacket. He wondered what Father Zale would say: *maybe 2 = 1 until you figure out where the mistake is.* When he looked back, Adam saw that she was on the cement pier, her arms up in the air, extended to the sky, just like the last time he'd seen Harry on the altar at the moment of the *Sanctus,* and he cried out to her against the force of the wind over the water, "Just call, call me, it could be a whole new life."

She kept standing with both hands in the air, fingers in the sign of two Vs, as he passed out of sight around the headland.

The Spanish verse chanted by Trigueño on page 147 is by César Vallejo. An English version, translated by David Smith, is:

And startled God is taking
our pulse, grave, mute,
and like a father to his little girl almost,
just almost, opens up the bloody cottons
and between his fingers takes hope.

Special thanks to Marilyn DiFlorio,
my typist, for her longtime commitment and assistance.